Hayden's Guild

P. Ryan Hembree

Heart Ally Books
Camano Island, Washington

Hayden's Guild
Copyright © 2014 by P. Ryan Hembree.

Contact the author at: www.pryanhembree.com

Published by:
Heart Ally Books
26910 92nd Ave NW C5-406, Stanwood, WA 98292
Published on Camano Island, WA, USA
www.heartallybooks.com

ISBN-13 (epub): 978-1-63107-002-0
ISBN-13 (paperback): 978-1-63107-001-3
Library of Congress Control Number: 2014934049

*To my brother, Danny, who's so wonderful
and adds so much
to our lives*

Friendship is one of the sweetest joys of life.

Many might have failed beneath the bitterness of their trial

had they not found a friend.

Charles H Spurgeon

Every good and perfect gift is from above,

Coming down from the Father of the heavenly lights...

James 1:17

1

00001

Lea Curtis scanned the blog one final time and posted it to run the next day. She rolled her head from side to side to work out a crick in her neck. As she shut down the program, her doorbell chimed. "One-thirty in the morning, who could that be?" she mumbled.

She glanced out the front window and spied Joe Wade's car parked in her driveway. "What in the world can he want at this time of night?" she groaned. Their relationship had been in off-mode for five months.

He pounded on the door with his fist. "Lea! Lea, open the door. It's about your mother."

Lea flung the door open. "What about my mother?"

"I'm sorry to show up like this, but your phone's going to voicemail."

When Lea worked on a deadline, she frequently turned off her cell phone. "What's wrong?"

"There's been an accident. Ronnie called me when she couldn't get you on your cell."

"Where is she?" Lea gasped.

"St. Luke's. All I know is that they admitted her to intensive care."

Lea grabbed Joe's arm to steady herself. "Oh, Joe, no!"

Lea snatched her keys and headed out the door. "I've got to go to her."

Joe escorted her back into the house. "Get dressed, first."

Lea glanced down at her nightshirt. In the bedroom she shrugged into a green tee shirt and jeans. She tied her long, brown hair back into a pony tail and slipped into her sandals.

On the way to the hospital, she tried to call Joe's sister, who was a police detective. She flipped the cell phone closed. "She's not picking up."

"We'll be there in a few minutes."

"Was it a car accident? I can't imagine what she's doing out at this hour."

"Ronnie didn't know what happened. She's working the graveyard shift and a call came in about two women found unconscious in Forked River Park off a hiking trail just after midnight. They found your mother's cell phone under her. They don't have confirmation of who the other woman is."

"Maybe it's not Mom." Lea speed-dialed her mother's house phone. It rang until it went to voicemail. "It can't be her. She wouldn't be out in a park this time of night. Joe, she goes to bed at ten-thirty every night after the news."

Joe pulled into the hospital entrance. "This late, we have to go in through the Emergency Room."

Lea raced into the hospital and confronted the desk clerk. "My mother, Hayden Curtis was just brought in."

The clerk tapped on her keyboard. "She's been admitted to the third floor Intensive Care Unit. Let me give you a pass."

Lea pointed to Joe. "He's with me. He's the detective's brother."

The clerk handed them passes, and they took the elevator to the third floor. As they stepped off the elevator, Lea spotted Veronica Ramsey outside one of the patient's rooms.

"Ronnie, is my mom all right?"

Ronnie stood straight and put her arm around Lea. "She has a concussion and a broken rib. The doctors just got the MRI report back, and there doesn't seem to be a skull fracture. They're going to keep her here for observation tonight."

"Is she awake? Can she talk to us?"

A nurse stepped out of a room. "Can I help you people?"

"This is Mrs. Curtis's daughter, Lea."

"Please, let me see her," Lea begged.

"The doctor is just finishing his exam. When he's done, maybe, and only for a few minutes."

"Let's sit on this bench." Ronnie escorted Lea to a bench and they took a seat. "Lea, do you have any idea what your mother was doing in Forked River Park," she glanced down at her iPad, "at night dressed in a Deanna Troi Star Trek costume?"

For a moment, nothing seemed to register in Lea's mind. "Ronnie, are you sure that woman in there's my mother?"

Ronnie nodded. "She's Hayden Curtis. Would you take a look at the other woman and tell me if you know her? She had no identification on her, and I've never seen her before. The man that called the police said her gaming name was Voyagess13."

Lea glanced at Joe and then back at Ronnie. This all just couldn't be real. "I know all of her friends. If it's someone she knows, I might recognize her."

Ronnie led Lea into the room next to her mother's. A woman lay in bed, her head bandaged and hooked to a menagerie of monitors. Lea took a close look. "Her neighbor. The woman across the street, Mary. Mary Johnson."

"That helps."

"Her house number would be eighty-nine-thirteen," Joe said.

"What happened to her?"

"Let's step out in the hall." Ronnie ushered Lea out of the room.

"Your mother and this woman were struck with something and knocked unconscious. A man from their guild found them and called the police."

"Guild? What guild?"

"Cody Ingham, the man who found them, claims they all belong to an ARG guild and they are competing for a $150,000 prize."

Tears formed in Lea's eyes. "Ronnie, I don't know what you're saying. I don't know what an RG thing is. And whatever it is, my mother wouldn't be involved."

The doctor stepped out of Hayden's room.

"Doctor, this is Mrs. Curtis's daughter." Ronnie introduced them.

"Your mother has some bruises, a fractured wrist, and a broken rib. The bones are in place, so she won't need surgery. She does have a mild concussion, and I'm recommending observation tonight. If her neurological signs are good in the morning, we'll transfer her to the medical ward. It's a good thing she was wearing that wig. It protected her from a worse head injury. I'd like you to work with our intern and provide him with your mother's medical history."

"Thank you. Can I see her?"

"For a few minutes. If you need anything, I'll be at the nurse's station."

Without thinking, Lea clasped Joe's hand tightly. They entered the room. Only one subdued light over the bed illuminated the room. The monitors recorded her mother's breathing. Her hair was caked with mud and scratches on her face were caked with dried blood. Two large cuts on her forehead had been cleaned and taped. Her left eye was swollen.

Lea took her right hand. "Mom," she whispered.

"Lea," she said weakly.

"Mom, I'm here."

Hayden blinked at Joe. "Joe. I'm glad you're back together with Lea."

Lea didn't want to confuse her mother, so she let the remark pass. She had a thousand questions for her mother, but they could wait. "Mom, do you know who hit you?"

Her mother looked puzzled. "No. I think I just fell down."

Lea patted her good arm. "I'm here now. I'll take care of you."

A nurse stepped into the room. "Because your mother was just brought in, I broke a few rules and let you stay, but she does need to rest. Ms. Curtis, can you step out to the nursing area and give us her medical history?"

Lea rubbed her mother's hand. "I'll be right back."

Lea completed the forms and handed them to the nurse.

The nurse scanned the forms. "This looks good. Your mother is stable now. Our visiting hours begin at eleven o'clock in the morning. I suggest that you go home and get some rest. We'll take good care of your mother."

Lea opened her mouth to ask a question—

"Code blue, ICU 329. Code blue, ICU 329."

Night-duty personnel converged on a room across from Lea's mother's room.

"It's okay." Joe folded Lea in his big arms. "It's not your mother." He put his arm around her shoulders.

"This is too much," Lea whispered, brushing her hair back with a shaky hand.

Joe walked her down to the waiting room where Ronnie had just finished a call and clicked off her cell phone. "I'll get us some coffee. Be right back."

Lea took a seat across from Ronnie, a friend from her college days.

"You okay?"

Lea nodded. "I can't for the life of me figure out what Mom was doing in a park this time of night."

"You didn't know that she was involved with an ARG game?"

Lea shrugged. "I don't even know what that is."

"Here." Joe handed her a cup of coffee and set a cup in front of Ronnie.

"Thanks." Lea flipped off the top and took a sip of the hot brew, letting the warmth work through her. "Joe, tell me this isn't real. Tell me I'm going to wake up, and everything will be all right."

"I'm having trouble believing this too."

"What is my tea-totaling, ultra-conservative mother doing in a park, in the middle of the night, in a Star Trek costume?"

Joe shook his head. "This isn't like your mother at all."

"Do you think she was kidnapped out of the house? Someone wanting her to get money out of an ATM card, which she doesn't have?"

Ronnie took a gulp of coffee and set the cup down. "Could be, but what explains the neighbor and the costumes? The neighbor was dressed as Captain Katherine Janeway of the USS Voyager. The man who found them said Hayden and this woman were regulars in the club and were top contenders for the $150,000 prize."

Lea shook her head slowly. "Mom can barely work her email. What exactly is an ARG game?"

"Massively Multiplayer Online Role Playing Game," Joe said. "An MMORPG, or she could just be part of a small Alternate Reality Game, are all played online. Some MMO games have millions of players world-wide. Players form small, local groups, called guilds or alliances, and sometimes a gamemaster sets up an alternate reality game where players compete for cash. That's probably what your mother got into."

Ronnie stared at her brother, her coffee cup half raised to her mouth. She furrowed her eyebrows. "You know this why?"

He raised his eyebrows at his sister. "Back in the day, I was pretty good."

Ronnie finished her coffee. "I'm beginning to understand your grades the first few years you were in college."

Ronnie put her hand on Lea's shoulder. "We can't solve this tonight." She closed her notebook and pocketed her cell phone. "In the morning, we'll interview the gamemaster of the guild your mother's in and get a list of players. We'll get a team to interview them and see who we need to focus on. Lea, you need to rest."

Lea nodded. "I just want to check on her before we leave."

Ronnie stood. "She's stable and conversing. I'm so sorry this happened to her, and I promise I'll find the person who did this."

"Thanks, Ronnie."

Lea and Joe returned to Hayden's room. A nurse checked her monitors and IV lines. She patted Lea on her shoulder. "She's doing fine."

"Thanks."

"Lea," Hayden whispered.

"Mom." Lea took her good hand. "Do you need anything?"

She shook her head slowly. "I remember a little bit. We just texted our solution to the gamemaster. I went up to check on the road that no one was there." She stopped for a few minutes. "When I came back to tell Mary, she was sprawled out on the ground in the mud, not moving."

Her mother stopped again and took a few deep breaths. "As I leaned over her. I heard someone behind me. When I stood and turned ..." She closed her eyes. "I just don't remember after that."

Hayden tried to raise up out of the bed, pulling her covers back. "I have to get our medallions."

Monitors beeped and squealed. The nurse bustled in. "Mrs. Curtis, you need to lie back."

"My head hurts." Hayden felt the bandage around her head.

The nurse rubbed Hayden's shoulder as she reset two monitors. "Just lie back. You're doing fine."

"We're going to leave," Lea told the nurse.

Lea leaned over the bed and whispered, "Mom, we'll be back in the morning."

Hayden grabbed Lea's hand. "Can you go over and feed Mary's little dog? Her house key's in the teapot. I always take care of her dog when she's away."

"Don't worry about a thing. Sure. I'll go over in the morning. You need to get some rest, now."

"I have to finish our game," Hayden mumbled weekly.

Lea kissed her mother on her cheek. "For tonight, game over."

2

00010

After a few hours of fitful sleep, Lea awoke at her mother's house. The clock registered only six a.m., but she couldn't fight trying to sleep anymore. She showered, dressed and was putting on a pot of coffee when the kitchen doorbell chimed. She glanced out the window. Joe. She didn't want to deal with him this early. She opened the door.

"You weren't at your house, so I came here. Just thought I'd check on you." He held up a bag from the bagel shop.

"Come in. I just put on some coffee. I stayed here in case someone called or came by with news of Mom's attack." She set two mugs next to the gurgling coffee pot.

"Thanks for coming to get me last night. It broke my heart to see Mom so battered." Lea set out plates on the dining room table while Joe toasted the bagels.

"Broke mine, too. You know, I think the world of her." He pointed to the dining room table. "I see she moved her computer here into the dining room," he said, setting the bagels on the table.

Lea dropped into a chair in front of the computer and booted up the hard drive. "She said she needed more room. Now I know why."

"Did you call the hospital?"

Lea checked her watch. "I'll do it later. The nurses will be changing shifts now, and I won't get any reliable information."

Lea spread cream cheese on a bagel half while she waited for Hayden's email program to thread through. She finger brushed her damp hair back behind her ear and slowly sipped her coffee as she thumbed through her mother's emails. "Mom and I frequently check each other's emails. I don't think she'll mind. That attack last night was brutal."

Joe sat next to Lea. He munched on his bagel while Lea worked through the emails.

"You never knew that she was in this group?"

"No. I called her every day. Got together a few times a week. Saw her in church on Sundays. There was always something going on with Edna or Frances, or her Bible study group. I thought she was fine." She glanced over at Joe and back at the computer. "I wonder why she never told me. We talk about everything. Why not this?"

Lea pointed to the long list of emails. "Get well wishes from this online gaming club she belongs to." She scoured the emails, looking for something that would point to why her mother was attacked. "I can't believe she's into a game contest."

"Word travels pretty fast through those chat rooms. You'll want to forward all of those to Ronnie. Have her team check for any menacing postings."

"Probably a good idea." Lea forwarded the emails to Ronnie's work computer and shut down the email program. She clicked through recent online searches. "I wonder where the game access is on this computer."

"Let me try," Joe said, taking over the mouse. He shook his head after a few minutes of clicking through programs. "My guess is that the game is loaded into Mary Johnson's computer and they both play from her house."

Joe checked internet URLs. "Here's something." He opened a Dylan's Games web address. "It looks like a trial game. Doesn't access the contest. Looks like she practices on the trial." He closed out the program. "Nothing more."

Lea finished her bagel. She sat back in her chair completely stumped by her mother's online capers. "I wonder what kind of hold this woman had on Mom that she would keep this such a secret. I think I'll call Edna later and ask her if she knew anything about this."

"I don't know," Joe said. "You're Mom's a pretty open book."

Lea sipped her coffee slowly, studying Joe. She'd had no contact with him for five months except for one brief visit to Lincoln for Ronnie's birthday. They'd all gone out to dinner together, and he left early the next morning. She wondered if he had planned to visit Mom. He might not contact her, but he wouldn't miss a chance to catch up with Hayden.

"So, Mr. Wade, why are you on vacation from your detective job in Kansas City?"

Joe carried the dishes into the kitchen and returned. He slumped down in a chair across from Lea. "No particular reason. I just wanted to visit my big sister."

"Ronnie said that you're on two weeks leave. I've known you for over fifteen years. You never take vacations."

He sat up straight and tipped his head slightly to the left, his out-with-it stance. "We got a new chief of detectives." He raised his eyebrows. "Let's just say that she doesn't like my detecting skills."

"She?"

He stared at her and drummed his fingers on the table. It was his unique way of making a point without saying anything.

"Your sister's a police detective—and a good one. Surely, you're not against women cops?"

"Ronnie does her job professionally. She isn't trying to prove anything to anyone. With this woman, every encounter with a man is a competition. She has to beat you out."

"So, when do you have to go back?"

"I took a few weeks off. I just got in last night. Had dinner with Mike and Ronnie. Then she called me around midnight. Your mother's such a wonderful person, I can't walk away from this."

"It's not much of a vacation for you."

"I don't have police reports to file and no one in particular to answer to. I do my best work when I'm not under pressure. It won't hurt to have two ace detectives looking into your mother's attack."

So, what's he not telling me? I'll call Ronnie later and get the rest of the story.

She was grateful for his help since he and his sister were expert detectives. He seemed appropriately restrained. Didn't throw himself at her. Maybe their status hadn't changed.

"Joe, I appreciate your help."

He leaned forward and spread out his hands. "Look, Lea, I don't want anything weird between us. About last winter, I should have given you a better answer when I walked away. I was wrong, and me, being me, I couldn't think of a way to repair the damage until too much time had passed. I really am sorry, Lea. I owed you more than, 'I'm too busy with cases now to get too much deeper into our friendship.' That wasn't fair to you."

Five months had passed since that last night they were together, and she'd worked through her anger and disappointment. She actually thought that night when he came over that he was going to propose to her. Instead, he ended their relationship.

Seeing him on the doorstep last night was a jolt. They'd have to find a way to work together.

Lea reached over, shuffled the mouse, and shut down the computer. He still hadn't answered the question of why he wanted out of their relationship.

Maybe there wasn't an answer. Maybe he just needed some space. She wasn't a video game you played with for a while and left idle on the hard drive for months until you were in the mood to play again. She needed him to help with her mother's attack, but she'd keep her distance.

"Thank you for telling me that. Let's just focus on one thing at a time. Which reminds me, I have to let Mary's dog out." She reached behind her and retrieved the key from the teapot on the buffet.

Joe stood. "I'll go with you. We still don't know any contact people for her."

Lea stepped up on the porch of the small, three bedroom house and heard the dog yelping. She opened the front door, and the small terrier jumped and barked.

"Hey, Bubbles. Good dog." She scratched behind her ears. The dog eyed Joe and barked, just to warn him. "I bet you need to go out." Lea headed for the kitchen door.

Bubbles sat in front of the living room door, waiting for Mary.

"C'mon, Bubbles. Mary's not coming right now."

Bubbles barked at the front door and bounded towards the kitchen. Lea opened the kitchen door and let the dog out into the large, fenced yard. As the dog chased a squirrel up a tree, Lea stepped outside the gate and retrieved the mail from the box. The dog seemed content with her morning surveillance of the yard, so Lea returned to the kitchen.

Joe examined the calendar on the wall. "No appointments. No scribblings. Do you know this woman well?"

Lea shook her head as she thumbed through the mail. "Apparently, she left the house yesterday before the mail was delivered." She held out an electric bill. "I'll call the electric company and see if they can hold off on this bill until we can locate her family." She set it by the house key. "I only met her briefly a few times. She and my mother went out to eat pretty often. Mom took care of Bubbles when Mary was out of town. She always sent Mother a nice gift basket to thank her. She impressed me as a kind, sweet lady." Lea opened and closed kitchen drawers. "I never guessed she would be involved with these online games. She didn't look the type."

Joe opened and closed kitchen cabinets. "She certainly doesn't fit the profile of a hard core online gamer. No wild hair do. No tattoos."

He stood with his hands on his hips glancing around the small kitchen. "It's kinda sparse. Usually, a woman that age would have cupboards packed with cookware and counters and shelves stuffed with knickknacks, salt and pepper shakers, decorative saucers—stuff."

Lea looked around. "That's true. But, if she fled an abusive husband or another bad relationship, she would have traveled light."

Lea went down the hall, ignoring the two small bedrooms on her right, and entered the master bedroom on her left. The bed was made. "One nightstand and a small dresser."

Joe stepped into the room behind her. He opened and closed the dresser drawers. "This all looks normal. But no pictures of herself or kids."

Lea opened the closet. She felt uncomfortable prying into this woman's life. She didn't know her that well. But there could be something here that would lead them to the attacker. "This is odd. One rack of clothes, not very many. A few suitcases. No airline tags. A few pairs of shoes. Not much at all. Like she's hiding." She closed the closet door.

"Anything in the nightstand?"

Lea opened the drawer to the nightstand. "Her Bible. Nothing in it. No notes. No special marked passages."

"How long's she lived here?"

"A little over a year." Lea scanned the room to be sure everything was put back. The bathroom was sparse. No pill bottles in the medicine cabinet. She entered the small bedroom next to the living room. Mary's computer sat on a long folding table with two rolling chairs in front of it.

"Whoa," Joe reverently approached the computer. "Suh-weet."

"Earth to Joe."

"No wonder she's winning all of these games. Falcon Northwest Fragbox. This is the ultimate gaming machine, with all the bells and whistles, and software loaded and add-ons, it can reach over seven thousand dollars. This woman was in to some serious gaming."

"Is that the mouse?" Lea pointed to the device on the table.

"It's a pricey Logitech G500 laser mouse. Kind of a mouse on steroids." Joe stood back and surveyed the set up and the huge monitor.

"Interesting," he said, pointing to the wiring supporting the computer and screen, "she had this house wired recently to accommodate the computer. Plastic casing around the wires. Probably to keep the dog from chewing them." He shook his head. "This woman's got more invested in this one room than she's invested in the whole house."

He picked up pads of note paper and leafed through them. "All game strategies."

Lea held up a steno pad. "Passwords to the games." She opened a cardboard file box. "House bills. Electric, gas, usual stuff. Work pay stubs from a clothing store at the big mall." She held out the last pay stub and closed the box.

"What I don't understand is why no one at the hospital knew Mary Johnson's name?"

Joe stroked the side of the tower. "It's got a liquid cooling system and huge fan pack."

"Joe, focus. Assault in the park. My mother in the hospital."

Joe stepped away from the gaming machine. "Anyway, I asked Ronnie about that. She was at the emergency room when they brought the women in and recognized your mother right away. When they started assessing your mother's condition, she was disoriented and couldn't tell them her own name.

"Apparently, as the first responders arrived at the park, a thunderstorm hit. Lightning all around. When the tornado sirens went off, they dumped the women in the ambulance as fast as they could and got to the hospital. The man in charge of the game was rounding up the rest of the group, who were scattered throughout the park. He corralled the people and drove them back to where their vehicles were parked."

"I was at a sensitive point in a blog design and re-member the sirens going off. I didn't hear any loud wind coming my way, so I kept on working. Didn't know anything serious was happening until you rang the doorbell."

"Personnel records at the mall store will have an emergency contact person," Joe said, opening the closet door.

"Mike and I were watching a baseball game on television. Didn't even lose our connection."

Joe searched through the closet. "Not much in here. Computer equipment. Cables and another laptop. For a woman that's lived here a year, I'd expect more clothes. Books to read." He closed the door. "I'll get Ronnie to send a forensic team over to check out the computer. Could be something in there that will lead us to the attacker."

"Dog wants in." Lea headed to the kitchen.

"Who names their dog Bubbles?" Joe asked, following her.

"It is an odd name." She opened the door and the dog bounded in. She barked at Joe and headed towards her food bowl.

"Here you go, Bubbles." She filled her dog bowl with dry food and put out a fresh bowl of water. She sat on the floor next to the dog and petted her. "I'm going to check on Mary and if she's still not better, you can have a sleepover at Hayden's house tonight. Won't that be fun?"

Bubbles continued crunching her food, ignoring Lea.

Lea stood. She turned on the radio on the kitchen counter and set it to a classical music station. "I've heard a radio is good company for a pet."

Bubbles hopped up on Mary's recliner, turned around, and sat down.

"You be a good dog; I'll be back later."

Joe had that look on his face, his usual perplexed look. "It's really sterile for a woman. Lots of dog toys and computer equipment in the bedroom. No pictures on any of the walls. No family photos. No parents. No siblings.

Lea scanned the living room again. "We didn't find anything scary like a hidden cache of weapons or drugs."

"Ronnie thought it could have just been a mugger in the park. We'll know more today."

"Could be she's hiding out from someone?"

Joe raised his eyebrows. "Someone who may have found her?"

"Why didn't he finish the job? If a person went through that much trouble to find the woman, he or she left her barely alive. I'm becoming more nervous about my mother befriending this woman."

"Or, Mary Johnson purposefully befriended Hayden," Joe suggested.

"That's a creepy thought. So, what does this woman want?"

Joe held the screen door for Lea. "All good questions."

Lea locked the house and followed Joe across the street. "Mom should know more about her."

3

00011

Lea entered her mother's hospital room. The shades were drawn and the lights were dimmed. Her mother stirred.

"You found me," she whispered.

Lea took a breath to control her emotions. Her mother's face was so swollen and bruised. It pained her to look at her. She stepped up to the bed. "They called me and told me that you were moved to a regular room. How are you feeling?"

Hayden pressed the control button and the bed raised. "A little better. I need a bath, and I want to wash my hair."

"I'll ask the nurse about that." Her mother's bruised face looked worse. Why would someone do this to her kind, gentle mother?

"Have you heard how Mary is?"

"I was just up there. She's still unconscious, but her vital signs are stable now."

"It was such an awful thing to happen. The club was so fun and so many nice people. I keep trying to remember what happened."

Lea didn't want to upset her mother too much, but they needed answers if they were going to find the person who did this. She stood and straightened her mother's blanket. "Mom, how did you get into this online game? I didn't know you liked them."

"Last fall, Mary had a bad cold, and I took her some soup. While I was there, Bubbles grabbed my house keys I keep on that leather strap and ran to the back room with them. I saw Mary's setup. I hadn't seen a computer that big. She showed me how to play a few simple games. At first I messed up a lot, but it was kinda fun. She said she belonged to a local club that had scavenger hunts. I always loved treasure hunts when I was a kid. Anyway, we went on one of the hunts at a park. She taught me how to use a GPS locator, and we won a one hundred dollar prize. We tracked the clues and came in first place. I was hooked."

"The few times I saw her," Lea said, "she seemed very nice. I don't remember seeing her in church."

"She works on weekends. Lately, she's been coming to church and a couple of the fellowship dinners."

The nurse brought in her mother's lunch. With her mother's wrist in a cast, Lea opened the juice carton and unwrapped the silverware.

"Those Swedish meatballs and noodles smell good." Hayden cut into the meat and took a bite.

"You probably haven't eaten since yesterday."

"I am hungry." Hayden dabbed her mouth with her napkin. "Lea, I hope you don't mind about me and Mary and the game. She's become such a dear friend, and I do enjoy the people at the club. The man that runs the club and his wife are church people. I wanted to do something on my own. When I won the big prize, I was going to tell you about it. Make you proud of me, how I was handling losing your father."

"Oh Mom, I am proud of you. You're so smart and have such a deep faith in God. You have so many wonderful friends. And, I'm glad you enjoy the club. Our first priority is to catch the person who attacked you."

Hayden rested her head against the pillow. "It's just that when your father died two years ago, the house was so empty."

"Mom, I can come over more."

"Lea, you've been so great. I didn't want to become like Mrs. Raimes down the street. She calls her daughter over every little thing. A few months ago, she called her daughter in the middle of that awful rain storm, and Helen got in that terrible wreck rushing over to Nancy's and all it was about was the garage door wouldn't close all the way. I don't want to be a problem to you."

Lea stood and gave her mother a gentle hug. "I love you so much. You're all I have now. You'd never, ever be a problem to me."

Hayden pulled a wad of tissue out of the box and dried her eyes. She grasped her daughter's hand.

Lea handed her the fork. "You need to eat all this so you can get well and go home."

"Did you let Mary's little dog out?"

"Yes. She was curled up on her chair when we left. I'll go over and get her tonight and bring her to your house. Mom, do you know anything about Mary's family? We can't find any contact information. There must be someone we can call. Do you know if she has children, a brother or a sister?"

Hayden finished her meal. "I asked her about her family once. She said that she didn't have any children and that her husband was dead. That's why she moved. She couldn't handle all the sad memories from where she lived." Hayden adjusted a pillow behind her back. "You know, I always thought there was something she was hiding. Something she wanted to tell me but never could quite get it out. Sometimes when I pray for her, I feel a deep sadness."

Her mother spent a long time in prayer every day. A flicker of guilt stabbed Lea's heart. She hadn't prayed for her mother or Mary today.

"Do you know where she lived before?"

"I think, somewhere in Southern California. Near Los Angeles."

Ronnie tapped on the door, and she and Joe entered. "How are you, Hayden?"

"Ronnie. So nice to see you. I'm much better. Did you catch the person who did this?"

"We're working on it."

"And Joe, it's so good to see you. Are you back for good?"

Joe leaned over and kissed Hayden's bandaged forehead. "I missed you. I came to visit Ronnie and Mike. But now, you're my first priority."

"Joe, you can always get a police job here in Lincoln."

"If you promise me you'll marry me, I might consider that."

Ronnie set a small bouquet of violets on Hayden's bedstand. "I just wanted to check on you. See if you remember anything that would help us in the investigation."

"I've been trying. We were in the park. It was raining. I remember an image of Mary texting the codes." She closed her eyes and shook her head. "Nothing."

"Don't worry about it. We'll figure it out. If you remember something, tell Lea and I'll check in to it."

"I'm going to leave now. Mom looks pretty tired." Lea said. She stepped next to her mother. "I'll be back tonight, and we'll get you a bath and get your hair washed."

"We'll be outside the door," Joe said. "Get well." He tickled Hayden's toes through the sheet.

Lea turned down the light and settled her mother back in bed. She held her hand and prayed for her. She kissed her hand and tucked it under the blanket.

Lea walked to the parking lot with Ronnie and Joe.

"I took Mary Johnson's fingerprints, and we'll run them through local Nebraska databases. She must have a sister, brother, or parents somewhere. Did she tell you anything more about Mary?"

Lea shrugged. "No. She doesn't know any more than we do. She looks tired, and I don't want to question her too much."

"Joe and I are heading over to the gamemasters who run the club. Do you want to come?"

"Definitely," Lea said. "I want to see what kind of geeks these are that lead people into virtual, real trouble."

4

0100

"It's up ahead," Lea pointed to a cluster of one-story office buildings. "Dylan's Gaming is to the right."

Joe pulled into the office complex and parked in the visitor's spot in front of Dylan's Gaming.

Ronnie sat for a minute, studying the building. "Clean on the outside. No druggies hanging around. Joe, I want to introduce you as Mary's nephew who just flew in from Los Angeles this morning. I think we'll get more cooperation if we all aren't cops."

"Got it," Joe said. "Do I get an alias like Captain America?"

"No. You get Joe Wade. Keep it simple."

Lea entered the reception area behind Joe and Ronnie. She wasn't sure what to expect. A young woman with long blond hair, wearing a blue tee shirt and jeans sat in a gaming chair, talking into a headset. She held up one finger and mouthed, "One moment, please." She continued speaking into the headset and tapping on a split keyboard.

"What do you think those blinking green lights are?" Lea whispered to Joe.

"It's a binary clock designed on a twenty-four hour time basis. The first lights show hours and second set of lights are minutes. The last column, which is forever changing are seconds. It's two twenty-five." Joe pulled out his cell phone and nodded. "Yep. Two twenty-five."

"I'll take your word for it," Lea said.

Large four foot by three foot framed posters on the wall depicted gaming scenes and frightening characters. A church pew was positioned under the posters. The room was bare except for a large, flat-screen on the wall directly across from the girl in the chair. No magazines on the stand next to the pew. The girl tapped on her headphone. "I'm sorry." She stood. "I'm Naomi Kendricks. What can I do for you?"

Ronnie flashed her identification. "I'm Officer Ronnie Ramsey. We're investigating the attack on two of your gamers last night. This is Lea Curtis, Hayden's daughter and Mary Johnson's nephew, Joe Wade."

"We're so sorry about what happened," Naomi said. "Our team is going over all of the game activity for the last few days. My dad's on the phone, and as soon as he's done, I'll take you back."

Lea pointed to the chair. "Is this a split keyboard in the arm rests?"

"Yep." Naomi shuffled the mouse and brought up a blank page on the screen on the wall. "Have a seat."

"I don't want to mess up anything."

"You won't."

Lea gingerly sat in the plush gaming chair. The thick leather seemed to suck her into a cloud. "Already, I can tell that I need new furniture for my home office."

"It's just like a regular typing keyboard—only half of the board is built into the armrest on the right and the other half is built into the left armrest. That extended area on the right is for the mouse."

Lea fingered the keys and focused on the large LED screen on the wall. She began typing her name, messing up a few times. The words appeared on the screen on the wall in large letters. "This is too weird."

"You get used to it in a few hours. It really reduces stress on your shoulders and hands. The phone light's out. I'll tell my father you're here."

Lea raised her eyebrows at Ronnie. "As much as I type, I could get used to this and that big screen. But, I'd have to do a lot of typing to afford it." Lea heard footsteps in the hall and hopped out of the chair.

A tall man with bushy brown hair entered the reception area. "I apologize. The call took longer than I thought. I'm Jon Mathers."

Ronnie introduced the group.

"I can't tell you how sorry I am. We've done this for years and never had a problem like this before."

"Maybe you can tell us about your contest, and we can figure out what went wrong," Ronnie said.

"I'll show you our shop," he replied. "Follow me."

"My wife, Shelly's office." He pointed to a room on the right. "She and Naomi do the accounting." A woman with short, black hair sat behind a desk talking into a headset, thumbing through data on a large computer screen on the wall.

They entered a room about forty feet long and thirty feet wide. Long tables held multiple hard drives with LED screens on the walls behind the tables. Six workers were positioned in front of computer consoles, flashing through gaming screens.

Joe pointed to the computer towers in the back of the room. "Cisco routers. You have your own internet hub?"

"We piggyback off a business for a high-level security program."

"Pricey gaming equipment," Joe observed.

"A few of the larger gaming hardware designers loan us new computers they've just built. We run them a while, reporting any deficiencies. Once the computers go on the market, we get to keep the loaners for free ads on our site."

Lea nudged Joe. "You're drooling."

"Our tech team here is looking for any emails or postings the last few days that may stand out as menacing. So far, we haven't found any. Let's go into the conference room and talk. It's quieter there."

Jon escorted them into a room with a round conference table and bookcases along the wall crammed with encryption books. "Please have a seat. I'll get us some coffee."

Lea took a seat across from Ronnie and Joe. She wanted to watch their facial reactions to the answers the gamemasters gave. She leaned toward Ronnie and whispered, "I thought this would be like a kindergarten classroom, with people on roller skates and bearded guys playing ball."

"It's handled more responsibly than I thought it would be," Ronnie whispered back.

Joe glanced around the room. "I thought everyone would be dressed in Zombie outfits."

The woman from the accounting office entered. "Good afternoon. I'm Shelly Mathers. Naomi's getting us some refreshments." The woman eased down in a chair across from Lea. "I can't tell you enough how sorry I am. Hayden and Mary are such wonderful people. We'd go out for lunch together whenever we could. When I got done here, I thought I'd scoot over to the hospital and check on them. How are they doing?"

Ronnie pulled her iPad out of her bag and set it in front of her. "Hayden's much improved and may go home in the next few days. Mary's stable, but still unconscious."

Jon and Naomi entered and Naomi set a platter of cookies and muffins in the center of the table. Jon set two coffee carafes on the table. Naomi poured the coffee into ceramic cups.

"Thanks, Naomi. Please hold my calls. I'll call you if I need anything."

Lea slowly unwrapped a poppy-seed muffin and let Ronnie do the talking. So far, these people had been nothing but polite. Whatever happened to her mother and Mary Johnson didn't begin in this building.

Ronnie took a sip of coffee. "Mr. Mathers, can you tell me a little about your gaming company?"

"Jon. Please, call me Jon. Our son, Dylan died seven years ago from leukemia. He was seventeen. That last awful year, gaming kept him going. I didn't like it at first, but I saw how it provided an escape for him.

"He wrote a program for an online game and wanted to use the money for cancer research. A local computer store got experts in a large MMO gaming group to donate their time to write the codes and got the game published. It went big really fast. All the money from the game was donated to child-hood leukemia research."

"So, this was the game the contestants were play-ing last night?" Ronnie questioned.

"Yes. Our software engineers design one MMORPG game a year. Gamers get sponsors just like marathon runners do. A pack of gamers, we organize them into guilds, participate in the game, and the highest scoring gamers compete in a final guild game for prize money. One hundred percent of the money raised by the competing gamers goes to childhood leukemia research. Most of our equip-ment is donated and those people in the next room are donating their time. All of the prize money is earned from royalties we get for online game designs we produce."

Shelly spoke up. "The current contest that Mary and Hayden participate in is only done once a year. We have other short-term games, but in this game, the four teams in the park last night won enough scoring points to play in the final leg of the game. Money from the online bets placed on the four teams all goes to our annual fund raising. There are only two more guild hunts, just two weeks left in the game."

"Wow," Lea said. "I can't believe my mother got this far, competing with so many skilled young people. She used to call me at least twice a day to help her with her Facebook page or her emails."

"Age isn't always a factor in these games," Shelly pointed out. "Older gamers use cleverly devised tactics to circumvent potential dangers to their characters. Also, the gaming computers have a lot to do with winning points. Younger gamers don't have the money for expensive setups and charge into situations in the games, where someone like Hayden would look before she leaps. Your mother and Mary Johnson are very skilled players."

Joe poured coffee into his mug. "I have to admit, I was jealous when she called me and said that she had the Falcon Northwest Fragbox. I game on the west coast, but don't have near the setup she has. I asked her to remember me in her will."

Lea finished her muffin and crumpled her paper. *So this is undercover. Build the lies. I didn't realize he was so skilled at it. I wonder if he ever lied to me that artfully.*

"This guild you run," Ronnie asked, "how many players total?"

Jon broke a cookie in half. "We started this event with 700 players. They compete in levels until they are whittled down to pairs in four teams. They're all local in the region."

"Can I get a list of the current team members with their home addresses?"

"Of course," Shelly stood. "I'll get Naomi to run you a copy."

The game seemed simple enough, but nothing here pointed to why her mother was attacked. What was she doing in the park? "If they're playing online, what was my mother doing in a park in a Star Trek costume in the middle of the night?" Lea asked.

Jon's cell phone buzzed. He checked the face and set it aside. "The teams play online games and score points. When they get enough points, a chest is downloaded to their game. Inside the chest is the general meeting place for the outdoor secret medallion quest. It's like a treasure hunt. We hide medallions in a specified area, and the teams are given the clues when they arrive at the site. Since all the gamers work, we schedule the quests for Friday evenings. In view of what happened last evening, I may change that to a Saturday, daytime quest next week."

"And that's the one the women were in?" Ronnie asked.

Shelly returned. "Naomi is running you a list."

"Yes," Jon said. "Team members, if they want, come dressed as their online personas. Your mother and Mary took their personas this week from key women in the Star Trek films. They can change from week to week."

"Did the others come in costumes?" Lea asked.

"The men, Cody and Brian did," Shelly answered.

"The quest begins at seven p.m. to allow for contestants to get home from work," Jon explained. "It usually ends around eleven p.m. When they arrive at the site, I give the signal, and they scatter out to find their medallion. When they find the chest, they text the codes on the medallion to me. The first text I receive, that team wins the big prize for that week. It's done to add fun to the game, and the children get to participate. The children help locate the medallions, but gaming rules prohibit the children from digging up the medallions or texting the codes."

Naomi entered the room and handed the list to Shelly.

"All the names of the current team members and their information is here." She passed the list to Ronnie. "I just ask that you keep that under lock and key. It's their names, addresses, and work addresses. We don't let that information out. Gamers from other guilds can harass the contestants."

"Got it." Ronnie set the paper aside.

"So, who was first to text you this past Friday?" Ronnie asked.

"Mary Johnson texted the correct codes."

"Who was next?" Joe asked.

Joe opened a folder in front of him. "Uh, Sam Preston. He has a twelve-year-old son who participates in outdoor quests. Because of the prize money, gaming rules prohibit the children from playing the online quests. Children are allowed on the outdoor quest but aren't allowed to dig the medallions, or retrieve other clues. Sam's teamed up with Lynn Foster."

"You have a copy of the guild members in the quest," Shelly said. "We sent an email earlier urging the players to cooperate fully with the police investigation."

"So, who's in first place?" Ronnie asked.

"Actually, Mary Johnson and Hayden," Shelly said. "They've been running ahead during the whole game."

"It's that computer of hers," Joe said.

"And her skill as a gamer," Jon added. "You can have the best setup in the world, and lose because you can't manage the tactical warfare."

Joe nodded. "I learn something new from her every time we talk."

Lea shifted uncomfortably in her seat. She'd never seen Joe at work before. His uncanny ability to lie unnerved her. The attack was starting to make sense to Lea. Her mother was in first place. "Hayden and Mary are out now because of their injuries," Lea said. "Who's in second?"

"Sam Preston and Lynn Foster have been running behind them all along. Cody Ingham and Brian VanDeer are third, and the Gleason's are last. They were sanctioned last week for farming."

"Farming?" Lea asked.

"Yes. We traced a bot program to her computer. She was harvesting weapons' caches, preventing other players from accessing weapons. There are certain behaviors we pounce on."

Joe rubbed his chin. "So, are Hayden and Mary completely out of the games now? Can people stand in for a player if the player can't continue, or is away on a business trip or something?"

"We have a provision that players can designate on their agreement form they sign with us a replacement, but the prize money only goes to the original player."

"Depending on how the teams register, the money is split equally between them," Shelly said. "All the teams have equal splits, except that Sam and Lynn are registered separately for the money, but play together as a team."

"Could Lea and I take Hayden's and Mary's place this week?"

Lea's stomach fluttered. What was Joe doing? She had no clue how to play these games. That huge machine in Mary's office scared her.

"Mary can't speak for herself yet, but since Hayden's registered as an equal half of the team with equal distribution of the prize money, she could designate you two to take their places. Our policies provide that half of a team, registered as a whole team, can make unilateral decisions for the other team member if one of them can't make decisions. Neither of you work in the online gaming industry, do you?"

"I definitely don't," Lea said.

"Not me," Joe said.

"Get Hayden to sign the form and get it to me tomorrow. I'll send out a request to the teams to allow for substitutes. We did this once before when a team member had a death in the family and missed a game. Shelly will give you the form for Hayden to sign."

Ronnie studied the list for a minute. She looked at Jon. "You know these people well? Any of them with a history of violence? Anyone in particular that we should be checking into their past lives?"

He shrugged. "Brian VanDeer was charged with an assault about ten years ago. He's since started going to church and made a lot of changes in his life. He's argued over points a few times. All the players get testy at the end of the game. He and his partner, Cody Ingham are near the bottom. Even if Hayden was eliminated, they'd still not win the top prize."

"We recently sold a game design," Shelly said. "We added a fifty thousand dollar second prize and a twenty-five thousand dollar third prize."

Joe pursed his lips. "That's motive if they're the bottom two."

"Or," Ronnie said, "a random mugger in the park who had no idea about the game in process. They spied two women in the park late at night in outlandish costumes and thought that they were easy prey."

"Possibly," Joe said. "What about previous gamers who have lost before? Would they disrupt the games for revenge?"

"I don't think so," Jon replied. "They could, but most of these gamers move on to other guilds in other games. This is a charity benefit, and it'd be rare that a misfit would camp around these games."

Ronnie stood. "Jon, Shelly, thank you for your time. We'll continue to look into this attack. You have another quest scheduled the end of next week. Can you find a more controlled environment for the quest until I catch the attacker?"

Jon nodded. "We'll run it at Morrow Running Park earlier in the day. I can't tell you how much I appreciate you looking into this."

Shelly passed a paper to Joe. "These are the code keys to enter the game Mary and Hayden use."

Ronnie shoved her iPad into her bag. "Thank you for your cooperation. The crime scene was disturbed because of the heavy rain and hail. We'll interview the players and get back to you."

Chuck entered the conference room after the detective left. "They know anything new?"

Jon shook his head. "They're just laying out their investigation."

"We've had problems before, but nothing ever like this. We've gone through all the postings from last week, and there's nothing out of the ordinary."

Jon studied his son-in-law. His intelligence tests were at a genius level. He was blessed to have this man in his family. No one would replace Dylan. Naomi's husband just added to God's glory in their lives. "We'll let the detective do her job. Let's focus on the games. We only have two weeks to go. Tell the volunteers that I appreciate them coming in."

"You got it." Chuck stood and patted Jon's shoulder on his way out.

Jon swiveled in his chair and faced the window. He picked up a picture from the bookcase under the window. He studied Dylan's face. He wiped a speck of dust off a corner of the picture. Dylan was healthier and stronger in this picture. He'd just scored a soccer goal.

If he'd lived, he'd be proud of the way the games developed and how many kids were helped because of the games. They'd pray their way past these troubles and keep the games going.

"I miss you, son."

Lea climbed up into Joe's pickup and they headed back to the police station to drop off Ronnie.

"Joe, I'd like to get you assigned to us for a few weeks, undercover. That way you'd get paid. I'll get a rental agency decal for your truck and license plates so that no one connects you with Kansas City. Tomorrow, let's interview the other six team players."

"Sounds like a plan."

Lea turned toward Joe. "Joe, I have no clue how to play these games. There's a lot at stake here, and I hate to mess up all Mom's hard work."

"We'll get you help. You'll be a pro in no time. Relax. Game on."

Lea leaned back in her seat. *Game on for him. So much for keeping my distance.*

Her mother had gone to great lengths to hide this activity from her. Why? She wouldn't have cared about her playing in the games.

Sure, if she showed up at her house one day sporting her new tattoos and riding a motorcycle—they'd have to talk. But Dylan's Games was a family-oriented business, and her mother seemed to fit right in. The couple who ran the business were committed to their son's legacy and committed to God. Her mother had earned the respect of other top gamers.

The key to all of this had to be Mary Johnson. Joe seemed to think it was that monster machine that Mary owned that won them the top spot. But why would a woman Mary's age be so obsessed with online gaming? Why not gardening or cruise shipping? Why had she gotten her mother into these games? Why was she in the game was a better question.

5

0101

Joe Wade pulled into the parking lot of Grayden Industry's warehouse where he and Ronnie were going to interview the first of the guild members. He shut off the engine and watched the ballet of forklifts pirouetting around each other, unloading a semitrailer.

His thoughts turned to Lea, as they so often did. He hadn't expected to be thrown together with her his first night home. He and Mike had just finished watching a Kansas City Royals game and were bantering over comments made on the post-game show when Ronnie called. Hayden Curtis was the closest thing he had to a mother after his own parents died in a car wreck years ago. Ronnie had met Lea in college and they had all bonded. Lea was Ronnie's maid-of-honor. Hayden and Lea's father had become like family. Both Ronnie and Joe were there for Hayden after Lou died two years ago.

He'd do anything for Hayden. It was her gentle manner that nudged him back to his faith in God.

He felt bad about the way he'd left things last winter with Lea. He'd come back to work things out, and he knew that it would take time to win her trust again.

First, he'd solve the attack. It had to be about the other woman. He'd been to enough crime scenes to know something wasn't right, an empty shell of a house. Hayden didn't have friends who would cause her to cross paths with someone who would beat her like he did. It had to be about Mary Johnson.

Then, he'd focus all his attention on Lea.

Ronnie pulled into the parking space next to Joe. Time to get to work.

Joe chirped the lock on his pickup and they stood on the sidewalk, eyeing the warehouse as another semi backed in. Forklifts danced around the loading dock, unloading pallets from the new trailer.

"Nice suit," he commented on her gray blazer, cream blouse, and gray pants. Her long, brown, frizzed hair was pulled back. Her brown eyebrows framed a serious face with a strong chin.

"Nice old slacks. You look like a homeless person."

"I'm on vacation. Besides, I'm undercover."

"Some undercover cops wear business suits."

He ignored her. "So, tell me about our first customer?"

Ronnie checked her clipboard. "Brian VanDeer. I started with him because he's been the most aggressive at the quest sites. He also has priors for assaults. One at a bar nine years ago and another assault charge filed by a neighbor. Just an argument; no physical contact. A street cam picked him up not far from where the women were found. His statement to the police that night places him two hundred feet from where the camera shows that he was."

Ronnie nodded. "That's him climbing down from that forklift." Ronnie called out over the noise of the equipment, "Brian VanDeer?"

The man stopped and turned toward Ronnie. "That's me. What can I do for you?"

"I'm Detective Ronnie Ramsey. This is Joe Wade, Mary Johnson's nephew. Is there someplace we can talk?"

Brian eyed the couple. He removed his cap, finger combed his hair, and replaced his cap. "Sure, follow me."

He led them into a small office with no door and pulled chairs up around a desk piled with folders and inventory sheets. He eased his large frame down in the chair behind the desk.

"I'm awful sorry those ladies got hurt. I hope you catch who did it. Last time I checked with Jon Mathers, he said Mary Johnson was still unconscious."

"My aunt's stable, but still in ICU," Joe said.

"What do you want to know?"

Joe knew Ronnie wouldn't play all her cards. She'd let the guy ramble on for a while to get a feel for his personality.

"Your game name is Bill Gates?"

He grinned. "We all adopt characters. I'm Bill Gates and my partner, Cody Ingham's Steve Jobs."

"Pretty creative," Ronnie said.

Joe forced himself to not laugh. Bill Gates, this guy wasn't. Thirty-five years old, he weighed at least two hundred fifty. Long curly black hair framed a round face with a scruffy short beard.

"You've played with this guild for nearly six years?"

"Me and Cody were the first to sign up. I was really messed up a few years back and started going to church. That's when I met the Mathers and heard about the game. Being with the guild kinda helps me keep myself in line."

"Is the pressure pretty intense as you get closer to the end of a game?"

"Yeah. You gotta make the points to stay in the game for the quests. It's real stressful. Working with a partner helps."

"You ever get aggressive at the quests?"

Brian's shoulders tensed up, and he was quiet for a minute. "Once, I was running to a spot where I thought the medallion was, and me and Sam Preston collided. It was more of an accident. I didn't mean to push him. I apologized."

Ronnie nodded. "I can understand how that would happen. What are you going to do with the money when you win? One hundred fifty thousand's a lot of money."

"I have to split it with Cody. My mom's eyes aren't real good, and her insurance doesn't cover much. That cataract operation will help her see better. She can't see all her TV shows real good."

Ronnie slipped her tablet in her bag. "That's a good plan. You've been on a number of these quests, did you see anything out of the ordinary that night? Anything make you wonder, what's going on there?"

Brian shrugged. "I been going over it in my mind. Our medallion drops were pretty close together. It rained earlier, so I didn't hear people crunching leaves under their feet. With the park lighting, I saw forms of other contestants through the trees. I didn't hear anything, and no one screamed. The people that I saw, I knew."

"Did you see Hayden or Mary?"

He shook his head. "As I was digging for our medallion, it started raining hard. I thought I saw someone with a flashlight up to our left. Sometimes gamers will try to draw you away from a dig to distract you to give the other team member more time to find their medallion. I told Cody that I'd keep digging. He went down the hill to check out the light. That's when he found the women."

"You didn't see anyone running away?"

Brian shook his head. "No one. The tornado sirens went off as I found our medallion. I texted the codes and headed back to the parking lot."

"Thank you for talking with us. Here's my card. If you think of anything at all, even if it seems insignificant, please call me."

Brian took the card, stood, and faced Joe. "I'm really sorry about your aunt. We're all taking up a collection to help with her medical bills."

"I appreciate that. Thanks."

Joe walked with Ronnie back to their vehicles. "You were pretty gentle with him."

Ronnie leaned against her car. "If I pressed him about his exact whereabouts the night of the attack, he'd just lie about it. I want an excuse to do a follow up interview at his home. I like to view a suspect at work and at home. Gives me a more complete picture of the person."

"That's a good idea. In Kansas City, we have so many cases piled up, we interview people where we can." Joe spotted Brian climbing back up into his forklift. He'd keep an eye on this man. "He was pretty up front with us about the assault charges years ago and his anger management."

"Yes," Ronnie looked perplexed. "Either he's being truthful, or he's trying to throw us off. Being honest, making us think he's got nothing more to hide."

Joe chirped his truck lock. "So, who's next?"

"Cody Ingham works near the mall. Why don't you drive to O'Leary's Restaurant, and I'll meet you there. We can take one car, then come back for lunch."

Fifteen minutes later, Joe parked in front of Engel's Foods. "They make food in there?" He pointed to the one-story, cinder block warehouse. The windows in the front were boarded up. Weeds grew in a gravely parking lot.

"Organic health food. Protein bars, stuff like that."

"This the man that found the women?"

Ronnie nodded. "Shelly Mathers says he's a little too friendly with the women, especially older women. Jason dug this up. Twelve years ago, Cody previously lived in St. Louis. Had two restraining orders against him for harassment."

"Interesting."

"All we have here are a few speeding tickets, all paid up."

Joe opened his truck door. "Let's see how he takes to you."

Joe entered the warehouse and held the door for Ronnie. No one was in the reception area, which was nothing more than a six by eight walled in area with two lawn chairs. They walked around a half wall into the work area.

To their left, a kitchen stretched out along one wall. Two stoves, a large double sink, two refrigerators and cooking pots and pans crammed into open shelving units. An assembly line of long tables held large kettles. Bare light bulbs at the end of cords hung down from the high ceiling. Three workers, wearing gloves and hats almost covering their hair, dipped spoons of something into bags, passing them down the line to a worker who sealed the bags by hand.

"Can I help you?" A tall, older man approached Joe and Ronnie. His long black hair was tied back in a ponytail. He wore a faded blue tee shirt, faded jeans, and sneakers. His dirty-white apron was splotched with old food stains.

"I'm Detective Ronnie Ramsey. I'd like to speak with Cody Ingham."

"I'm Cody. This about the attack Friday night?"

"Yes. This is Joe Wade, Mary Johnson's nephew. I'd like to ask you a few questions about the night Ms. Johnson was attacked."

"Sure. Man, I'm sorry about what happened to your aunt. She's a really great lady. How is she?"

"Stable," Joe said.

"What is it you make here?" Ronnie asked.

He hooked his thumbs under the straps of the dirty apron, and his chest swelled with pride. "Let me show you." He led them to the work tables.

"These big kettles have trail mix we made up this morning. We're packaging it. I don't have any fancy equipment, but it's all done real clean. Here's some bags you two can have."

He handed Ronnie and Joe sealed bags of Healthy Trail Mix. As he was speaking, Joe noticed a cockroach scurry out from under the table and dart into a crack in the concrete floor. One thing he didn't see was any health inspection notices.

"Thanks." Ronnie said.

"Tomorrow, we'll start on snack bars and Friday is sweet potato chip day."

"Where do you market these?" Ronnie asked.

"All around the area. Mostly, small restaurants and convenience service stations."

"I'll grab a chair, and we can talk out front." He turned to his workers. "Glenn, finish up the last of this trail mix, and box them for delivery."

"Sure thing, boss," a burly man replied.

Ronnie and Joe took their seats in the lawn chairs while Cody straddled a chair. Joe watched another cockroach crawl out from between a crack in the concrete floor, its feelers feeling along the crack. It darted back into the hole. He made a mental note to take two baths when he got home.

Ronnie began, "I'm just talking to all the game players to figure out what happened that night— where everyone was, so I can eliminate them and concentrate on possible vandals in the woods in the park."

"Sure, it makes sense." He tugged at the collar in the front of his tee shirt. "Me and Brian were getting close to our medallion dig. The gamemasters try to keep the digs far apart, but since it was night, they wanted to keep all the digs near street lights in the park. Brian started digging, and I thought I saw something to my left down the hill. Someone with a flashlight was watching us. Sometimes, other gamers try to stop you from digging. It gives their partner more time to find their medallion. I told Brian to keep digging, and I'd check it out. It started raining real hard. That's when I found the two women passed out on the ground. I didn't know what happened."

"You called nine-one-one at eleven-fifteen?"

"I called the GMs first and then nine-one-one. We were always told that if anything happens at a dig site, call the gamemaster right away. Everybody was having trouble finding their clues. We're usually done before eleven."

"Did you see anyone at all as you approached your dig site or where you found the women? Hear anything at all?"

Cody shook his head. "Couldn't hear nothing because of the thunder. When I found Mary Johnson, I turned her over cause her face was in the mud. I didn't touch Hayden. I tried to talk to them, but they didn't answer."

"You did all the right things. I understand you've played games with this guild for six years?"

"Yeah. They're a nice group of people. Real smart. Competitive, but nice."

"Your game name is Steve Jobs?"

He smiled sheepishly. "Yeah. We all took characters names. Kinda makes it more interesting. After playing together for so long, we already know everybody's real names."

Joe listened quietly as Ronnie built a profile of the man. He definitely isn't a Steve Jobs' type. Probably late forties, early fifties. A large man, not obese, but muscular, who obviously worked out. Slowly going bald. He wore red-rimmed glasses and persistently tugged at his tee shirt.

Joe didn't like the way the man's eyes rolled over his sister.

Ronnie glanced at her iPad and up at Cody. "What are your plans for the prize money if you win?"

"I gotta split it with Brian, but my share, I'm going to expand my operations here and get more modern equipment."

Joe studied the old, torn menu hanging on the wall, which listed food the company produced. *Maybe invest in some modern cleaning equipment. Plug up the holes in the concrete. Fumigate.*

"I appreciate you taking the time to talk with us." Ronnie stood and handed him her card. "If you think of anything at all, please call me. Sometimes after an attack like that, something comes to you later."

He took the card. "Sure. Glad to help."

Cody watched the pair drive off. He didn't like the police snooping around. He'd been through this before in St. Louis. That stupid girl he'd met online. She claimed he was stalking her, then got her girl-friend to lie and say he was stalking her, too. Yeah, he sat outside her apartment house a couple of times, but he'd never been to the door.

The way cops work, they keep digging and digging until they found something, and if they couldn't find anything, they'd plant evidence. That's why he left St. Louis. The cops there were bigger crooks than the guys in jail.

He'd stayed away from trouble here. Started his business and got into the games. He did like Mary. She was older, but looked young. Boy, was she smart with the games. She knew more about gaming than anyone he'd ever met. He asked her out a couple of times, but she always refused. Once, he and Brian saw her in Chili's with Hayden. She invited them to sit with her.

He waited in the mall parking lot and followed her home from the restaurant. Every now and then, he'd take the long way home from work just to drive by her house. See if she was home.

He wondered how deep the cops would dig into the investigation. Would they hack into the gamers' home computers? When he got home tonight, first thing he'd do is clean out all the pictures of the women in his photo folder.

Joe drove to O'Leary's Restaurant. They pitched their bags of trail mix in the trash can in the parking lot. Inside the restaurant, they scooted into a booth.

Ronnie ordered iced tea and shepherd's pie. Joe ordered a roast beef sandwich and a soda.

"So, what do you think?" Joe asked.

"We're just starting. I'm trying to not draw any hard and fast conclusions. I can make a case for Brian. He has a violent streak. He says he wants to help his mother. I'd have to see him interact with his mother to decide if that's valid. I can also make a case for Cody. Maybe he made an advance on one of the women, and she stood her ground against him. Of the two, he's physical enough to have attacked the women. Two gamers down and four to go."

"When did my big sister get so smart?" Joe said. "It did seem kinda rehearsed to me. They gave almost identical explanations to your questions."

"I noticed that. We'll wait until we interview all the gamers to decide what's rehearsed and what isn't."

Ronnie's cell phone chirped. She answered the call and clicked off. "As of now, you are officially attached to our precinct as an undercover investigator. If a homicide case comes up, I'll be pulled away from this."

"Thanks," Joe said.

"After lunch, let's squeeze in Sam Preston. He's off today because he worked last Sunday. Since you're going to be around for a few weeks, we should squeeze a trip in to visit Uncle Jim."

"Good idea. I got an email a few days ago. He's got seven new horses."

"Thirty years as a U. S. Marshall, he deserves his retirement."

The server delivered their meals. Joe spread mustard on his sandwich. "I agree."

Ronnie stirred a packet of sugar in her iced tea. "So, how's it going with Lea?"

Joe blinked his eyes and raised his eyebrows. "Going? Meaning?"

"You two split up. You never dated anyone else, and she's not looking."

"This an interrogation?" He took a healthy bite of his sandwich.

"I just want the best for you and my best friend."

Joe swallowed. "If you must know, I got spooked— the whole commitment thing. I messed up. Even if we don't get together again, she deserves an explanation from me. Workout some kind of amiable friendship."

"Amiable? You set your sights too low."

"When I came home last winter, I'd worked three back-to-back grisly murders. I shouldn't have tried to talk to her when I was at my lowest point. She deserves my best, not my worst. I just... just realized that I didn't know how to be a cop and not bring my job home with me."

"It's a learned process, Joe. I constantly have to work on that. Some cops make a firm decision to never bring work home in their heads. It's always there. That's not realistic. If something's really got me down about a case, Mike and I talk it out. I don't mention names or any sensitive details about the case, just how I'm feeling. The tension evaporates, and we go on with our lives. You just have to work at it."

"It's just that I want the best for Lea. Maybe me being a cop will start to drag her down later in life. Maybe she'd be better off with some guy who doesn't work with a gun all day."

"Some boring computer geek, married to his hard drive? A guy with no goals? You've got drive and ambition. You two are perfect for each other."

He shrugged. "I just want to find the guy or guys who did this to Hayden. Keep it professional for now. Then we'll see about the rest." He pointed his fork at her. "Don't you go getting everything out of control."

"Me? I'm the model of moderation," she smiled.

Joe waited while his sister made a quick trip to the ladies' room. They had always been honest with each other. Because of their parent's untimely death, they'd forged a deep bond between them few other brothers and sisters shared.

They could talk about anything, occasionally stepping on each other's toes, knowing when to back off. Their Uncle Jim, who owned a ranch outside of Omaha stepped in to help when he could. As a U. S. Marshall he spent a lot of time on the road. It was Ronnie's friendship with Lea that brought a sense of family and stability in their lives. Hayden took the orphans under her wing and provided the wise nurturing only a mother could give. God had been good to them.

Ronnie was right about Lea. He couldn't imagine her with anyone else. When he was with her, the rest of the world wasn't even there. He constantly tried to analyze their relationship. That was his problem. He needed to admit to himself that he loved her, and then admit that to her.

6

Brian VanDeer stopped in the diner near his house on the way home from work. He ordered grilled chicken, a baked potato, and carrots for his mother. While he waited for the order, he called next door and ordered a large pizza. Cody was coming over, and they were going to work on their game points together.

He went over in his mind what he had told the detective this morning. Yeah, he had a violent history, but since he'd been going to church, he'd worked real hard on staying in control. The anger started with his alcoholic father. All those beatings as a kid, not to mention the beatings his mother took. His father was hit by a car and died when Brian was in his last year of high school. Go figure—killed by a drunk driver. Served him right.

He watched out for his mother and helped her all he could. She got a good job working as a nurse and retired a few years ago. He noticed last year that she was forgetting things. He went over one day, and they had lunch together. She was making their sand-wiches and was having trouble placing the meat between the bread.

He took her in for tests. The doctor thought it was early Alzheimer's, which is nothing more than a generic term for dementia. Brian thought it was because of all the beatings she took from her husband to protect him. His dad caused this dementia, but he wasn't going to win. Brian moved in with his mother to watch over her. That's why he needed to win this contest. Get her eyes fixed so she could enjoy her television programs. When she'd go days without speaking, he'd sit and watch an *I Love Lucy* video with her. Then he'd get her to talk about Lucy and Desi. She'd go on for hours. She'd be all right. He'd see to it.

He paid for the meal, went next door, and picked up the pizza. When he got home, it was getting dark. There were no lights on in the house. His mother was dozing in front of the television, which hadn't been turned on.

He turned on the lamp and picked up the remote. He thumbed through to the old movie channel. Bing Crosby and Bob Hope. That would cheer her up.

"Hey Mom." He kissed her forehead.

She sat up straight. "Hi, honey. You're home early."

"I got you some dinner." He pulled the TV tray over and set the plate of food down. He'd heated it in the microwave and served her on a plate. He wanted to keep things as normal for her as he could.

"I'm not hungry. I just ate a few minutes ago."

A note on the kitchen table from the lady that delivered Mom's lunch from Meals-on-Wheels said that she sat with his mother to be sure she ate. She had eaten nearly all her meal. Brian knew that it wouldn't be much longer before he wouldn't be able to leave her alone during the day. He'd asked Jon Mathers about learning online game design, and he put him in touch with a guy that would train him—but it was pricey. If he won this competition, he could get his mother's eyes fixed and have enough for the training. Once he started selling games, he could stay at home with Mom.

He put a load of laundry in the washing machine. A nurse his mother was friends with for many years came over four times a week to visit her and gave her a bath. He felt guilty not paying her, but she refused any money.

He set his mother's hot tea on her stand. "Mom, you have to eat."

"I'm watching Bing Crosby. I'm waiting for him to sing."

"You can eat and watch the show at the same time." He sat with her a few minutes until she started eating. Once her mind tracked into an activity, she usually stayed with it. The front doorbell chimed. He glanced at his watch. It'd be Cody.

"Who's that?"

"My friend, Cody. We're going to work together tonight. I'll be in the den if you need me."

Brian let Cody in and they set up in the den with pizza and sodas. "So, where are we in the standings this week?" Brian asked.

Cody shook his head. "I can't believe Hayden and Mary got their medallion codes off before they were clobbered. They're in first. Lynn and Sam are in second place, we're in third, with the Gleasons bringing up the rear. I don't want to end up at the bottom next week."

Brian didn't always like Cody's attitude, especially about Hayden and Mary. Sometimes he was sarcastic about them and other times he was respectful. Sometimes he flirted with the women. He thought Cody was following Mary. Once he slipped and mentioned driving by her house once. He never could read Cody right.

The attack on the women started before he sent Cody to check out who was following them. Patty usually sent Carl to distract other players. Where Cody flirted with women, he didn't think he'd ever hurt Hayden or Mary.

He wondered what the other players were telling the police about that night. What the other players saw. He and Cody were having trouble finding the last medallion. Cody sent him over to distract Sam and Lynn. "Just flash a light around. Make them think someone was watching them." He watched them digging and tossed a few rocks into the brush to their far right. They stopped and went check out the noise. He flashed his light beam around behind some boulders, and got them off the trail.

Then he made it back to their own dig site to help Cody when they spotted the lights to the left of their dig site. He thought it was the Gleason kids trying to distract them, but Cody said he'd go and check. That's when Cody found the women.

Brian liked Mary—she was brilliant with the games. She knew how to use the clock and not rush the game. When the contest was over, he wanted to sit with her and pick her brain about game strategies that would enhance games he designed. He hoped she pulled through okay.

Cody studied the computer screen. "A cop came over and interviewed me today. Had Mary's nephew with her. I didn't know she had any family."

"Yeah. They talked to me, too."

"You think Mary's nephew will take over her place in the games? If a player can't continue this close to the end, they're allowed to bring in someone to finish the game. If he doesn't take their place, that narrows it down to three teams. "

"I don't know. We've got one more quest and then the final one. That's always the toughest."

"I wonder if her nephew's any good. You remember when we first started? Those two guys at the bottom the whole four weeks won first place."

"We're going to have to work hard to do that. Our computer's so old. If we win and want to stay in these games, we'll have to get a faster computer."

"Dream on, Dude."

Brian shook his head. "I got no idea about if Mary's nephew knows how to play the games. We'll have to wait and see. What's the focus of this next game?"

"From what I can see, it's all about the terrain. The last game quest had rogue bands of attackers, but this one has hidden terrain traps. Some traps send you back to the fray, and you have to battle your way out before you can follow your route."

"I see what you mean. I'm better at the battles than terrain, but if we're going to win this quest, we better get wise."

If they won this quest, the game and the outdoor quest, they'd be ahead. Even if they didn't win the one hundred fifty thousand, they'd be in line for the fifty thousand. It'd still be enough to help his mother and give him a boost for online game design. He had to win, no matter what.

7

0111

Joe pulled up across from Sam Preston's duplex. He wasn't home earlier, so they had to come back. "Someone's home. Lights are on. What do we know about him?"

"What I learned from the gamemasters, he's thirty-four. A pharmacist. Works for Randall Drugs. His wife died six years ago from cancer. Has a son, Kevin, twelve."

"His wife was young. That's sad."

"Twenty-seven."

Joe rang the doorbell of the duplex. A young boy with short, curly black hair opened the door. "Hi."

"May we speak with your father?"

"Yeah. He's on the phone."

A tall man with short cropped hair came up behind the boy. He clicked off his cell phone. "May I help you?"

"I'm Detective Ronnie Ramsey. This is Mary Johnson's nephew, Joe Wade. We'd like to ask you some questions about the attack the other night."

"Sure. Come right in. The GMs said you'd be around."

Sam led them to a small living room. The room was neat. A text book and papers were strewn across a coffee table. A long table on one wall held a gaming computer.

Joe studied the setup. "Digital Storm system."

Sam stood next to him. "It's an earlier version. Kevin and I splurged this past Christmas and updated our game mouse. Be nice to win this game and upgrade the whole system. These days, gaming's all about speed."

Joe shook his head. "Boy, that's a nice system."

Lea and Joe took a seat on the couch.

Joe picked up a paper. "Quadratic equations?" He glanced up at Kevin. "How old are you? You've got to be old enough to drive to solve these problems. You got a driver's license?"

Kevin grinned. "I'm twelve."

Sam sat in a chair across from them. "He was advanced to seventh grade because his math and science skills are so good."

Joe shook his head and handed the boy the paper. "Fellow, you're way ahead of me."

"Kevin, why don't you make us some coffee?"

"Sure, Dad."

Sam picked up the papers and book and laid them out on the kitchen table. He returned to his chair. "I'm real sorry about the women. Mary's really smart. She wrote a recommendation that got my son in a science clinic for a month last summer in St. Louis. How's she doing?"

"She's still unconscious, but stable."

"I wish her the best. She and Hayden are wonderful. I've never seen women their age so knowledgeable about gaming. They're amazing."

"Thanks." Joe said. He could hear the coffee gurgling through the pot in the kitchen. For two males living together, the house was clean and neat.

Ronnie glanced at her iPad. "We just have a few questions. Maybe someone heard or saw something that would help."

"Sure. Anything I can do."

"From what Jon Mathers said, your area was the opposite end of where the women were found."

"Yes. We were the farthest away. I'm teamed up with Lynn Foster. I didn't know anything was happening. Lynn and I just found our medallion half and texted in the code when I saw police cars converging on the park. Tornado sirens went off. It was raining pretty hard, and we headed back to my car in the parking lot to get out of the rain. I called the GM and Shelly to report police cars in the area. We've always been trained to report any unusual activity during an outdoor quest."

"Did you see anyone in the area you didn't recognize?"

Sam shook his head. "I knew who the people were around me. The gamemasters get permits from the park service and seal off the area we're all working in until the game is over. Kinda like they do for marathon runs. I suppose, since it's a public park, someone could get by the security, but they're pretty careful about that."

"You've played with this guild for a while?"

"Five years now. I got into it after Karen died. Something Kevin and I could do together. They have a great kids' setup. Do a lot of math and science clinics. Run short quests for the kids during the year. They write a lot of math into the GPS location drops. Kids have to solve equations to find the next clue.

"The games kinda helped me keep my sanity. Because of all the medical bills, I lost the house. I got this small place so I could put all the money I got into Kevin's education."

"You've set some really good goals for yourself and your son. Did you ever hear Hayden or Mary talk about anyone bothering them? Any scary emails?"

Kevin brought in two cups of coffee and set them on the coffee table in front of Joe and Ronnie. He returned with a cup for his father and a tray of cream, sugar, and cookies. "I just made these peanut butter cookies a little while ago."

Ronnie bit into a cookie and rolled her eyes. "They're really good."

"It's my mom's recipe," he said. He picked up a picture off an end table and handed it to Joe. "That's my mom."

A lump formed in Joe's throat. This young boy shouldn't know this much sorrow. He looked at the pretty woman laughing with the sun in her face. "She's gorgeous." He handed the frame to Ronnie.

"Everybody thinks she's beautiful," Kevin said.

"She is beautiful," Ronnie said. "You have her lovely eyes and curly, black hair."

Kevin smiled as he took the picture and returned it to the end table.

Sam nudged his son. "How about you work on that next problem by yourself, and I'll see how you do. Take some cookies with you for brain food."

Kevin grabbed three cookies and headed to the kitchen.

"He's amazing," Ronnie said in a low voice.

"That, he is," Sam said. "If it hadn't been for God's love and mercy, I don't know how I would have survived these past years. Uh, you asked me a question, and I forgot what it was."

"Mary ever mentioning any threats?"

"Oh, yes." He shook his head. "I just can't think of her mentioning that. We live pretty isolated lives during the week. That's why Jon has the social gatherings. He knows what nerds we can become if we don't get out."

"We'll keep digging. Something may turn up. My next question hits a little closer to home, but someone stands to gain a lot of money at the end of this game. Do you think any one of the team members would have done this?"

Sam seemed surprised by the question. He was quiet for a moment.

"Absolutely not. I've known some of these people for years. It was probably some mugger in the park that wasn't connected to the game at all."

"Well, we've taken up enough of your time." Ronnie slipped her purse strap over her shoulder and handed Sam a card. "Please call me if you think of anything you heard or saw that night, also if you remember her mentioning someone they were afraid of."

Sam stood and took the card. "Of course."

"Kevin, thanks for the coffee and cookies," Ronnie waved.

"I make good chocolate chips, too," he said, looking up from his problem.

Joe waved as they went out the door.

He and Ronnie climbed into the pickup.

"He's at the bottom of my suspect list."

"I agree," Joe said, starting the pickup.

"The Gleasons live eight blocks from here. You want to drop in on them?"

"Why not?" Joe started the engine and headed toward the Gleasons' home.

"I don't see that guy attacking the women. He's in the running for second prize." Ronnie said.

Joe put his blinker on to make a turn. "He's too devoted to his son to do anything to risk something happening."

"I agree."

"Who are the Gleasons?"

"Carl and Patty Gleason. Two kids, fifteen and seventeen. Joined Dylan's Games three months after Mary Johnson. They were on a quest to the left of Hayden and Mary."

Joe parked in front across from a split level home and parked. "Were the boys involved on the quest?"

"I don't remember Jon mentioning that. I was focused on the gamers themselves and didn't think to ask about the kids. Nice home, clean yard," Ronnie observed.

"Where are their standings in the game?"

"Sam and Lynn are below Hayden and Mary. The Gleasons are at the bottom."

"So, Brian and Cody are in third place. The bottom two teams could be the most aggressive."

"According to Shelly Mathers, Patty has been very aggressive online. She's been known to hack into other gamers' computers. Also, farming resources. I don't understand what she was talking about, but anyway, she's been sanctioned twice in these games. A third sanction, and they're out of the game. That's why the Gleasons are at the bottom. They're trying to make up for lost points."

Joe opened his truck door. "I smell motive."

"I'll take the lead, you backup," Ronnie said.

Joe rang the doorbell. A petite woman with short, blond hair answered. "Yes?"

Ronnie introduced themselves and gave her the reason for their visit.

"Please, come in."

She ushered them into a pristine living room. Ronnie noticed that the woman was perfectly trimmed. Her short, platinum blond hair, her make-up, right down to her peach short-sleeved blouse and tight shorts, with smoothly tanned legs presented a carefully manicured image.

The dark wood furniture accented the beige carpet. The carpet had been vacuumed and showed no footprints. The furnishings were modest. It was the dinner hour, but there were no dinner aromas from the kitchen. Ronnie figured that she probably fed her family health biscuits she got from Cody. Ronnie thought that with two teenagers in the house, the room should have looked more used.

"I'll get my husband. Make yourselves comfortable," she said curtly.

Joe bounced a few times on the stiff couch. He mouthed, "Like new. Never sat on before."

Ronnie put her finger over her lips to shush him.

"Good evening," Carl Gleason said, entering the room. He was a few inches shorter than Patty. Clean shaven with a friendly demeanor. He took a seat in a stuffed chair across from Ronnie and Joe. Patty sat in a chair next to him.

"I don't know what we can tell you," Patty blurted out in a high-strung voice.

It had always been Ronnie's belief that when a suspect took control of the interview from the get-go, something was amiss.

"The police already asked us about that night."

"We're just doing a follow up," Ronnie said. "Sometimes people remember things later. Do you remember hearing or seeing anything out of the ordinary that night?"

Carl opened his mouth, but Patty put her hand on his and said. "I have this."

She turned and faced Ronnie. "Nothing at all. It was a completely normal quest except for the rain and until I heard police cars screaming into our area. The cars were up on the road above where we were digging. I was quite annoyed because it was pouring down rain, and we needed to find the medallion to get our codes texted in."

It didn't concern you that one of your friends might be injured? Ronnie focused on Carl. "So you didn't hear anything?"

"I think I just answered that question," Patty said abruptly.

No touchy feely here. Maybe I should pass my iPad to Patty and let her finish the interview.

"How long have you two been playing online with Dylan's Games?"

"My family and I started last summer. This is our second quest," Patty replied.

Short, crisp answers. "Do your boys go on the digs with you?"

"My boys have nothing to do with this. And no, they aren't allowed on the digs."

"During the time you've had social gatherings, have either of you heard Mary Johnson mention any threats? Threatening emails?"

"No," Patty replied curtly.

Carl shrugged and shook his head. "I don't know them very well. We talk at the social gatherings. They both are really smart—"

"Detective Ramsey," Patty cut in, "the police aren't going to try to stop the games, are they? We only have two weeks left, and there's a lot at stake. This money I need for my boys education."

Or, to keep up your Botox injections. "I don't see any reason to stop the games as long as no one else gets hurt."

Ronnie wanted to get a look at the rest of the house, but would save that for another time. Ronnie rose. "Thank you for speaking with us."

Patty opened the front door. "Good night."

As Ronnie cleared the door, did she think it was slammed behind her?

Patty turned on her husband. "You need to learn to keep your mouth shut when the police interrogate you. Anything you say, you just sneeze, they'll take that as a sign of guilt."

"We got nothing to hide. You need to learn to be more polite."

Patty turned the light out in the living room and peered around the blinds. The cop's truck pulled away from the curb.

What were the others saying? She knew the gamers didn't like her much; she didn't care. She didn't like them either. But she hated it that she didn't know what they were saying about her.

That stupid gamemaster constantly picked on them because they were new in the area. She'd caught Cody and Brian farming a half dozen times, and reported it. Jon ignored her. Everybody was probably pointing fingers at them. The gamers probably told these cops that she had something to do with the women being hurt.

It irked her that they caught her in a lie about the boys. She got ahead of herself and said the boys weren't at the digs. She'd shrug it off as nerves. If the cops questioned her again, she'd just say that they were ordered to stay in the car. She didn't know they were out roaming in the park.

She'd be careful and not give them any new fodder. No farming this week. Keep it clean. When they won the one hundred and fifty thousand dollar prize, she'd show them all how she was better than they were.

Joe pulled over to the side of the road a few blocks up from the house. "Whoever you have as a number one suspect, cross out his name and pencil in Patty Gleason."

Ronnie tapped on her iPad. "Already done. She may not have had anything to do with it, but what a character."

"Did you notice that she's the only one we've spoken to that hasn't asked how either woman was doing?"

"Yes. Hayden and Mary are in the lead. With them out of the way, that just leaves Sam and Lynn blocking their prize money. I don't see Brian and Cody as much of a threat since they fluctuate between third and fourth place."

"Who's next?"

Ronnie glanced at her phone face. "It's almost seven thirty. Lynn Foster isn't far from here. Let's finish with her."

"Lead the way."

8

1000

"That's her apartment building across the street." Ronnie pointed to a house on a large plot of land.

"From what I can see in the dark, it looks clean. No junk cars or junk in the yard."

"The house is divided into four apartment units. The owner, an older woman lives downstairs."

"What's with this woman?"

"Lynn Foster. Has a twelve-year-old daughter. Shelly Mathers says Lynn has above average intelligence. The daughter is a year ahead in school. Really smart. No problems with the gaming. She was working with Sam, far from the women the night of the attack. Her apartment is downstairs on the right."

Ronnie knocked on the door.

A young woman answered. She was medium height, short brown hair, held behind her ears with a headband. She wore a long-sleeved tee shirt and shorts. "What can I do for you?"

"I'm Detective Ramsey. I'd like to ask you a few questions about the attack at the park."

Lynn opened the door wider. "Please come in."

She and Joe entered a long living room. The room was clean and sparsely furnished. The furniture was used. The old carpet was stained but clean. A book case on one wall housed dozens of computer code books. The kitchen table was against a far wall, with a computer tower and cables strung along the back of the wall to surge protectors.

"Your gaming system?" Joe asked.

Lynn stood in front of the computer. "It's a few years newer than Sam's, but it seriously needs to be upgraded. Today, it's all about the speed."

"I hear you," Joe said.

She pointed to the couch. "Please have a seat."

Ronnie and Joe took a seat on a long, lumpy couch.

"This is Joe Wade, Mary Johnson's nephew."

"I'm so glad to meet you. How are Mary and Hayden?" The woman took a seat across from them.

"Hayden will be released from the hospital tomorrow. Mary is still in a coma."

A young girl entered the room and stood next to her mother. She was tall for her age. Her long brown hair was in a long braid. She had pretty long eyelashes. Ronnie got the impression that she was a bright, happy child.

"These people are trying to find out who hurt Mary and Hayden."

"Are they okay, now?" She sat on a foot stool next to her mother.

"This is my daughter, Terrie. They're doing better."

"Kevin just texted me that you were at his house. He said he gave you some cookies. He makes the best peanut butter cookies in the world."

"I apologize," Lynn said. "She gets a little ahead of herself."

"I got something for Mary and Hayden." The girl jumped up and disappeared into a room down the hall.

"She's very close to Hayden and Mary. Did Hayden remember what happened?"

Ronnie shook her head. "She has no memory of the attack."

"That's so awful. I've been with this group for years, and nothing like this has happened before."

Terrie returned with two envelopes. "Mary taught me how to make these beaded bracelets. She held them up to show Ronnie. I want to give one to Mary and Hayden to remind them we care about them."

Ronnie examined the bracelets. "This is really nice bead work." She handed them back to Terrie who dropped a blue, rose, and green bracelet in Hayden's envelope and the yellow, green, and rose bracelet in Mary's envelope. She passed the envelopes to Ronnie.

"These are lovely. We're going to stop by the hospital on our way home. I'll see that they get them."

"Thank you."

"You go back and finish your homework, and I'll check it when you're done. I want to talk to this detective."

Terrie waved and disappeared into a room down the hall.

"She's very sweet."

Lynn tugged nervously at the sleeves to her sweater. "Yes, she is."

Ronnie studied the girl for a few seconds. A tightness around her eyes, she was definitely on edge. Ronnie relaxed in her seat. She'd learned that if she relaxed, people she questioned would relax. "We won't keep you, but do you remember anything from that night? See anything unusual?"

Lynn shook her head. "Me and Sam were working far from their site. Each team has a designated area to work. We usually keep an eye out because gamers try to interfere with the digs, but we didn't see anyone we didn't know."

"Anyone in particular interfere more than the others?" Joe asked.

"Sometimes Patty sends her husband or her boys. They haven't done that lately. If they get sanctioned again, they're out of the game."

"Do the Gleason boys often go on all of the outdoor quests?"

"Oh, yes. Patty rules them like a drill sergeant."

"Do the kids work on the online games with the adults?"

"No. Jon doesn't allow that. Kids can't participate in an online game with a large prize like this one. It's kind of an honor system. I suppose kids can use their parents' passwords, but the kids aren't very good and a player could risk losing a lot of points.

"The outdoor quests, kids can help look for clues, but they can't dig for the medallions. They're not allowed to text in the medallion codes. It's kinda weird, but Jon said there are laws restricting the kids from certain activities surrounding the games. Again, it's an honor system. Sam and I are real careful about following the rules."

"Did you ever see the Gleason boys dig for medallions?"

Lynn laughed. "Patty Gleason's such a control freak. I think she only allows the boys on the quests so they can disrupt other gamers."

Ronnie glanced down at her iPad and up at Lynn. "I just have a few more questions, and I'll be done. Did Mary or Hayden ever mention any threatening emails or phone calls? Anyone at the socials bother them?"

Lynn's eyebrows went up. "Wow. They're so nice, I can't imagine anyone threatening them or hurting them. The chat room chatter can be brutal to gamers, but gamers treat Mary and Hayden with respect."

"We're looking into Mary's work records to see if there's a problem there. Something may turn up unrelated to the games."

Lynn paused and tugged nervously at her sleeves.

Something's thrown her off. I wonder what?

"So, you've been with this gaming guild for several years now?"

"Uh, me, Sam, and Brian all started together a little over five years ago. They've got great programs for kids. When Jon Mathers gets extra money, he runs clinics for kids for computer programming, math, and science. Sam Preston's son and my daughter have been bumped up ahead in their classes in school because they're so smart."

"I've heard a lot of horror stories about tightly-knit gaming groups. This is my first introduction into the online gaming world," Ronnie said, "and I'm impressed with these people."

"I think a lot of it's Shelly's doing. She really pushes for family involvement."

"So, you and Sam are in this together. What are you going to do with the money, if you win?"

"Sam and I—it's all about the kids and their college funds."

Ronnie stole a glance at Joe. "I have a younger brother I put through college. It's expensive."

"I want the best for Terrie."

"You work at Crescent Gardens during the day?"

Lynn tugged at her sleeves. "I work while Terrie's in school. I build websites for people at night. Computing is my income, but gardening is my passion. Someday, I want a place of my own with a huge yard I can garden in."

Ronnie shouldered her bag. "We won't take up any more of your time," she said, standing. "Here's my card, and if you think of anything that would help find the attacker, please call me."

She held up the envelopes. "I'll get these to Hayden and Mary. Thanks."

After they left, Lynn called Sam.

"Hey, it's me," she said.

"Whatcha got going?"

"The police were just here asking questions about Mary and Hayden."

"Yeah, they were here, too. They're just trying to find out who attacked them."

"I guess that I just don't like so much outside involvement in the games so close to the end."

"I hear you, but I want them to catch this guy so no one else gets hurt."

"Who do you think did it?"

He sighed into the phone. "I don't know. I'd hate to think it was one of the gamers. Could be someone already in the park and they followed the women because there weren't any men present."

"What about Cody or Brian. They were working close to the women."

"I don't think they'd do it. They like those ladies."

Lynn was silent for a moment.

"You okay?"

"Just tired. You want to get together tomorrow night and get in some gaming?"

"Sure. Kevin and I'll be there at five with health food pizzas."

Lynn clicked off and slumped down on the couch. Maybe Sam was right. It wasn't anything to worry about. Probably just some druggies in the park rooting for drug money. Still, she hoped they didn't check too deeply into their backgrounds.

Joe climbed in the truck. "I'm thinking Sam and Lynn are at the bottom of the list."

Ronnie nodded. "Me, too. She was awfully nervous. Something I said shook her up. I can't remember what it was I said. I wish I could videotape each and every interview that I do."

"Completely innocent people get nervous around cops," Joe said. "Besides, we'd read too much into what we were watching."

"You're right. The plot thickens. Patty Gleason lied about the boys."

"Lies are the best clues we have in this business, almost as good as DNA," Joe said. "I wonder why she lied? She'd know that we could verify if the boys were there or not."

"As obnoxious as she was during the interview, I like it that her lie will haunt her day and night."

"Why don't you call the Chinese place, and we'll get carry out and go to Hayden's house. Lea's staying there tonight."

"Good idea. Mike's in Memphis until Friday presenting some kind of business deal."

"Hope he gets back soon. We got a lot of sports team catching up to do."

9

1001

"Knock, knock. We got food!" Ronnie called out, entering Hayden's kitchen.

"Ruff. Ruff." Bubbles bounded into the room and barked twice at Joe.

Ronnie held the bags down so that the dog could get a good whiff of the food. "This smells good doesn't it? You're not getting any." She set the bags on the kitchen table.

"I'm back here," Lea called out.

Ronnie and Joe entered Hayden's bedroom. "I just cleaned and changed her sheets. She's coming home tomorrow."

"That's good news," Joe said. "How's Mary?"

Lea shook her head. "Still out. They removed the ventilator, and she's breathing on her own. The doctor said she may wake up in a few days or a few months. You can never tell with a head injury. Once they're sure she has no other internal injuries, they may move her to an extended care facility. Did you have any luck finding a next-of-kin?"

"Not yet. Let's just keep praying that she wakes up," Ronnie said.

"How did you two do with all the interviews?"

"Let's get some dinner and strategize," Ronnie started down the hall towards the kitchen.

Bubbles was on a chair, sniffing at the bags on the table. "Get Down!" Ronnie commanded.

Bubbles hopped down and scooted under the table for safety.

"She chewed up one of Mom's new bedroom slippers this morning."

Ronnie washed her hands, pulled plates out of the cupboard, and set the table.

Lea made a pot of tea and set it on the table. "Joe, I need you to do me a favor."

"Anything."

Since their talk yesterday, he was being extra conciliatory. "Can you dismantle Mom's treadmill in the basement? The first thing she'll do when she gets home tomorrow is try to tread a marathon to make up for all the exercise she missed the last few days. The doctor doesn't want her exercising for a few weeks."

"I'll unplug the motherboard and the cable that runs the machine. That'll stop her."

"Let's pray," Ronnie said. They bowed their heads and Ronnie offered a heartfelt prayer for the women to recover and for wisdom to solve the attack before anyone else got hurt.

"This looks good," Joe said. "We should have brought some of that Healthy Trail Mix for dessert."

"Trail Mix?" Lea asked.

"Don't ask," Ronnie replied.

"No chop sticks?" Joe asked Lea.

"I'm too hungry to play pick-up sticks with my food. So, who's your number one suspect?"

Ronnie shook her head. "Six people with one hundred and fifty thousand good reasons to knock off the top contenders for the prize. If it were a random attack, why did the leaders get hit? This was planned. It's just too bad that it rained so hard. No evidence was left at the crime scene."

"I don't know about Brian VanDeer, but Cody Ingham concerns me," Joe said, chasing his noodles around his plate with the sticks.

Ronnie nodded. "Brian's got a history of violence and a desperate need for the money. Shelly said he got into a shouting match with Jon about his scores last week. He thought he had more points. So, I'm not ruling him out completely, but we can't zero in on Cody just because he's a creep. I've learned that sometimes it's the ones with the weakest motive who commit crimes."

Joe picked the noodles up with his fingers and dropped them in his mouth. "I don't see Sam Preston or Lynn Foster as primary suspects. They were too far away to have attacked the women, returned to their dig site, dug up the medallion, and texted their code to the gamemasters."

"But Lynn was really nervous during the interview," Ronnie pointed out. "Something I said unnerved her. However, I can't see any motive. College tuition for the kids is not an issue at this time."

"A lot of innocent people freak out when they're questioned. What about the Gleasons?" Joe asked.

Ronnie finished her egg roll. "Now, there's a suspect. She never asked how the women were. Wouldn't let her husband say anything. She's concerned that the games will be stopped—and she lied about her sons participating in the outdoor quests." She texted a note to herself to call Jon and ask how many times the boys participated in the quests.

"Who could have done it?" Lea asked. "Left their dig, attacked the women, and returned without anyone seeing them?"

"The Gleasons were working to the women's left, across a dirt road, maybe one hundred feet away," Ronnie said. "They could have attacked the women and returned to their area. With the heavy rain, it would have been impossible to keep track of other players nearby. She's a classic, textbook narcissist. She doesn't need a motive."

"Brian and Cody weren't that far to their right," Joe said. "One of them could have attacked the women and gotten back to their dig."

"I'd hate to think one of the guild players did this and can still win the prize money," Lea worried.

"We'll figure this out before that happens," Ronnie said, stabbing the last egg roll with her fork and dropping it on her plate before Joe could get it. "Jon said that in the agreements the players sign, if anyone is involved in a felony of any kind during the game, the person is automatically disqualified at the time the felony was committed."

"So if they find out later that one of the gamers attacked Mom and Mary, they can't win the prize?"

"Yes," Ronnie said. "If someone attacked the women and wins the prize money in a few weeks, if it's later proven he or she was the attacker, they forfeit the money and have to pay it back. They don't award the prize money for six weeks after the game ends. He said this rule keeps a lot of druggies out of the game. Keeps the games clean."

Joe narrowed his eyes, watching Ronnie eat the egg roll. "You don't get any fortune cookies."

"What about someone from the outside?" Lea asked. She cut her egg roll in half and dropped the other half on Joe's plate. "Remember we talked about Mary's house, how empty it was? What if she were running from someone, and he found her?"

Ronnie took a sip of hot tea. "That's possible, but absolutely no one knew where the dig sites were until that night. The GPS coordinates are passed out when they arrive for the quest."

"I forgot to tell you, they drove Mary's car home and parked it in her garage."

Ronnie nodded.

"You know, the attacker could have followed her to the park," Lea suggested.

"That could be," Joe said. "They're still going through footage of cameras in the park looking for people not part of the game."

"Bubbles is at it again." Lea jumped up. "Where are you going with that?"

The dog slinked into the living room and hid behind a chair. Lea retrieved the shoe and put the shoes on the top shelf of the closet.

She returned to the table. "The problem is that the closets have sliding doors, and she noses them open, roots around until she finds something to chew on, and goes to work."

"That's why Hayden's house was so empty," Joe laughed. "The dog ate everything."

Joe picked up the bags from the table and stuffed them in the trash. "I think our best suspect is linked to Mary Johnson." He faced the women. "I think if we find out who Mary Johnson really is—we find the attacker."

Bubbles crept into the kitchen and slouched next to Ronnie's chair. Ronnie rubbed the dog behind her ears. "What do you two think about going under-cover in the games as stand-ins for Hayden and Mary?"

"We could do it," Joe said. "I played a lot of those games in college."

"Yes, and your grades reflected that. All my hard-earned money went to gaming?"

"Not all of it. I got good grades in sports."

"I've no idea how to do those games. I hate it that Mom and Mary worked so hard to get where they were and then I mess up and they lose after all."

"I can get one of the techs from work to coach you," Ronnie offered. "I need to keep Hayden at the top to watch the other players' reactions."

"You're right. I mean, Mary could still die. That means one of those players is a murderer. Yeah. I'm in."

"I don't like that look on your face, Joe. Whassup?" Ronnie asked.

"There's got to be something in the Johnson woman's past that caused this. I'm going to focus on her. She's the reason this happened."

"I'm going to rule out a mugger," Ronnie said. "Muggers are fearful, lazy people. They wouldn't have worked the park once the thunderstorm began. I'll keep the idea it was a mugger in the news reports. That will steer the interest away from the gamers. It's one of those gamers."

Joe shook his head. He and Ronnie stared each other down.

"Gamer," Ronnie nodded.

Joe raised his eyebrows. "I sense a little friendly competition here."

"You've been around your new boss too long. If I were a betting woman, I'd place a bet on one of the gamers."

"And if I were a betting man, I'd place my bet on Mary Johnson."

Lea gasped, "What are you two doing?"

"We're just challenging ourselves," Ronnie grinned.

"Game on," Joe mouthed to Ronnie, who mouthed the same words back to him.

Lea crossed her arms and shook her head at Joe and Ronnie. "I can't believe you two."

"Lea, you look completely used up, and so am I. I'm going home, call Mike, and go to bed. Joe, you coming?"

"Let me unplug the treadmill. Give me two minutes."

Ronnie and Lea put the dishes in the dishwasher. "Lea, you get some sleep tonight. You're no good to your mother as exhausted as you are. The doctors won't release her until some time after ten o'clock."

"I'm all done in. I'm going to let the dog out for a run around the yard and turn in early."

Lea climbed into bed in her old room and buried herself under the covers. Bubbles hopped up on the bed and snuggled in next to Lea. "At least if you're sleeping here, you aren't eating the rest of the house."

She prayed again for her mother and Mary, that Mary would wake up and Ronnie would find the person who attacked them. Deep under the covers, Lea shivered. One of her mother's new friends brutally attacked her. Or, someone from Mary Johnson's past. Why would she drag her mother into this? They were close in age—maybe she needed the companionship of an older friend.

Please, God, who did this?

10

1010

Early the next morning, Lea let Bubbles out back and she immediately chased a squirrel up a tree.

A few minutes later, Joe tapped at the kitchen door and entered. "Breakfast." He held up a pastry bag.

"Morning. Thanks."

Lea had taken a shower and her dark hair was wet and straight. Her dark eyebrows framed big brown eyes.

She counted scoops of coffee into the basket and closed the lid, fighting how comfortable it felt to have Joe stop by in the mornings. "You want to let in the dog?"

Joe opened the door and Bubbles scooted past him, dashing to her food bowl.

"Coffee in a minute."

"I brought blueberry muffins this morning."

"I love blueberry muffins," Lea said, setting out bread and butter plates.

Bubbles sat next to Lea, with her paw up, begging.

"You can't have this," Lea said. She reached behind her and pulled a bag of dog treats off a shelf and dropped some on the floor.

The dog sniffed the treats and backed away. She trotted off to the living room.

"She really is in to people food and fine leather." Lea pulled the paper off the muffin. "Problem is, when I can't see her, I don't know what she's eating."

Joe sipped his coffee. "You look better this morning." Actually, beautiful.

I did get a good night's sleep."

"Sleep's a powerful weapon. I get going on a case, and forty-eight hours have gone by before I realize that I haven't slept. I'm trying to change that. Find a way to work a normal life cycle into my job."

"I do that when I'm developing a media program for one of my clients. This age of technology will kill us all in the end."

Lea gazed at Joe and grinned. "You going to shave or is your razor broken?"

"I'm on vacation."

"We need to get you some new clothes."

"What's wrong with my clothes? I love this Husker shirt."

"That's the same shirt Mom bought you for your birthday eight years ago."

His face brightened. "And, it still fits."

Ronnie had called her after she got to work this morning, and they had a long talk. At least she wasn't going into this blind. "So, why did you really come home, now?"

"I kinda came home to talk to you."

She figured as much. She wasn't sure she wanted to hear what he had to say. She didn't trust her responses. He touted his cop, poker-face persona, thinking she wouldn't be able to read him. But she sensed his pleading her to listen to him. *We've been friends for so long, I owe it to him to listen.*

"Talk about what, Joe?"

"Lea, it's about last winter." He set his mug down. "When I left, I panicked. I lost my parents so suddenly, and I deal with people every day who are thrust into sudden tragedies. I let that fear of suddenly losing someone that I loved get tangled up in our relation-ship. I had to sort it out." He studied her face for a few seconds. "I should have let us both figure it out together."

She could play games, too. "That's all it was? Not another woman?"

"Absolutely not." He sat up straight in his chair. "It was me. It was just about me reacting to fear. Our love should conquer our fears, shouldn't it?"

"Some things take time to work through. Joe, all kinds of things can happen to you or me. Your parent's tragic accident. My father had just had his annual physical, complete with an EKG and chest X-ray. The doctor said that he was in perfect health. He dropped dead two weeks later. In life we have God's deep love for us and love for each other. You can't go through life not trusting God. Building walls around yourself so nothing bad will happen to you."

Joe's shoulders sagged. He tipped his head to the left. "Your right."

The clock on the wall ticked away the minutes. "Can we… can we try again?"

Lea set her fork across her plate and looked up at Joe. "Yes. Slowly."

"I'm really sorry."

She reached across the table and took his big, calloused hand in hers. "I forgive you."

Lea and Joe arrived at the hospital at nine o'clock. She stopped at the nurses' station and filled out the release forms while the nurse briefed her on home care. Armed with pages of instructions, Lea entered her mother's hospital room.

Hayden was sitting on a chair, fully dressed. "Let's go."

Joe picked up Hayden's overnight bag. "She's ready to bust out of here."

A nurse entered the room, pushing a wheel chair. "I have to take her down in a chair."

Hayden stood. "I'm perfectly fine."

"Hospital rules," the nurse said.

"I want to stop and see Mary before we leave."

Lea helped her mother into the chair. "We can do that."

Lea pushed her mother into Mary's hospital room. She'd been moved to the medical floor. The shades were drawn, and a dim light was on over her bed. A wound on the side of her forehead was covered with a smaller bandage. Her face was splotchy red where the ventilator had been taped. Hayden got out of the wheel chair and stepped up to the bed. She clasped Mary's hand. "She looks like she's just asleep. Like she'll wake up any minute."

Hayden patted her hand. "Mary, you're going to be all right. I've been praying for you. Little Terrie made us both bracelets." Hayden held her bracelet up to Mary's face. "I see you got yours on. Everyone's praying for us.

"Don't you worry about Bubbles. She's at my place, and I'm gonna take good care of her. She's sure eating all right. Already ate through one of the bedroom slippers you bought me for my birthday last fall." Hayden stroked her hand gently. "You're gonna be all right."

Lea watched her mother interacting with Mary. So loving. So caring, the way that she was with everyone. But did Mary deserve all of that love? What had this woman gotten her mother in to? It had to be more than the games.

Hayden sat back down in the wheel chair. "Let's pray before we go." She led them in a prayer for Mary and for Ronnie to find the person who did this so no one else would get hurt.

A half hour later, Hayden entered her kitchen. Bubbles yelped and bounded up to her, licking Hayden's hand and wagging her tail.

"Good dog. Good dog." Hayden scratched behind Bubbles' ears. "Somehow, we have to figure out a way to sneak you into Mary's hospital room. If she sees you and hears you bark, I'm sure she'll wake up."

Lea eyed all the food dishes on the counter and kitchen table. "Looks like your friends were here."

"I do miss the girls," Hayden said, lifting the foil on a casserole dish. "Shepherd's pie. My most favorite."

"We can heat that for your lunch," Lea said.

"First, I want to walk on my treadmill. Then, we can call the girls and invite them for lunch. We got plenty of food—"

"Hold on there, lady." Lea held up her hand. "Doctor's orders. No strenuous exercise. The house dark and minimal stimulus."

"Honey, I'm not dead. Those orders are just for dead people."

"Why don't you get a hot shower and change into your sweats. I'll make lunch."

"I guess I gotta start somewhere, so a shower sounds good."

Lea taped a plastic trash bag around her mother's cast on her left arm. "You're good to go."

"You're going to have your hands full," Joe said, settling at the dining room table. He booted up Hayden's computer. "Jason Wilkes from Ronnie's precinct is coming over later to give us lessons on this game. I brought that folder of instructions from Jon Mathers with pass codes to get into the site."

Lea put the casserole in the oven and set the kitchen table for lunch. "How many points do we need each week to get into the outdoor quest?"

"Each team needs a minimum of ten thousand points to qualify. Last week, Hayden and Mary had twelve-thousand sixty-two points. It's already Wednesday. We'll have to catch up fast. What we really need is Mary's computer. We need speed."

"I seem to remember something in the Bible about not coveting your neighbor's goods."

"I'm not coveting…exactly. Just stating a fact. And, I think I recall it was coveting your neighbor's wife."

"It's both."

Lea stood next to Joe as he entered the Dylan's Gaming site. "It's kinda cheating if Jason helps us."

Joe scrolled down until he found this week's scores. "Everyone's in the four thousand range. By the way, it's kinda of cheating to bash two women's heads in so you can get ahead."

"Point well taken." She heard her mother turn off the shower. Bubbles sat in front of the door, her ears cocked, impatiently waiting for Hayden to emerge.

Lea found her mother's blue sweats and laid them on the bed. It was comfortably strange having Joe around again. She was remembering why she was attracted to him before. His easy-going manner. Since she'd met Ronnie in college and they became friends, Joe was always part of the family. It wasn't until a year ago, that they had begun seriously dating. She honestly thought he was going to propose. Then he gave her the speech about focusing on his work, and he was gone. She wouldn't let that happen again. She'd keep her emotions in check. He'd leave when this was over to go back to his job in Kansas City.

Hayden entered the bedroom wrapped in her terry cloth robe. "It's so good to be home."

"I laid out your clothes. Let me help you with your sore arm."

Joe thumbed through the first two games the women played, getting a feel for the game layout. He thought it would be more difficult. He'd cut his gaming teeth on World of Warcraft and then ventured into other games.

He could hear the women talking in the bedroom. Hayden quizzed Lea about all of her myriad of friends. She'd only been away three days.

He studied the women's personas. For the outdoor quest, Mary Johnson's persona was Captain Katherine Janeway and Hayden, Deana Troi. In the online quests, Mary Johnson was Gibborot and Hayden, Abbirah. He sat back and drummed his fingers on the table. Who assigned the names, and what did they mean? He searched through their online profiles. Maybe something there would be a clue as to why they were targeted. Jon Mathers said one of his men studied the profiles and didn't see any warning flags. But these men didn't have police investigative training.

He could hear the women talking in the back of the house. A sense of déjà vu swept over him like old times coming home from college. It was good to be home, but it wasn't what he'd planned. Since he returned to Kansas City, he'd paid closer attention to the people he worked with. Why was his new chief so distant? So militaristic. But a lot of law enforcement were militaristic. Totally locked into the job. They had police scanners at home so they wouldn't miss one call. And the police like that were cold. Unshaken by the most violent attacks.

Joe worked with another detective, investigating the death of a mother and her three-year-old daughter. The violent crime scene brought tears to his eyes. At the police station the next day, the detective was completely unmoved by the pictures taken at the crime scene.

If he wasn't careful, he'd become sociopathic just like the people he chased down.

After solving the murder of the mother and baby, he started going back to church. Through a lot of prayer, he realized that he had to set things straight with Lea. That's why he came back. He'd planned to meet her for lunch at SouthPointe Pavilions, something relaxed. He'd apologize for the way he left things and see how that went.

The problem was, he was crazy about Lea. When he returned to Kansas City, hard as he tried, he couldn't get her out of his mind, feeling guiltier every day that he'd left her. If she didn't want anything to do with him, he'd understand, but he had to try. He'd wait until this business with the games was over, then deepen the relationship.

After lunch, Hayden stretched out in her recliner in the living room. With Bubbles snuggled next to her, she drifted off to sleep.

Lea joined Joe at the table. "I'm hoping she'll get a good sleep. It's hard to sleep in a hospital."

"I called Jason and told him to come in the kitchen door and to not ring the doorbell. I don't want to wake up Hayden."

"Thanks. I'll get some note tablets."

Lea settled at the table in front of Hayden's computer, which Joe had linked to Hayden's laptop.

"Click on the Dylan icon," he instructed her.

Lea clicked on the icon, and the home page opened. She clicked on the contest and logged in under Hayden's name. A woodsy forest scene opened.

The kitchen door opened. "Hey, guys," Jason said, entering the kitchen, carrying his computer bag.

Joe nodded. "This is Lea. Hayden's asleep…"

"Ruff. Ruff."

Bubbles bounded into the kitchen, growled at Jason, and continued barking.

Jason bent down. "Hey, little girl, I'm friendly."

Bubbles sniffed the back of Jason's hand and began licking it.

Hayden stepped into the kitchen. "I heard the dog bark."

"Oh, Mom. I was hoping you'd get some sleep."

"I never really sleep good during the day. If I sleep at all, I won't sleep tonight." She focused on Jason. "You must be Jason Wilkes."

"I'm honored to meet you. You've racked up some pretty amazing scores."

Hayden pulled a chair around and sat at the end of the table. "It's all Mary's doing. She's the expert."

"I bet she is," Lea said under her breath. *An expert manipulator.*

"Joe, I need your help. A friend of mine's at a profiler training course in Virginia for two months. He said we could use his gamer since he won't have time to game for a while. His wife, a gaming widow, said we could keep it for all she cared."

Joe helped Jason carry in the computer system. They plugged in the cables and Jason coded in the Wi-Fi connections.

Joe stood back admiring the computer. He glanced at Lea, grinning from ear to ear, and pointed. "The ultimate gaming experience. A Marauder. Check out the gaming mice. Logitech G 500, like Mary's. It's laser operated."

Lea saw a side to Joe she hadn't seen before. "This is why, Joe, we separated." She pointed to the machine. "You never looked at me like that."

He put his arm around her. "I look at you with my heart."

"Sure, you do," she said.

"It's a little like Mary's," Hayden said, looking over the computer.

"Mary's is faster, but this one's more than adequate," Joe said.

Jason and Joe carried Hayden's computer into the spare bedroom and hooked it up for her so that she could check her emails when she needed to.

Jason set his laptop up at the other end of the table and cabled to the new computer. "I'm going to monitor you, Lea, and give you pointers along the way. There's a trial game you play to orient yourself to the next level, so we'll start with that. Then we'll play and get you some points logged in."

"It's all very daunting," Lea said. She was scared of the huge tower, thinking it could suck her inside any minute. She tried to palm the mouse and the cursor shot across the screen in a crazy pattern. "I can't use this."

"You'll get the hang of it. It's ultrasensitive. That's why it works so well for gaming."

Lea sat back. "This mouse isn't going to work for me."

"Just use the regular mouse. Joe can compensate with the gamer mouse." Jason plugged in the regular computer mouse.

Joe brought up the trial game. "Okay. We're in." He clicked on Gibborot. "You click on Hayden's game persona."

Lea finally positioned the mouse and clicked on Abbirah, who appeared bigger than life on the huge screen the men had set up.

"Hayden, you're smokin'!" Joe exclaimed, gaping at the tall, thin woman with knee-length curly, black hair and a voluptuous body.

Lea glanced at Joe. "You do know that's my mother you're talking about."

"I mean, attractive." Joe looked at Hayden and mouthed, "Hot. Very hot."

Hayden laughed. "Thanks for the compliment."

"So, who are Gibborot and Abbirah?" Joe asked.

"Gibborot is Hebrew for Mighty One. Mary thought it would give her a tough image."

"What's Abbirah?" Lea asked.

"It means Strong One. We added an "ah" ending to soften it a little. We're known in the chat rooms as the Mighty and Strong Ones."

Joe oriented Lea to the screen. "Every player has their own duffel bag, which contains objects you'll need to complete this week's quest. Yours is hanging on that peg up top. Lightly, double click to open it and move the items to your backpack." He worked with Lea to practice using the arrow keys to move her figure and practice with the mouse to phaser any unwanted guests or objects blocking their path. He let her make a few forays into the woods to get the feel of the controls.

"How's it feel?"

"It's kinda odd, but I'm getting used to it."

"So, you two ready to get through the trial? You'll need to work in tandem with each other. I recommend that Joe, you take the lead and let Lea cover you."

"That's what we did every week," Hayden said. "Mary focused on the quest, and I went after anything in her way. I covered her in battle. If someone was going to be sent to the mountain, it would be me. Mary went on ahead, and I'd catch up."

"If you get attacked and can't physically recover fast enough," Joe said, "you'll be sent to a mountain top and have to navigate through treacherous rock slides to return to the game."

Lea sighed deeply. "Oh, my."

"I'll fix you all some sodas," Hayden got up slowly.

Joe glanced at Lea and raised his eyebrows. "Ready?"

"Lead the way."

Joe entered the Kingdom of the Yalefs. Wild animals roared and big birds cawed as they soared across the computer screen. An open area led to a forest with a canopy of tall trees.

"Watch for the packs of wild dogs. You usually see one, but there're more hiding behind trees or rocks," Jason cautioned.

Joe moved Gibborot at a comfortable pace towards the hunter's lodge. "We have to get to the hunter's lodge where we'll receive our quest. Attacks at this point are minimal. Nuisance stuff. Watch out!"

At first it was difficult working the keyboard to move her character and using the mouse, all the while, keeping her eyes on the big screen. She was accustomed to her laptop. Eventually, she was able to keep up with Joe. Lea moved Abbirah into position, palmed her mouse, and phasered her first vicious dog. "Gotcha." She picked up her mouse, blew on it, and set it on the pad.

"Good girl."

The trail grew more narrow, and the trees taller. The canopy darkened the route. Seedy, yellow eyes peered at them through the dense foliage. At first, Lea had trouble keeping Abbirah moving behind Gibborot and watching for the dogs, but as she adjusted to the controls, it got easier.

"Lodge is up ahead. Stay alert."

A sleek black puma dropped down from an over-hanging branch in front of Joe. Its fangs glistened. Joe was blocking her way, and she couldn't maneuver fast enough to get at the cat.

"Got it," Joe said, eliminating the animal.

"Pshew. That was close." Lea couldn't believe that her heart was thumping with fear, her eyes glued to the screen.

"It was a clean kill," Joe observed. "No blood dripping from the fangs."

"I did a shorter quest with this group three years ago. To keep the games open to all family members, Jon nixed bloody, gory scenes. No dismemberments. Creatures or humans just evaporate. It's still a chal-lenging, interactive game."

To their left, several woodsmen worked on felling trees. "Are they a threat?" Lea asked.

Joe shook his head. "So far, only animals. The quest instructions will alert us to the threats."

Abbirah made her way through the clearing and moved next to Gibborot. A woodsman exited the lodge and handed Gibborot a scroll.

"Your quest." He turned and disappeared into the lodge.

Working the arrows, Joe clicked on the scroll icon. "A Yalef village is being attacked, and we're to go to their assistance. Our route is north and east."

"Let's do it," Lea said, impatient to show Joe what she could do.

She worked her arrow keys and followed Joe into the forest. As they followed the compass, the trees grew denser. "Those fallen trees ahead may hide dangers."

"I've got my weapon." Joe slowed.

With no warning, two large packs of wild dogs flanked them on both sides.

Gibborot aimed her weapon. "I'll take the ones on my right. If you get attacked and end up on the mountain, I'll continue on and you catch up."

"Gotcha." Lea focused on the dogs on her left. Joe phasered the dogs and began to move around the obstacles ahead. Lea tried to keep up, but the dogs came after her. She eliminated three dogs, but one dog rushed her.

Splat. She was down. Suddenly, Abbirah lay curled up on the side of a high mountain. She double-clicked her mouse and stood.

"Open your backpack," Jason said.

Lea clicked on the backpack, and the contents were displayed on the screen.

"Choose the two walking sticks and take it slow down the mountain. Approach it at an angle."

A field of loose rock and boulders stretched out ahead of her. She carefully picked her way over the rocks, sliding and loosening boulders, which careened down the mountain. Finally, she made it to the foot of the mountain. Using her arrow keys, she raced along the path towards Joe.

It was too much work to recover. She'd be more careful and not get caught again.

"I'm behind you," she said to Joe.

"Good work. Our quest is up ahead. In this trial, the other teams would have eliminated some of the threats."

Working through the trees, eventually Abbirah and Gibborot emerged from the forest at the edge of a hill. Down below, a village was under attack from gorilla-like animals.

"Those ape-like creatures are the Gorribogs," Jason said. "You'll need to work together to eliminate enough of them that the survivors will feel threatened and retreat."

"Let's take the ones near the forest. I want the survivors running out in the open so we can keep an eye on them. You ready?" Joe asked.

Lea was in control of the game. It wasn't as hard as she thought. She hadn't anticipated becoming so competitive. Did she want to best Joe, or was it the game? She didn't have time to figure it out. Joe had moved ahead toward the battle. They worked together for another hour removing Gorribogs and freeing villagers.

Gibborot headed to the next village, which was larger than the last. Abbirah skirted towards her right and when she was within striking distance, she began firing. Two Gorribogs advanced towards her. She phasered them.

Gibborot surged ahead and made quick work of a cluster of six Gorribogs. Lea worked Abbirah towards four of the apes that were converging on a cabin.

"Until you get the feel of the mouse, you can use your keyboard. Double-click the "d" key to duck if they throw something at you, or the "j" key to jump if you have to."

Lea nodded. No sooner were the words out of Jason's mouth, a Gorribog grabbed a log and hurled it towards her. Lea clicked on the "d" key and dropped down, the log sailing over her head.

"Click on your figure," Jason said.

Lea clicked and Abbirah stood. "You're toast." She took out the ape and his friends. In a few more minutes of battle, the Gorribogs retreated to the west, across the plains.

"I think we did it," Joe said.

"Congratulations. Quest Successfully Completed," flashed across the screen.

Lea dropped her mouse. "Yeah. We did it." She hopped out of her chair, hugged Joe, and planted a kiss on his lips.

"Mom, did you see that?" She pointed to the screen. "We did it."

"Yes. I did see it." Hayden puckered her lips and then smiled.

"I guess I did get a little carried away. Sorry, Joe."

Joe grinned. "Don't apologize,"

"Let's take a break and get into the real game. We've got some points to catch up on."

Lea could tell Joe was fired up. Was it the game or her impulsive kiss?

"We've got a nice vegetable lasagna and a salad for dinner. Jason, I hope you can stay for dinner."

"Thanks, Mrs. Curtis," Jason said, checking his cell phone and texting a message. "My girlfriend." He kissed the phone and set it next to the keypad.

"Jason, would you mind letting Bubbles out in the back?"

"Sure."

"Mom, why don't you rest? I'll set up the kitchen table."

Joe asked Lea, "What can I do?"

"This will only take a few minutes. She already heated the casserole. Why don't you keep her occupied so she'll rest? Tell her all about your new boss."

It took Lea a few minutes to set out dinner. Maybe she could do this after all. The game didn't seem that hard, but it was a trial run. If they could keep the points up, her mother's attack wouldn't be in vain.

And, oh, please God, heal Mary, whoever she is.

Lea took one final look at the table. "Food's ready," she called out.

They settled at the table and Jason, a Bible teacher at his church, prayed God's blessing on their meal and for Mary's recovery.

"Jason," Hayden said, "don't be shy. You have to help us eat all this."

"Don't worry. Veggie lasagna's my favorite." Jason's cell phone face lit up. He quickly texted a message and set it down. "Only way I can keep up with her with all the hours I work."

Hayden took a helping of lasagna and salad. "Joe, I have a small favor to ask."

"Name it."

"I put some clothes in the washer downstairs, and I couldn't get my treadmill to work. Could you take a look at it?"

Joe shot a look at Lea.

"Mom, the doctor said absolutely no exercise until he clears you. You had a bad head injury."

"Honey, I'll walk real slow." She wiggled her shoulders. "I feel all itchy inside if I don't exercise, and I don't like feeling deficient."

"You're not deficient, just temporarily out of order. You have a doctor's appointment next Tuesday, and if he clears you, we'll reconnect the treadmill."

"You don't trust your own mother," Hayden grumbled quietly.

Lea figured she better change the subject. "So, tomorrow is the awards dinner."

"Yes. It's very informal. It's an award for winning the weekly quest. It's usually a gift card at a restaurant. Just wear jeans and tee shirts. Some people come dressed as their characters. By the way, Mary's costume's in the wash. I think it would fit you, Joe."

Jason grinned at Joe. "Shoes might be a little tight. Is he going as Katherine Janeway?"

"Very funny. Thanks, Hayden, but I'll pass. However, Lea would look great as Deanna Troi."

Lea poured more tea. "Not happening."

Jason looked puzzled. "Aren't those two different Star Treks?"

Joe helped himself to more lasagna and passed the platter to Jason. "Janeway is from *Star Trek Voyager* and Troi is from *Star Trek The Next Generation.*"

"We wanted strong female characters," Hayden said. "Tomorrow, the couples will have their kids with them. It's a lot of fun. Mary and I are at the top?"

"Yes," Joe said. "Lynn and Sam are next with Cody and Brian following and the Gleasons last."

"They cheat a lot. Mary says that Patty's so desperate to win and be on top that she takes too many risks. Then when she can't win, she starts farming or spamming other players. Jon's team always catch her. Maybe we can keep our lead. I enjoy playing the game with Mary and the people in the group. But for Mary's sake, I'd like to win the prize."

Lea marveled at her mother. Where did she pick up all of this vocabulary? She never could learn foreign languages. As far as doing anything to *help* Mary, Lea wasn't so sure about that. If this woman was hiding from someone, why did she draw her mother into her life and put her in such grave danger? Lea had her reservations about Mary Johnson.

Joe sat back in his chair. "What do you think of the group as it is now? You don't think it was one of them who attacked you?"

Hayden shook her head. She closed her eyes. "Makes me dizzy." She held onto the table until the dizziness passed. "Oh, no. Probably some mugger in the park. I'd think if it was someone I knew, it would have come back to me in my dreams or my mind. No. It was an outside attacker."

"You and Mary get along with everyone okay?"

Hayden nodded. "The Gleasons are a little off. That woman, Patty's hard to get to know. Her husband's okay. Cody makes passes at the women. Even asked me out once. But, I do like Brian VanDeer. He takes good care of his mother. Sam Preston and Lynn Foster are really great. Sam came over here one night and gave me and Mary pointers with the game. Their kids are fun. I've been secretly hoping they'd get together—you know, married."

"Ronnie and I met everyone. It is a great group."

"All of them but the Gleasons and Cody go to church. The gamemasters have a deep faith in God."

Lea stabbed a bit of lasagna and shoved it in her mouth. She fumed quietly, following the conversation. Her mother's face was still bruised, her eye swollen. A cast engulfed her left wrist. Her beautiful, gentle kind mother, who did so much for other people, the victim of a violent attack. Her mother would never think ill of anyone that she knew. In her eyes, everyone was a saint until they prove to be otherwise. One of those people in that group did this, and she was going to find out who, and win this game for her mother.

"Now, Jason, the ladies from the church baked us six pies. You just help yourself."

"Thanks, Hayden. I may wait a while. That lasagna's delicious."

Hayden cocked her ear to the window. "I hear Bubbles. Her barking might disturb the neighbors." Hayden started to stand.

Lea got up and stepped to the kitchen door. "I'll get her."

Bubbles bounded into the house, shook herself, and growled at Jason.

"Hey, girl." Jason scratched the dog behind her ears. "You and I have to work on our relationship."

"Mary and I used to walk her every evening after dinner around the neighborhood."

"Why don't you get the game set up to play, and I'll take Bubbles for a quick spin around the block. We'll be so close when we return, it'll make my girl-friend, Cassie, jealous."

Joe and Lea loaded the dishwasher and cleaned the kitchen.

Joe tied the trash bag to take it out. "I don't ever remember us being that way. You know, calling and texting every few minutes."

"When we got serious, we weren't in our twenties. I think it's cute. I hope she's the one for him; he's such a great guy." She wondered if it was a sign. Jason and his girlfriend were fun in love with each other. That wonderful crazy stage. Her and Joe's friendship had always been more serious.

Hayden settled in her recliner in the living room. When Jason returned, Bubbles snuggled next to Hayden.

Lea dropped down in her chair. "So this is real time?"

"Yep," Joe said, studying the instructions. "Everything's same as before, only notes to pay attention to are obstacles embedded in the landscape."

Lea felt confident. She was itching to show Joe her stuff. "Let's do it."

Jason booted up his laptop. "This game closes down at noon, Saturday. You have to complete your online quest by then. Your competitors have roughly five thousand points now."

Lea studied the gaming screen. "We've got a lot of catching up to do."

"Play smart," Jason warned. "Being the victor of large engagements, nets you big points, but if you're whacked in the attack, you'll lose points getting back to your place in the game. I'd engage in a few large events and build points up in the smaller events."

Lea nodded, nervously palming her mouse, eager to begin.

Joe opened the game screen and checked his backpack. He double-clicked his character and shouldered the bag. "Got your pack?"

Lea nodded.

"Same as before. I'll lead. If you get whacked, I'll continue on ahead."

"Works for me."

Jason scanned the screen. "Welcome to The Kingdom of Zahay. Woods all around. That cabin in the valley below is where you get your quest."

Joe worked his keys and the Mighty One's figure moved down a path toward the cabin.

"Mm. Mm."

"What?" Joe asked.

"Oh, I'm just wondering."

"Keep up."

She worked her arrows, and the Strong One surged ahead.

"Wondering about what?"

"What your new boss in Kansas City would think of you on Saturday masquerading as Katherine Janeway in a public park."

"Not funny."

"Look out behind you," Jason shouted.

A log rolled down the hill towards them.

"Jump!" Joe worked his mouse.

Lea clicked on the "j" and Abbirah jumped. The log rolled under them and out of the way.

"Pshew. I better open my eyes more."

They made it to the cabin and Joe received the instructions for their quest. Joe read to Lea. "The Tarelkons have invaded the woodland Kingdom of Zahay. Each team group is responsible for clearing the Tarelkons out of a specific sector of the city. We have sector two, which is to the north."

"We're burning daylight." Lea smiled at Joe.

Joe moved the Mighty One ahead. They made good time. A few dog attacks, but nothing they couldn't manage.

Lea worked her character over obstacles. The terrain was densely wooded and hilly. As they worked to the top of the hill, a valley spread below them.

"According to the compass, we're at the eastern part of the community," Joe said. "We'll have to track in a northerly direction. Keep an eye on the compass in the corner up top."

Abbirah and Gibborot moved carefully towards their destination. "Where should we start? There're only two of us and a hundred of the Tarelkons."

"They're grouped in clusters of six," Jason observed. "Also, they don't have the weapons and skills you have, only their size and numbers."

"There's a cluster up ahead. Let's get in some practice. I'll take the first two, you the next two, we'll both get the last two."

Lea sucked in her breath, her finger tapping the mouse. Six, dark brown, hairy Tarelkons were huddled over prey they'd killed to eat. Joe surprised two, and eliminated them quickly.

The four remaining beasts surrounded Joe too quickly for Lea to fire her phaser. She shot wildly. Gibborot crumpled to the ground. "Oh, no!"

"Keep firing," Joe yelled.

The four beasts advanced toward Abbirah. She eliminated all four.

She sat back and glanced at Joe's screen. He was pulling himself out of a huge beaver's dam. He climbed out of the hole and shook himself off.

"I don't want to go there again."

"I'm sorry."

"We're fine. Move ahead to the next cluster, but don't engage them."

Lea gingerly moved Abbirah ahead through the woods, all of her confidence gone. A Gorribog lunged out from behind a huge tree. She barely managed to take him out. Two marauding Torelkons emerged from a cave. Lea moved Abbirah behind a tree as the Torelkons passed by, not noticing her.

"Lea, you're going to have to be more aggressive," Jason said. "If you don't attack, the characters will not sense you as a danger and not attack you. You'll lose huge points if you don't engage."

Lea nodded. Gibborot arrived and they surged forward again. Together, they managed to take out three more clusters. As they liberated several cabin families, they gained allies.

"These allies will help you if you get captured or run low on food or weapons in future games."

For hours they worked back and forth through the woods and freed more Zahayins. Abbirah and Gibborot crept around a hillside strewn with boulders.

Jason, checking a text on his cell phone, laughed out loud. "She sent me a joke." He checked Lea's computer screen. "Watch out for those boulders. If they come loose, wait until they're near enough and jump."

He began texting Cassie.

"Incoming!" Joe yelled.

Lea held her breath as a huge boulder bounced towards her. She tapped the "j" key just in time, and the boulder bounced under her. She slumped back in her chair. "That was too close."

"We've built up to seven thousand points," Joe said. "How about we break for tonight?"

"I'm ready," Lea said. She glanced at the clock. "Midnight!"

"You can get lost—completely lost in these games." Joe closed out the game. "You did great. I'm proud of you." He patted her back.

What? No kiss?

Lea set her mouse aside and shook out her hands. "It's harder than the trial."

"What do you think?" Jason asked, as he slid his laptop in its bag.

Joe pushed his chair back. "Not bad. I do like this monster computer and mouse. But, I'm used to aggressive games where foes come at you from all directions. However, this was more challenging than I anticipated. I wonder why the contestants don't compete with each other? It'd be more exciting."

"They tried that for the first two quests years ago. It got too personal. Game chatting became too vulgar. Almost had fistfights during the weekly social gatherings. Farming was uncontrollable. It wasn't the vision Jon had for this. Friendly competition among players and money raised to fight cancer. Jon backed off and beefed up the action in the games."

Joe stood and did some stretches. "There's a lot of money at stake. It's supposed to be hard. How about let's have some pie and ice cream? We need to strategize about the award's dinner tomorrow. Who we're going to focus on and what information we want to get out of them?"

Jason left to be with his girlfriend. Joe scooped vanilla ice cream on warmed apple pie and handed a plate to Lea.

"I'm proud of you," Joe scooped his ice cream onto his pie.

"I didn't think I could do it. It's hard to watch out for everything at once, the creatures and the terrain."

"You're doing great." Joe finished his dessert. "We've got a big day tomorrow."

"I dread all this. I know one of those people attacked my mother. Somehow, I have to keep my emotions under control."

"It's a nice group of people. Ronnie's going to spread the rumor that she's focusing on someone from outside the group, for now. And there is a remote possibility that someone was in that area of the park we don't know about." He stood and petted the computer tower. He leaned down and said, "I'll miss you until I see you tomorrow."

"Should I be jealous?"

He glanced at the computer and at Lea and nodded his head. "Probably."

"Good night," she said as he went out the door.

She put the dishes in the sink and checked through the house. The doors were locked. She passed by the computer. "You've got nothing on me," she said, and turned out the light.

She crawled into bed. A few minutes later her cell phone buzzed. She opened a text from Joe. "Pleasant dreams."

She texted back, "Good night."

11

1011

Early Thursday morning, Lea heard Bubbles whimpering. She didn't want her mother to have to get up, so she called to the dog and let her out back. After a minute, the dog danced around the fence on the side of the yard, barking at something on the front street.

Lea hadn't turned any lights on in the house, and she peered out the front window. She thought she saw a light flashing inside of Mary's house.

Bubbles went crazy barking and growling.

She got Bubbles back inside. The dog paced through the house, whimpering, unable to settle. Thankfully, her mother had slept through the whole event. It was five thirty. The sun would be up soon. Knowing Joe was an early riser, she called him.

A deep voice answered, "Joe, here,"

"Joe, someone's in Mary's house."

"I'm on my way. Stay in your house, keep the lights off. Keep the back door unlocked, so I can come in."

Joe arrived a few minutes later and entered the kitchen.

"Where's your truck?"

"Parked in the next block. Jason's on his way over." Joe peered out a front window. "Yeah, I just saw a flash of light. Someone's in there."

"Jason, coming in the kitchen," Jason whispered, coming through the door.

"Lea, stay here. Don't turn on any lights," Joe said.

She peered out the front door window at the figures of Joe and Jason running across the street. Lea could see in the dim street light that the men had drawn their weapons.

Jason quietly opened the screen. The kitchen door was already open. They entered the kitchen, weapons drawn. Mary's flat screen television had been unplugged and sat next to the door. Joe pointed to the hallway. He could hear movement in the back of the house, but he didn't know how many people were in there, or if they were armed.

"Don't forget to grab the printer," a voice said.

"They're after the computer equipment," Joe whispered.

He and Jason silently eased down the hall. Joe quickly looked into the back bedroom the computer was in. A small penlight flashlight sat on a bookcase. Two men were packaging up the Fragbox.

Joe stood in the hall. He held up his left hand and counted with his fingers. One. Two. Three.

Joe stepped into the room and flicked on the light. Jason screamed, "Down on the floor, now!"

The men were taken completely by surprise.

"I said, get down!" Jason kicked one man's legs out from under him.

The man dropped to the floor. Jason and Joe handcuffed them. Joe called on his radio and two police cars pulled up out front of the house.

Joe turned the men over to the police officers.

"Got a guy on the other street sitting in a pickup," an officer said. "It's a three-man team."

"Thanks for your help," Joe said. "We'll go through the house and then lock it."

Joe and Jason went through the whole house and basement. He locked the door. Jason headed home, and Joe crossed the street to talk to Lea.

He entered the kitchen, coffee gurgling through the pot. "We got some guys trying to take Mary's gaming equipment. The local police have them."

"Was the house all right?"

Joe nodded. "Everything's fine."

Lea poured him coffee and set out a tray of muffins. She sat across from him, sipping her coffee. "Joe, this is all getting too much."

"Information about Mary's attack has been in the newspaper and all over the chat rooms on the gaming sites. They know she would have good gaming equipment, or she wouldn't be in first place. Can we box up her gaming equipment and put it in your basement?"

"Sure. There's plenty of room."

"I'll stop by the hardware store later and get some motion sensors for the side and front doors. I'll start sleeping over there at night until we can find some family member of Mary's who will take responsibility for her home. Let's not tell anyone about the break-in."

"Sure. Thanks for coming out, Joe."

"Not a problem." Joe finished his muffin and gulped down the last of his coffee. "Got to get home. My big sister's making me pancakes."

"You spoiled brat," she teased.

Thursday afternoon, Lea drove Hayden to the hospital to visit Mary. They entered Mary's hospital room and Hayden spent a few minutes tucking Mary's blanket around her and watering the flowers people had sent. Dozens of cards were positioned around the flowers in the window.

"Sounds like she's breathing all right," Hayden said, gently stroking Mary's hand.

"Her face looks better. They took that big bandage off."

A nurse bustled in and checked Mary's IV line. Hayden was beside herself. "I feel so helpless. I wish there was something we could do to help her."

The nurse put her arm around Hayden's shoulder. "By visiting her and talking to her every day, you are helping her. When she wakes up, think what a comfort it will be to her to know that you were here."

Hayden sat in a chair next to the bed. The bruises were fading and she had more color in her face. She held Mary's hand and looked over at Lea. "I've lost family and dear friends to illnesses." She turned her gaze to Mary. "This is all so unnecessary for her to end up this way. She didn't deserve this."

Lea reached over and rubbed her mother's shoulder. "She's blessed that she has you for a friend."

"I suppose," Hayden said. She patted Mary's hand. "I brought some emails people sent to read to her." Hayden looked up at the nurse. "Do you think she's doing better?"

The nurse nodded. "Her vital signs are stable now. She's breathing on her own, which is a good sign. I must say though, that this could take several more days or months. There's just no way to know. But you being here is important."

The nurse got a call and left.

Hayden pulled the emails out of her purse. She held Mary's hand. "I just want you to know that Bubbles is fine. We're taking good care of her. Everyone in the guild misses you. Joe and Lea are keeping our points up and will accept our award tonight. You just need to work on getting well."

Hayden read four short emails and sat back in her chair. "She looks like she's just asleep. Like if we talk too loudly, she'll wake up." She rubbed Mary's hand and looked over at Lea. "Let's pray some more."

Lea nodded and joined hands with her mother. She listened as her mother poured out her heart to God on her friend's behalf. Lea prayed at home, but not with the fervor that her mother had. She hoped that some day she would mature to that level of communication with God.

Hayden sat quiet for a few minutes. "Well, you've got an awards banquet to attend."

At home, Lea showered and dressed in her best jeans and tee shirt. Her mother's friends were coming over for the evening while they were out. She didn't feel comfortable leaving her mother alone since she still had dizzy spells, but she trusted that Edna could keep her under control. She determined to study every person in that guild and figure out which one attacked her mother.

Lea's cell phone chimed in the living room.

"I'll bring it to you," Edna called out.

"Here," Edna bustled in Lea's bedroom and handed her the phone.

"Thanks." Lea checked the face. Linda Washington. The only crabby client she had. Another text for more changes in the web design.

"Later." Lea dropped the cell phone on the make-up table.

"You need anything?" Edna asked.

Edna was her mother's closest friend since grade school way back in the last millennium. Edna's husband died six months after Lea's Dad. Her mother and Edna worked through their grief together.

"Edna, how well do you know Mary Johnson?"

"Not real well," Edna said, folding Lea's tee shirt and shorts she'd been wearing earlier. "We had lunch a few times. You know your mother, always gathering stray chicks under her wings."

"Did she go to church?" Lea dropped make-up into her bag.

"No. Just a few times, lately. Hayden brought her to a few of the senior socials. Mary didn't know anybody. Kinda kept to herself.

"The ladies all pass around pictures of their grandchildren on cell phones or tablets. She took no interest. She seemed kinda sad to me."

"I'm just trying to figure out who she was and how my mother got to know her."

Edna shrugged. "I think she's harmless. A lonely, unhappy woman who needs God's love to fill the empty spots in her life—a lot like all of us."

"Thanks Edna."

Lea heard the doorbell chime in the kitchen.

Frances had arrived at the same time as Joe. Lea combed back her short hair. In her mother's mind, and her friends', they already had her married to Joe and on their honeymoon. How was she going to keep these women under control?

Joe didn't want her; he wanted his job. She was afraid that when the investigation was over that he'd leave again.

Lea entered the kitchen and shouldered her purse. "Mom you all set for tonight?"

Hayden sat at the kitchen table with Edna and Frances. Hayden had a sweatband around her head. The women had their laptops open. Joe set a platter of chips and dip in the middle of the table.

"You won't let me exercise my body, so we're going to exercise our minds. I hope that bang on the noggin didn't damage my brain so I lose my high Lumosity score."

"You'll do just fine," Edna said, entering her password in the website. "Lea, you don't have a thing to worry about. We're going to work on our Lumosity games and improve our minds. Then we're going to feast on casseroles in front of the television. We got six movies to pick from."

"I appreciate you two so much. Our numbers are taped to the fridge if you need us. Be back in a few hours."

Twenty minutes later Lea and Joe entered Burelli's Pizza Shop and made their way to the banquet room in the back.

"Welcome," Shelly greeted them, clutching her clipboard. Her pretty eyes seemed to do all her smiling for her. "I'm so glad you could come. How is Hayden?"

"She's fine," Lea said. "She thinks she's completely well and wants to start jogging again. I may have her in a straightjacket by the end of the week. She's home working on her Lumosity program."

Shelly shook her head. "I admire her and Mary so much. They're so active. I did stop by the hospital for a few minutes today. Mary's still out."

"I'm afraid so. I took Mom over. She read her some emails from the group."

"We're praying for a complete recovery."

"Thank you."

Lea scanned the room full of the top gamers in the city. She determined to study every person in the room. Joe was law enforcement and had to follow the rules. Lea didn't. She planned to divide and conquer.

Joe escorted Lea around the room, introducing her to the other players. "And finally, this is Lynn Foster and her daughter, Terrie. Terrie made the bracelets for Hayden and Mary."

"I'm pleased to meet you," Lynn said. "I'm glad your mother is doing better."

"Miss Curtis, I made more bracelets for Mary and Hayden," Terrie said, holding up two beaded bracelets. "They're new ones. I just want them to remember that we love them."

Lea took the bracelets and turned them over in her hands. "They're lovely. And you can call me Lea."

"Lea. I like that name. Do you think they'll let Mary have the bracelets while she's in the hospital?"

"She's wearing the one you sent a few days ago. My mother won't take hers off. When we go to visit Mary tomorrow, we'll add the new one and give the nurse instructions that they're not supposed to be removed."

Terrie smiled a sweet smile. Lea was moved by how pretty the girl was. Soft, brown hair. Pretty, long lashes. A beautiful smile. She carried herself gracefully. Lea remembered her grade school years. Lanky, big crooked teeth, fixed by years of wearing braces. Freckles. Always unsure of herself.

This girl was lovely inside and out.

"May I have your attention," Jon Mathers bellowed.

The group took their places around the tables. Lea noticed that in a large crowd, Kevin tended to be shy. Terrie had a way of pulling him out of his reticence.

"Please sit with us," Terrie begged.

"Thanks," Joe said as they settled with Lynn and Sam and the two kids.

"This is the next to the last awards dinner for this game series. At the next dinner, I'll be announcing the winners and awarding first, second, and now, third prizes. A group of gamers in California put up money for a third prize, twenty-five thousand dollars."

The group clapped and cheered.

"Before I get into the award this week, I'd like to give an update on the attack last week. We do everything we can to keep you safe, but somehow an attacker got through our security net. The police believe it was a mugger already in the park. There was a similar attack on a couple in a park in Omaha the week before.

"Hayden Curtis is home and recovering nicely. Mary Johnson is still in a coma. The doctors say she can wake up at any time. We're praying for her. Hayden has asked her daughter, Lea Curtis and Mary Johnson's nephew, Joe Wade to take their place in the contest—"

"Jon," Patty Gleason interrupted. "I thought we agreed that no one could come in after the second week. Do they enter the games under the same scrutiny we did when we applied?"

"Those are fair concerns," Jon replied. "Our contest rules do account for a contestant not being able to complete the game due to family illness, accident, or illnesses. The contestant can designate a stand-in. Neither Joe nor Lea are part of any other gaming group. Hayden has a fractured wrist and can't work the controls."

Patty sulked back in her chair. It was clear to Lea that she didn't like what Jon had said.

"When we're done here, I can show you that clause. Anyway, security will be beefed up at the next outdoor quest Saturday afternoon. Now for the past week's winners."

Jon adjusted his glasses and held up a sheet of paper. "Before the attack, Mary Johnson did text the correct medallion number and did win the quest for last week. So, first prize goes to Mary and Hayden. A one hundred dollar gift card at Chili's."

Shelly handed the envelope to Lea. "I hope they can both use this real soon."

"Thank you."

"Going into the final week, Mary and Hayden are in first place. Sam Preston and Lynn Foster in second. The Gleasons nudged up to third, and Brian Van Deer and Cody Ingham in fourth. Don't be discouraged. I've seen these standings completely reversed at the end of a game.

"Game points end Friday at midnight. The quest destination will be announced an hour before it begins. We'll start promptly at three o'clock. The final game will be uploaded by Sunday at three o'clock. That will be your last week for game points. We won't have a banquet next Friday. The quest will be Saturday with the final awards banquet on Sunday. Please enjoy your pizzas."

Restaurant servers set out pizzas and the contestants filed down both sides of the table filling their plates. As agreed before, Lea and Joe would split up. Since Cody responded to women, he was her assignment. She dropped a slice of pizza on a plate, grabbed a soda, and crossed over to where the men were sitting. "May I join you?"

Cody eyed Lea and grinned from ear to ear. "Sure." He pulled out a seat for her next to him.

Lea took a seat across from the men. In her mind's eye, every one of these people were suspects. She focused on the men who could have beaten her mother. It was tough getting past Cody's slick, black hair and red-rimmed glasses, but she'd try. Cody may not have had anything to do with the attack since he was supposedly digging with Brian. Joe thought that Brian had the most motive of the two. Her stare bore into Brian. Her heart palpitated with anger. If she were going to accomplish her mission, she'd have to control herself. She took a few deep breaths.

Brian finished off a slice of pizza and wiped his greasy hands on a small paper napkin. "I'm glad Hayden's better. You tell her I asked about her."

This didn't sound like a statement from a man who bludgeoned her mother. "Sure. Thanks."

Cody slurped down his soda. "I saw your scores this morning. You're pretty good."

"Hayden coached me." She was terrified she'd accidentally say something wrong, like Jason was helping her, or the police were on to them all.

Cody stood. "I'm going to get some more pizza. You want anything?"

Lea shook her head.

"I'm fine," Brian said.

Cody and Brian were equal partners. If one of them was disqualified, they'd both forfeit the prize money. She'd put pressure on them to take care of business themselves. If one of them voluntarily dropped out, then the police investigation would only be focused on the other two remaining teams.

While Cody grazed through the food tables, she leaned forward and asked, "What do you think about the attack last week? Who do you think did it?"

Brian shrugged. "Somebody from the outside."

Lea checked around her. Cody was engaged in a deep conversation with Carl. "I heard they're focusing on Cody because he found the women."

"Couldn't be," he said defensively. "He wouldn't hurt them."

Lea sat back. "All that money would make a person do things he or she never thought of before."

Brian's eyes narrowed. "He didn't do it."

Maybe she'd gone too far. Lea glanced at a back table. Jon was teasing Terrie and Kevin. Terrie's vivacious personality lit up the room. She was good for Kevin, who tended to be an introvert.

Cody dropped down in his seat with a fresh plate full of pizza.

She focused on the men. She needed to lighten the mood. "Does it get easy at all?"

Brian shook his head. "Sunday, when they put up the new game, it'll be tough." He slapped Cody on the back. "Separate the men from the boys. One week, you gotta watch out for the creatures, another week, the terrain, but the last week, everything's mixed in. I practice the trial a couple of times before I start playing—"

Cody nudged his arm. "Don't give away our strategies!"

"I'm not telling them anything the others aren't doing."

Cody studied Lea for a few seconds and leaned forward. "So, you and this Joe got anything going on?"

Terrie called out something to Jon at the back table, and the whole group erupted into loud laughter.

What a jerk Cody was. She pretended to not hear him. "These games are so unpredictable," Lea said. "According to Jon, you could move to the top by next week."

Cody nodded his head. "I got some ideas how that can happen. Three years ago, two guys at the bottom all along won first prize. It could happen again. Someone can be disqualified at the last game. If a team doesn't find all the quest clues that could drop them back in points."

She concentrated on Brian and Cody's faces. "Even an attack on the leaders, could move someone up."

Did Brian flinch? Cody's eyes shifted to the left.

Joe settled at the table with Sam and Lynn. Kevin and Terrie had their heads together looking at a program on Kevin's tablet.

"I hear you kids are pretty good with computers."

"Lynn and my dad help us a lot," Kevin said.

"Mom's teaching me about programming, so I can make up some games to play," Terrie said.

"I can barely play the game here," Joe said.

Lynn sighed. "This one's been really challenging. I can usually get the animal and people attackers, but I go charging after the people and completely forget about the terrain."

Sam sipped his soda and put the can down. "Especially, those invisible spider webs. I walked into six of those this week. You'd think I'd learn."

"I got caught in one of those, but spent most of my time climbing out of the beaver's dam," Joe said.

Joe focused on Sam. "Hayden says you helped them with the games when she started."

"Yeah, and now they're ahead of us. I may ask her to come over and give us some pointers next week."

Joe didn't sense either Sam or Lynn had any reason to attack the women. They were standing in second place. He didn't see any tangible motive here.

Terrie made a move on a chess game that she and Kevin were playing on her tablet and sat back while Kevin studied the game. "Mary and Hayden are fun. I like Mary's little dog. Where is her dog?"

"She's at Hayden's house," Joe said. "Lea and Hayden are taking care of her. She's more comfortable with Hayden than me."

"I'm glad. I was afraid they'd put her in the pound," Terrie said, returning to the game. She made a move. "Checkmate!"

"Not again," Kevin groaned.

Sam rested his arms on the table and nodded, glancing around the room. "It's a fun competition. Nice group of people. It helped a lot when I lost my wife. Kept Kevin and I together."

Joe eyed the table with the Gleasons. Patty was making quite a statement to Jon with her long finger pointed at his face. Were those two just annoying game players, or was there something else going on with them?

Lea stood. "Thanks for the tips, guys. We'll see you Saturday afternoon."

"Good luck," Brian said.

As Lea walked towards Joe, she heard Cody say, "I'd do anything to win this contest. Need that money for my biz."

Anything? Including eliminating other players?

Joe joined her. They snagged fresh sodas and crossed over to the Gleason's table. "May we join you?"

"Sure." Carl Gleason pulled out a chair for Lea.

Lea tried to not let the disconcerted look on Patty's face get under her skin. Patty had just finished some kind of argument with Jon, and Lea was sure it was about her and Joe. Her two boys got up and sauntered over to the games arcade.

"I'm glad your mother is better," Carl said.

"Thank you."

"Do any of you have game experience?" Patty asked.

Digging for dirt, are we?

Lea didn't like this woman. "Solitaire, mostly."

"I did World of Warcraft in college until my grades started slipping," Joe said, raising his eyebrows.

"I hear you," Carl said. "That's how I met Patty— through a local gaming guild. We were living in Minneapolis at the time."

Patty shot Carl a hard stare.

Lea wondered what that was about.

"So they think it was someone from the outside?" Patty asked.

"That's what we heard this morning," Joe said. "Detective said a couple in a park last weekend in Omaha were hit in the head and robbed. Detective thinks that with all the gaming security in the park, the man didn't have time to rob the women, not that they had anything on them."

Patty was clearly in control of Carl. She'd have to come up with a different plan to smoke out Patty. She wasn't as gullible as Brian. If Patty did this, it was for greed.

"Let's hope they keep a better eye on us this week," Patty snorted. "I don't want to end up in the hospital and miss the final quest."

Lea let Joe fish for a while, but the couple were tight-lipped about their jobs and where they lived before. Maybe Ronnie should check out this couple more.

Shelly sat across from Patty. "So, did you try out that garden shop I recommended?"

"Yes. I saw some flagstones in there I wanted for our patio As usual, Carl didn't like them. Honestly, men don't know what they want. If I didn't make decisions for us, we'd never have anything." She raised her head in an air of superiority. "I bought them anyway."

Lea exchanged glances with Joe. She smiled pleasantly at Patty and texted Joe. "Time to go."

They said their goodbyes and in minutes were in the parking lot. Lea sat back against the plush seat as Joe threaded his way through cross-town traffic. "So what's your take on the evening? Who's our top suspects?"

Joe waited at a traffic signal. "If it was a gamer who attacked the women, I can't decide between Cody, Brian, or Patty Gleason."

"Brian has the most desperate need."

"True," Joe said, moving through the intersection. "Could be motive there."

"Cody is the one who claims that he found the women that way. FYI, he hit on me tonight."

"Did you crumble under the spell of his red-rimmed glasses?"

"No interest. He thinks that he's so hot with all the girls. The guy's a bottom feeder."

"What about the Gleasons?" Joe asked. "Motive?"

"Greed. Money. Status. How would she look as the winner of Dylan's Games?"

"Pretty good," Joe replied.

"But that's all at risk if she's caught," Lea said.

"A pure narcissist never considers failure an option. In their minds, they never lose. They're cautious, very cautious, but they do make mistakes."

Joe pulled in Hayden's drive around eleven. "I'm going to stay at Mary's house tonight. Anyone else after that gaming equipment, I'll be waiting."

"Do you think it was something to do with the attack?"

Joe shook his head. "Mary and Hayden's names have been in the newspaper and on the television. Someone knew the house was empty. If it had to do with the attack, I would think they would have gotten in there before now. It wouldn't surprise me if more people don't try to break in."

"I agree. Mary's sofa's long enough, but if you want, we've got a camping blow-up bed in the basement."

Joe went in with Lea. Hayden and Edna were sound asleep on the couch, Bubbles snuggled in between them. The television was still on, the DVD had long ended.

Joe drove Edna home, while Lea helped her mother to bed.

Lea tried to sleep but couldn't, her mind still buzzing by the late night activity. The guild people seemed nice enough. Jon and Shelly were genuine. She did like Sam and Lynn and the kids. If it really were one of the contestants who attacked her mother, it had to be Cody or the Gleasons. Brian didn't seem like a person who'd do that, although he did have a past history of violence. But he seemed genuinely concerned about Hayden. The Gleasons? Motivation? In order to win the big prize, they had to move up in the standings. Patty didn't strike her as the type that would settle for anything less than first prize.

How did Ronnie and Joe learn to read people? Patty Gleason was a snob and competitive, but that didn't necessarily make her a mugger. Brian had a gentle, thoughtful side to him, but was he hiding a more aggressive nature? Cody wasn't hiding anything—he was just plain weird. Lynn and Sam, there wasn't anything in their character that concerned her. She couldn't figure it out. She and Joe would talk it out tomorrow.

She whispered a prayer for Mary's recovery. *Please, God, don't let her die. Help her find a way through the fog in her mind to wake up.*

It was a selfish prayer. She needed the woman to wake up so that she could find out who she really was. Be sure that her mother was out of danger.

12

1100

Lea pulled on her mother's Deanna Troi costume. She wouldn't be caught dead in the getup, but her mother insisted she wear it. If someone attacked her, her mother was sure the wig would protect her better than any hard hat. Her mother had asked Ronnie if they could borrow some bullet-proof vests for the outing. Ronnie said that she couldn't get them.

She fitted the long wig. It was tight. She'd have a headache before the day was over. How was she going to find the GPS locations with all this hair flopping around her face? Joe had adamantly refused to wear a Captain Picard costume. He had asked Jon to design him a Captain America figure for the online game.

"You look great," Hayden exclaimed when she saw Lea.

"Wow," Joe exclaimed. "Just like her online persona." He turned to Hayden and mouthed, "Smokin'."

Joe had selected a red Husker shirt and black cargo shorts as a quasi-costume.

Hayden pulled Edna aside. "Listen, she had a really serious head injury. You can't let her talk you into a run or a walk until the doctor clears her."

"Don't worry about a thing. I've got our inside activities all charted out."

"Thanks."

A half hour later, Lea greeted the other contestants gathered at Morrow Running Park. It irked her that no one else was in costume, except Brian VanDeer wearing a Bill Gates face mask and Cody Ingham with a Steve Jobs mask.

Cody gawked at her, not taking his eyes off her long hair.

The park was huge with well-marked running and walking trails. A kid's play area was to the east. Trees and hedges provided privacy and marked the trails. Outdoor exercise equipment was sprinkled throughout the trails.

"Everyone gather around, and I'll give you some pointers," Jon called to the group.

Once they had gathered, he explained the layout of the park. "Some of you have been here before, and running and walking trails are branched out from this point like spokes on a wheel. The red trail is running and the green trail is for walking. Exercise obstacle courses are embedded throughout the park. Each team is assigned to a north, south, east, or west area. Those are marked on your topographical maps Shelly is handing out, with your cell phones.

"When it's time, I'll send a text, and you look at the GPS marking I give you, mark it on your map and take off to your first dig. The next clues will be in the treasure chests you locate. Remember, fill in the holes you dig. Points will be deducted from your gaming scores if holes aren't filled in. Good luck, and God bless you."

Although it was a warm, May day, Lea shivered. Where Joe, as a contestant, had no direct input in the game, he did make security recommendations to Jon. Joe and Jon had set up the deployment scheme earlier. Since Sam and Lynn were not a threat, but next to win, they were west, with extra security along their path. Joe and Lea were north with the Gleason's to the east near the children's play area. Cody and Brian were given the far southern route.

Joe's cell phone rang. He pulled up the text and marked the GPS location on the topo map. "Keep up," he said as he trotted up the red, running trail.

Where Lea was accustomed to running with her mother, she had to regulate her pace to keep up with Joe's long strides.

"We have two goals—win the quest and watch the other gamers."

"I'm with you," Lea replied.

After a six-minute trot, Joe slowed and stopped by the half-mile marker. He pointed to the map. "First clue's around here." He put his hands on his hips and scanned the ground in front of him. "Where would you hide a clue?"

Lea studied the ground on the other side of the trail. "Your detective training using the process of elimination won't help you here."

Lea looked closer at a clump of leaves. She squatted down. "This could be it."

"Squirrels," Joe said. "It wouldn't be that easy."

"No. The dirt's been recently disturbed."

Joe stood next to her. "Squirrels."

She pulled her trowel out of her pack and poked the dirt. She dug up the small, wooden chest. "Found it." She said triumphantly, standing, holding the small chest high above her head.

Lea unscrewed the top of the chest and handed the paper to Joe, who punched the coordinates into the GPS locator.

They quickly filled in the hole and tamped the dirt down.

Joe pointed. "Dead ahead."

Lea took off skipping beside Joe and then settled into a run, trying to match his steps. Maybe they'd win this for her mother. She deserved to win after what she'd been through. She caught something in her peripheral vision.

"Someone's flanking us on our left."

Joe turned and ran backwards for a minute and turned forward again. "Security."

Lea wondered. *Or the attacker in a security outfit.*

After being sent on redundant loops around a green and red trail, a half hour later, Joe slowed his pace and pulled the map out of his jacket pocket. "It's up there." He stopped where the red path inter- sected with the second circle.

Joe studied the grass on both sides of the trail. "Problem with GPS is that it can be anywhere within a twenty to thirty-foot radius. That covers a lot of ground."

"It may not be in the ground," Lea reminded him.

They worked through the area looking for where the chest could be. "I don't see any grass or dirt disturbed," Joe said.

They searched another ten minutes. Lea checked under a picnic table and then climbed upon the table and scanned the area closely. "Bushes. No ground upturned. I see it."

"Where?" Joe asked.

"The lamp over the emergency call station."

"I've been on Easter egg hunts harder than this." Joe stretched and reached the bag hanging from the back of the call station. "It's either the game chest or somebody's stash of drugs. Remind me what the purpose of these quests are?"

"Kids get to participate if parents allow them. Shelly said that gamers asked for shorter quests during the year. They want more challenging city-wide quests in the future."

"Given the security concerns they're facing now, that doesn't seem an option." Joe opened the bag and pulled out the chest. He unscrewed the top and pulled out the paper. He punched in the coordinates. "Two down, two to go."

Lea dropped the small chest into her back pack. She took out a bottle of water and gulped it down. She returned the bottle to the pack slung the pack over her shoulder.

"Let's do it."

They set off to the far end of the northern trail.

Joe's mood seemed lighter today. Maybe it was the outside activity. He loved being outdoors. They used to take four-day weekends and drive to Colorado for hiking trips in the mountains. Ronnie and Mike would come when they could. She had wonderful memories of them camping and hiking. Before her dad died, they rented a motorhome and traveled to Colorado. Her mother and father kept up with them on the most challenging hiking trails.

She missed those times. Now that Ronnie and Joe had been on the police force longer, they rarely got away from work long enough for vacations like that.

Joe was more of himself around her today, not guarded like before. She grinned as she ran alongside of him. *He thinks he's won me over. Has he?*

A little, she admitted to herself. She could understand his insecurity about plunging into a long-term commitment. He'd have to push past the fearful ghosts of his parent's deaths. He couldn't let that accident inhibit him forever.

She had always enjoyed being with him. He wasn't like other men she'd dated. When they were together, they talked long into the night. Couldn't get enough of being with each other. It jolted her, like a lightning strike when he left. Like Joe, she needed to push past last winter.

She scanned the area as she ran. "I haven't seen or heard anyone else."

Joe scanned around him. "The park's officially closed, except for the kids' area, and these spokes are set pretty far apart farther out. It's not a bad running park. I never knew it was here. I'll bring Ronnie and Mike out here."

"Where is Ronnie today?"

"She got a call. Some kind of gang shooting. This town's getting as bad as Kansas City with the gangs."

Lea kept up with Joe. She figured they had another half mile to go. When he showed up Saturday night, she was annoyed having him so close at hand. But now, she was remembering why she was drawn to him. When he was in the midst of an investigation, he was all business. Short, to-the-point conversations. She could tell when an investigation was done. He'd get on the phone, or posting on Facebook for hours.

She knew that Joe was crazy about Hayden. Never forgot her birthday. It was because of Ronnie that they all met. Ronnie had started college, and her parents were killed in a car wreck. She dropped out for two years to get Joe through high school. Once he was in his last year of high school, she started back to college.

Lea remembered meeting her at a coffee shop they both visited each morning. She had sold her parents' house so that she could pay for her and Joe's college tuition. They had become good friends. Hayden took Ronnie and Joe under her wings, remembering their birthdays, inviting them for Christmas. Hayden had seen Ronnie and Joe through their graduations from the police academy and their first jobs. It wasn't until last year that she and Joe had become serious.

Then he was gone.

Ronnie said it was the commitment thing. They had a long talk and determined to not let Mr. Wade's behavior impact their long friendship. She and Ronnie had become closer after that. Joe had come back a few months ago for Ronnie's birthday. They all, including Hayden, who still considered Joe the son she never had, went out to dinner together. It was awkward at first, but Hayden and Mike had a way of putting everyone at ease. He left again the next day. She hadn't seen him again until he showed up at her doorstep Saturday night.

The big question was, if he wanted to get back together again, did she? As she ran, her shoulders drooped. She did like him—a lot.

"The fitness equipment's the next marker."

"Ugh. It could be hidden in any of the equipment."

"Or," Joe stopped and took a bottle of water out of his pack, "the equipment could be a decoy."

Lea glanced around. "You take the equipment, and I'll check out those bushes."

Joe nodded and examined the ab/crunch machine.

Lea poked around a fifteen-foot long row of shrubs. She carefully studied the ground around the shrubs. They wouldn't hide something where digging would disturb roots. This group was eco-friendly. They had a team go through the parks and re-seed any areas that were dug up. She got down on her knees and crawled along the grass next to the path. She stood. "Nothing over here."

Joe was under the rower machine. Lea crawled around the leg stretcher and push-up bar. She stood and clapped dirt off her hands. "I can't find it."

"Deanna Troi's telepathic. Use your mental gifts."

"Joe, you're not funny. Not while I'm nervous and hot and tired."

"Got it." Joe stood. "The rowing bar comes unscrewed. It was in the handle." He held up a map with the next coordinates. "That's the trick, they've eliminated the chest."

Lea marked the last stop while Joe threaded the handle back onto the rower. She handed the map to Joe. "We're doubling back. A two mile run to the last stop."

"Let's water up."

They finished a bottle of water. Nearing five o'clock, it was getting hotter. Joe had shed his jacket. Lea pulled the huge mop of hair off her head and stuffed it in her backpack. "Let's go." She took off running towards the hub of the spoke.

He pointed to the wig, curly black tresses hanging out of Lea's pack. "Hayden's not going to like that."

"She'll get over it. Especially, when we win."

As they approached the half-mile marker from the hub, Lea caught a glimpse of Sam and Lynn to their right. "Competition's gaining on us."

"We're here." Joe stopped.

Shoulder-high bushes hedged the red path on both sides. Lea pointed. "There's a drop-off to those picnic tables to our left and a water fountain to our right."

Joe adjusted his cap. "Or, it could be in the bushes."

"It's the last clue. They're not going to make it easy for us."

"To err on the side of caution," Joe said, "let's stay together. We'll start with the table."

They walked around and around the table. Checked under it twice and studied the ground.

Lea pulled trash out of a can and dropped it back in. She took out a small bottle of hand sanitizer and dumped a glob in her hands, rubbing them together. "Nothing in the trash can. Just paper."

Joe nodded to their left. "Sam's onto something over there." Joe rechecked the table and pulled the trash out of the deep can Lea had just finished examining. "Here." He held up a piece of waded paper he'd opened. "Hold this." He whipped out the cell phone and texted the codes to the gamemaster.

Lea and Joe stood, paralyzed. Lea couldn't breathe. The phone buzzed. Joe opened the text. "Congratulations! You've won the quest."

Joe raised his arms to heaven. "Yes! Yes!" He threw his arms around Lea and they hugged and kissed and hugged.

"Good work," he said, slapping her on the back.

They put all the trash back into the can and filled their holes. He put his arm around her and they started back to the hub.

Joe's phone buzzed again. "What's this?" He opened the text. "A message that Sam and Lynn just came in second."

13

1101

"Nicole, I have to go to the bathroom," Lila said, working across the footbridge to the slide.

"Mom said not to go to the bathroom at the park. We'll have to go home," Nicole said, climbing the ladder again.

"There's a lot of policemen here because of the joggers," Lila said. "I have to go now."

Nicole slid down the slide. "I guess it won't hurt this once."

She checked the area out around the restrooms and went in with Lila. When Lila was done, Nicole looked outside. She didn't see anyone near the row of hedges in front of the building.

"Let's go," she said to her little sister.

As Nicole started toward the play area, she heard a man shouting, "Don't hit me."

"Get down," Nicole ordered her sister.

Nicole crawled over to the bushes and pulled them apart just enough to see the running trail. Lila scooted next to Nicole. A man across the running path was kneeling on the ground, his hands raised covering his head. Another man stood over him with a bat.

Lila pulled the bushes apart and watched the men.

Nicole gasped as the man swung the bat and hit the other man in the head. The man on the ground fell over.

Lila leaned against her sister. Nicole pulled her cell phone out of her pocket and snapped a picture of the man with the bat. He hit the man again. She ducked as the man looked their way. After a few seconds, she raised her head and was horrified that the man with the bat was running towards them. Nicole and Lila huddled under the bushes as they heard the man's footsteps running so close to them that she could reach out through the bushes and touch him.

As his footsteps grew faint, she peered through the bushes trying to see the parking lot.

"Stay here," Nicole ordered Lila, who was crying.

Nicole crawled over to the bushes along the parking lot a few feet away. She saw the man talking to a woman. She snapped another picture. The woman ran across the lot and onto a hiking trail. The man got in his car and drove out of the lot.

"Nicole, I want to go home."

"We can't tell Mom. If she knows what we saw, she'll never let us come here again."

"I won't tell anybody. I just want to go home."

Lea and Joe took their time walking back to the hub to meet the other gamers. It was a nice afternoon, and they enjoyed the time outdoors. Joe's cell phone buzzed, again. He read the text that Jon had sent out.

"Brian VanDeer's been attacked. Everyone report to the parking lot, immediately."

Lea and Joe sprinted to Joe's pickup and drove around the service road to the southern, red trail. An ambulance was already at the site.

Jon was talking with two policemen. Shelly stood on the road watching the EMTs load Brian, who was conscious, into the ambulance.

"What happened?" Joe asked.

"I can't believe another gamer was attacked," Shelly said, wringing her hands. "Cody was working one side of the hill, looking for the last clue, and Brian was on the other side working behind the bushes. Cody called out to him, and when he didn't answer, he went over to investigate and found him unconscious. He called us right away."

"He didn't see anyone? Hear anyone?" Lea asked.

Shelly shook her head. "He smelled something funny. It burned his eyes. Police think Brian was pepper-sprayed. Because they were the farthest out and they were men, and also the lowest scorers, we didn't have as much security on them."

Lea nodded toward the road. "Ronnie's coming."

"I just got the call," Ronnie said, out of breath.

Shelly crossed the road to speak to her husband.

Joe turned to Lea. "Because I'm undercover, I can't be involved in the investigation here."

"I understand. It's going to be hard for you to not be involved, but you may find out more from the contestants if they don't know you're a policeman."

"You're right."

"I heard the call come in," Ronnie said, "and came right over.

Joe filled her in on the attack. "It's kinda odd," he added, "that Cody Ingham found both victims of the attacks."

Ronnie shrugged. "I don't know what to think. These boys weren't in the run to win. Why them?"

Lea spied Sam and Lynn approaching the group.

"I'm going to talk to the policemen," Ronnie said. "Joe, keep your cover. I know how hard this is, but you need to act like a contestant."

"I hear you."

"Who was hurt?" Lynn asked.

"Someone attacked Brian just like they did my mom."

"Is he all right?" Sam asked.

Lea watched Ronnie for a few seconds then turned back to Sam. "He was unconscious when Cody found him, but was conscious when they took him away."

"We only got one more of these quests," Lynn said. "They're going to have to issue hard hats to us."

Shelly stepped over to the group. "The police are going to search the area, so they want us to leave."

"Is everyone finished?" Ronnie asked.

Shelly nodded. "The Gleasons texted their codes. Brian and Cody didn't get a chance. We're done here. I want to get to the hospital and check on Brian."

Lea put her hand over her mouth. "His mother. Mom knows where he lives. Someone needs to take care of his mother. She can't be in her house alone."

"I forgot about that," Shelly said.

"You go to the hospital," Lea said. "You have enough to deal with. We'll take care of Mrs. VanDeer."

"We've been playing this game for over five years," Lynn said as they walked back to their vehicles. "We never had any trouble before."

Lea tossed her backpack into the back of Joe's truck. "They'll catch the person."

She climbed in Joe's pickup. "I hate to tell Mom someone else was attacked."

Joe pulled onto the main road and headed to Hayden's. "I don't like the way this is going. There's only one week left, but is the game worth someone dying over?"

"No, it isn't. For sure, it's got to be someone in the game."

Joe waited at a red light. "Or, one of the online betters hedging his bet. But you could be right. They had four extra policemen in the park. It's looking more like one of the gamers. I'm going to owe Ronnie dinner after all."

"Tell me that you two are not competing over who is proved to be the attacker. I hadn't thought of an online gamer hedging a bet. But, security was so tight, and the boys couldn't have won. We'd already texted the winning codes and Sam and Lynn were next."

"I don't know. I'll wait to see what Ronnie tells us later."

When Lea entered the living room, Hayden and Edna were sitting in front of the television. Bubbles was stretched out in a spot of sun on the carpet.

"Where's your hair?"

"In my pack. Mom, it was too hot."

"It'd keep you safe."

Lea sank down in a chair next to the sofa. "Mom, Brian VanDeer was hit over the head. He's in the emergency room now."

"Oh, no," Hayden gasped. "Not again."

"Is he bad?" Edna asked.

"He was conscious when the ambulance took him away."

"What about his mother? He told me about her, and she can't be alone at night."

"I don't know what to do. If we take her out of the house, she may become disoriented, especially if he isn't around."

"I can get some of the girls together," Edna said. "Two of us can stay with her tonight and two others stay with her tomorrow. If he's going to be in the hospital a long time, of course, we'll have to make other arrangements."

"I hate to ask people to do that. Mom's still under doctor's orders to reduce her activity. The only reason they let her come home is that I promised them she'd stay calm and uninvolved."

Edna pulled her cell phone out of her purse. "I'll call Frances. You've got some casseroles in the fridge. We'll take one over and stay with her tonight. What's her first name?"

Lea looked at Joe and they both shrugged. "We don't know."

"Mrs. VanDeer will work for now," Edna said.

Edna left to pick up Frances.

"That woman's a saint," Lea said. "She's been taking care of people in the church for thirty years."

"She's my dearest friend," Hayden said. "I'm just so upset about Brian."

"Mom, I'm starved. I'll make us some dinner."

"We still got two casseroles left," Hayden followed Lea to the kitchen.

Joe clicked off a cell phone call. "I'm going to Ronnie's to shower and change."

"You get back over here and help us eat these pies," Hayden ordered. "We got vanilla ice cream and pumpkin and apple pie."

"Be back in a few," Joe said, going out the door.

Forty minutes later, Lea had dinner on the kitchen table. Joe said grace and prayed for Brian. "This looks good."

"I bet you don't eat this good at home," Hayden said, scooping a huge helping of beef and potato casserole on his plate.

"I'm a bachelor. Microwave or Chinese take-out."

"It's sure been fun having you back," Hayden said, raising her eyebrows at Lea.

Yes, it has been fun having him around again. But he'd be gone in another week. Focus, I commanded my heart.

"Who do you think did this?" Lea asked.

Joe shook his head. "Sam and Lynn were next to us when it happened. They couldn't have run ahead, attacked him, and double backed. We'd have seen them. I can't think what the advantage is for Cody to incapacitate his partner—"

"So, where were the Gleasons?"

"They were on the far, east side, but all of us were working back toward the hub. I'll find out more from Ronnie later. I still feel in my gut that this all goes back to Mary Johnson. We haven't found any family of hers. She had to have had parents. Must have a brother or sister, aunt, cousins—someone." Joe shook his head. "She's involved; I just can't make the connection."

"Now that she's out of the game, why is the person still attacking?"

Joe ran his fingers through his hair. "I don't know, but there's something there with that woman."

After dinner, Lea cleaned up the kitchen. Hayden had talked Joe into watching the *Red II* movie with her. It was a bit violent, but her mother thought Joe would like all the shoot-'em-ups. It was all getting too much for Lea. If they continued the games through next week, who would be hurt next? They hadn't been able to prevent another attack. These games were supposed to raise money for childhood cancer research, but people were being violently attacked.

Her mother fretted over Mrs. VanDeer being alone. Lea had never thought about it before, but what if something happened to her? Who would look after her mother?

Edna and Frances. Ronnie and Joe. Ronnie's Uncle Jim. All of the women at the church her mother had attended since she was a little girl. Her mother was well covered.

14

1110

Lea nodded to the other contestants and took a seat next to Joe. The gamemasters had called an emergency meeting. During the annual gaming event, no participants were allowed in the Dylan's Games' building. The owner of the restaurant, whose daughter had successfully recovered from cancer, donated the banquet hall every year for the four-week event. Everyone assembled at the banquet room of Burelli's. Lea noted that Patty was nervous, ordering her boys to sit still and fussing at Carl.

Lynn nodded as she dropped down next to Sam. The two kids took seats in the back of the room, huddled over their tablets. Cody arrived last with a man Lea hadn't seen before. Cody hadn't shaved, and his eyes behind his red-rimmed glasses looked puffy from lack of sleep. Lea almost felt sorry for him.

"Thank you all for coming on such short notice," Jon Mathers began. "After what happened yesterday, I felt that I had to meet with you face-to-face. In the seven years of gaming, we've never had trouble like this. That's why we have such strict codes in our gaming family, to weed out troublemakers. My dear son wouldn't like what's going on. Wouldn't like it at all.

"Just to let you know, Brian VanDeer will be released this evening. Hayden's friends and some of our church members are caring for his mother. Brian asked if Kenard Baylor could stand in for him this week for the online gaming. Brian's still experiencing a lot of double vision and can't work on the computer."

The gamers nodded their heads and mumbled their approval. Lea was surprised that even Patty approved.

Jon ran his fingers through his hair. "I'm tempted to end this gaming event and award everyone on the basis of your current standings. But I'm going to leave it up to all of you. What do you want to do?"

The room was quiet for a few minutes. Cody shrugged. "I'm in. Me and Brian aren't quitters. I talked to Brian this morning, and he's hoping we can finish the game."

Patty spoke for her family. "We're not ready to stop," she said determinedly.

"Why am I not surprised?" Lea whispered to Joe.

Sam crossed his arms on the table and leaned forward. "Jon, do the police have any leads?"

"The police investigating the possibility that it's someone from the outside. Maybe a former gamer who lost and is trying to disrupt the games."

"I don't know how you can do it, but can you add more security for the last quest?"

"We'll figure something out by Saturday. I know this last outdoor quest wasn't very challenging, but we tried to scale it back for security concerns. We have an indoor place in mind for the next quest, we're just waiting on approval."

Lynn narrowed her eyes. "Someone's determined to stop this game, and I'm not quitting."

The gamers rumbled their agreement.

"We only have this week to finish. We'll have the final online game uploaded by six tonight. I'll notify you of the time that the final quest will be held. We'll keep it on Saturday. Don't forget to keep Brian and Mary Johnson in your prayers. Mary's condition is unchanged. There're refreshments offered. Thanks for coming."

Lea felt bad for Jon. As good and big as his heart was, he didn't deserve what was happening to his dear son's legacy. Benefit online competitions were catching on around the country. After finishing the game next week, she'd probably never play the games again. It wasn't her thing. But these people had earned her respect.

Shelly dropped pizza slices on a plate and sat in the back of the room with Jon, watching the gamers interact.

"They make good pizzas here," Jon said, finishing his slice.

"They put more sauce on them than other places do," Shelly said. "People seem to be enjoying themselves."

Jon nodded.

"Who do you think's doing this?"

Jon shrugged. He scooted the plate away and rested his arms on the table. Terrie shot him a paper airplane she made out of a paper plate. He reached down on the floor and shot it back to her. "Could be one of the gamers we sanctioned before. They usually move on to other games, but maybe somebody can't let go."

He took a gulp of soda. "Remember that woman and her two sons four years ago? Boys were shooting pellet guns at the gamers on the digs. She was going to take over our operation."

"How could I forget her?"

"Once in a while, someone strays into the games. We'll figure them out." He eyed Patty Gleason complaining to Cody about the point system. "I'm kinda putting my money on that new family."

Shelly eyed Patty ordering her husband to clean the table off.

"She's a troubled woman. Carl's a hard worker and provides well for his family. She never cuts him a bit of slack."

"We only got one more week. I'll get with the guys when the game's all over, and we'll figure out a way to make it safer. I'm not giving up. We're bigger now and raising more money. Bound to be some setbacks. But I don't like it when such nice people get hurt. We'll find a way to make it safer."

When Lea entered the house, she found her mother resting in the living room. She and Bubbles were alternately snoring. Joe had gone to Mary's to sleep. He was basically trespassing, but given the break-in and the brutality of the attack on the woman, plus the fact that Mary could still die, they needed to keep up the appearance that he was related to Mary.

She booted up her laptop and quickly worked through blogs that she was responsible for. It was hard to concentrate. All twelve of her bloggers were in good shape. Mrs. Washington posted that she wanted out of the contract. Lea was only too happy to let her go. The woman was never satisfied with any designs. What Lea had sent her, the woman had tried to recode the design herself and wrecked the blog. She sent her a polite email cutting her loose.

The kitchen door opened. "Knock, knock." Ronnie entered the kitchen.

"Come in," Lea said.

"I didn't want to ring the doorbell in case Hayden was sleeping."

"She's asleep in the living room. Have a seat. Did you eat?"

"Earlier."

Lea opened the fridge. "We've got apple, pumpkin, who makes pumpkin in May? And, check this out." She set a chocolate silk pie on the table. "I'll put on some coffee."

Lea poured Ronnie a mug of coffee and one for herself. She cut slices of the pie.

"After the day I had, this helps," Ronnie said, stretching out her long legs.

"I can't believe someone else was attacked." Lea sent one last email and closed her laptop. "I thought with all the police presence, no one would have the nerve to go after any of the gamers."

"It was kinda odd. Brian doesn't remember the actual attack, but the doctor says he was pepper sprayed. He's a big guy, a forklift operator. The only way a woman could take him down is to use something like pepper spray first, then club him. I feel responsible. I should have had watchers on all of the teams. I figured two big men, they could take care of themselves."

"Don't be so hard on yourself. You did have spotters throughout the park. This is all getting too much. I get a knot in my stomach every time I look at my mother to think someone she knew did this to her. She's such a kind person, how could you get to know her and nearly clobber her to death?"

"I agree," Ronnie said, pulling her long, frizzed brown hair behind her ears.

"Have you come up with anything at all on Mary Johnson's true identity?"

Ronnie raised her eyebrows and shook her head. "Nothing from her job at the mall. She quit the job months ago. We looked at the personnel file there, but no new information that we didn't already know. Fingerprint check in California criminal database came back negative. What concerns me is that a check on her social security filings reveal nothing. Her card was only issued six years ago."

"I can't help myself, but I'm starting to hate that woman. Through some sick, twisted agenda that only she knows about, she drew my mother into her web. And we've no idea what she's really up to, except that it almost got her and my mother killed."

"We don't know, Lea. They both could be innocent victims of a mugger in the park."

"If it weren't for her, my mother wouldn't have been in that park." Lea thought for a few minutes then sat up and rested her arms on the table. "For a woman Mary's age, you'd expect a social security card issued years ago. Ronnie, this isn't a random mugging. We can't find anything about her. How did she even get a driver's license without a valid social security number? If she doesn't work, where does she get money from? She has to buy groceries and pay utilities. That gaming equipment and software is worth over seven thousand dollars."

"She's got a valid Nebraska license. We checked. She's got one hundred thousand dollars in her checking account."

Lea furrowed her eyebrows. "Something's not right with her. Witness protection?"

"I was wondering about that today. Usually in law enforcement databases, there's a flag on data that tells us to quit searching. You know, I'm going to call Uncle Jim. Thirty years as a U. S. Marshall, he'll figure this out."

Ronnie called her uncle and explained the situation about Mary Johnson. She called her office and asked them to fax all the information about Mary Johnson, including her photo to her uncle.

"He's going to check into that social security number. He doesn't think she's in protection. The handlers would have seen the television news coverage and notified us by now. If there's anything there, Jim will find it."

Ronnie cut another piece of pie. "How's it going between you and Joe?"

Lea sat back and took a long sip of coffee. "He wants to start over, like nothing ever happened. What do you think is going on with him? He made up this story about a renegade police chief. He's not one to shy away from trouble. Not Joe Wade."

"I know that woman. Met her at a few training seminars. P.C.D. Power, control, and dominance. She'll crush anyone who blocks her way to the top. Joe's a great cop. Savvy. He'd stagnate under her domain, never make rank. By the time she's moved on up the ladder, it may be too late for him to advance. He's smart to get out from under her rule.

"I've seen her type before. They find a couple of guys under them to pick on. Makes them look good that they can police their unit all by themselves. No. He's better off moving out from under her."

"You think he'll apply for a position in Lincoln?"

"He's been making inquiries." She paused for a few seconds. "Lea, he's still in love with you. He hasn't said anything, but I can tell."

She toyed with a piece of crust on her plate. "I know. But he's going to have to make a stand. I can't do this off and on thing."

"I know. I wouldn't let him get away with that either. Just give him some time."

"I'm not going to make it easy for him."

"I wouldn't either."

"Just so we understand each other," Lea smiled. "Where's Mike tonight?"

"Salt Lake City for two days. He's in for a promotion at work, and if he gets it, he won't have to travel again."

"Wow. That'll be great."

"We'll be training some new rookies this summer. We've got budget approval to take them on permanently if they pass the trial period. That'll reduce my work load." Ronnie yawned. She pulled at long strands of her frizzed hair. "I'm thinking of going straight. Getting my hair straightened."

Lea shook her head. "It wouldn't be you. You'd look too harsh. Too old."

Ronnie sat up straight. "I definitely don't want to look too old."

She stood and shouldered her bag. "I just stopped by to check up on you. After we get this solved, you and I are hitting the spa for a whole day."

"You're on. Spa date."

15

1111

Early the next morning, Lea dragged into the kitchen.

"I got coffee going," her mother said, glancing out the kitchen window. She tapped on the window to distract the dog, hoping it would quit barking. "I don't know what she's barking at."

"I don't think she needs a reason." Lea dropped down in a chair at the table.

"How late did you work last night?" Hayden opened the door and Bubbles bounded inside, shaking herself.

"You've got too much energy for me this morning."

"Here." Her mother set a steaming cup of coffee in front of Lea.

"Thanks. We got eight thousand points. This game's really hard."

Hayden opened the oven and pulled out an egg and sausage quiche. She set it on a warming plate on the table. "That smells good."

"Mom, I'm supposed to be taking care of you. What's with all the cooking?"

"Honey, I'm fine. I called Joe to come over for breakfast. Frances dropped off this quiche on her way over to check on Brian and Donna. His mother's name is Donna."

Joe tapped on the kitchen door and entered. "Morning. Smells good in here."

Bubbles barked twice at Joe and disappeared into the living room, her nails scratching on the hardwood floor.

Hayden took her place at the table and prayed for God's blessing on their day. She took a sip of coffee. "Tomorrow, we go to the doctor. Maybe he'll clear me to start running again. My insides feel all itchy. And all that food people have been bringing—I got to take off a few pounds."

"Mom, that was a serious head injury," Lea reminded her for the hundredth time. "You need to take it slow."

"You rest; you rust. I'm being careful. Do you think we can squeeze in a visit to Mary today?"

"Sure," Lea said.

A cell phone chimed.

"It's mine," Lea stood. "It's in the living room. Excuse me."

"Frances said Brian's doing real good." She passed Joe a chocolate chip muffin. "He's a man. Must have a hard head."

Joe laughed. "Men's heads are harder than women's?"

"Trust me, Joe. I was married almost forty years. I know—"

"Bubbles!" Lea yelled.

"Uh oh," Hayden whispered.

"Give me that!"

Bubbles scampered into Hayden's bedroom with Lea in hot pursuit.

"Don't think I can't see you under there."

Hayden smiled. "She's under the bed."

"Shame on you."

Lea entered the kitchen and dropped down on her chair.

"I'm afraid to ask."

Lea plopped Hayden's new leather bag on the middle of the table. She dug into her eggs.

Hayden picked up the bag up and examined it. The strap had been bitten through and the dog had worked a hole through at one corner. "Honey, she's just upset at Mary not being with her. It'll pass." Hayden opened her wallet and took out a fistful of bills and a credit card. "She didn't chew up my money or my credit card."

Joe took a gulp of coffee. "You know, I just thought of something."

"Yes," Lea said. "Think real hard what we're going to tell Mary when she wakes up about how her dog died."

Bubbles scratched into the kitchen, slinking away from Lea and settling next to Hayden's chair.

Hayden scooped a spoonful of egg on a saucer and set it on the floor. She petted the dog's head. "I forgive you."

"You know," Joe said, "Mary's been real careful about her identity, but maybe we'll find something at her vet's office. She's very protective of the dog. It's had a recent rabies vaccination."

"It might be worth checking what information the vet has," Lea said. "Maybe there's a family member that would just love to take care of precious, little Bubbles."

Hayden raised her eyebrows at Lea. "Her vet's just a few blocks from here. I went with her a few times. It'd be good if we could find out if Mary has a sister or brother."

Lea stood. "Let's clean up here and get to the vet's. We've got a full afternoon of gaming ahead of us."

Lea, Joe, and her mother converged on Adkin's Veterinary clinic. An older man sat in the waiting room, leafing through a dog magazine.

He looked up at the group. "I'm just waiting. You go ahead."

"May I help you?" A young woman behind a desk in a blue apron set aside a stack of folders.

"I'm Hayden Curtis. I was in here before with Mary Johnson."

"I remember. That's Bubbles." She pointed to the dog in the carrier Joe held.

"Yes. Anyway, Mary had an accident and is in a coma in the hospital. I've been taking care of Bubbles. I can't locate any family of hers to call.

Mary mentioned once that she had a pet finder chip in Bubbles. Can you scan the dog and see if the identification chip is active? Maybe she's listed another family member's name."

"Set Bubbles on this low table here," the veterinary assistant said. "I'm so sorry to hear about Mary's accident. Will she be all right?"

"We're hoping she'll come out of it in a few days," Hayden said.

The technician pulled out her wand and waved it over the dog's neck. The wand beeped. "She's got a chip." She pressed a key on the computer. "You can put her back in her carrier."

"Let's see." The girl punched a few keys. "You're in luck. Most pet finder groups only list a number you key in with a password before we can access the information, but this one gives us all of her information."

The three of them stepped around and studied the fact sheet. Hayden pointed to the computer. "That's her address and phone number, but under additional owner, I don't remember her ever mentioning a Turner."

"Turner," Joe read out loud. "Fifteen-fifty Blue River Road. That's an odd address. No first name, just Turner."

"I'll pull Bubbles' chart."

The vet entered the waiting room, carrying a small dog. "Mr. Watson, Buster's just fine. I cleaned the wound. You can take this sleeve off in a few days."

"I appreciate it. I saw all that blood and thought he'd cut his foot off."

"We'll keep it clean then check it later in the week."

"Thanks a lot."

The man stepped over to Lea. "That's a storage place. Turner's Storage on Blue River Road. Fifteen-fifty sounds like a unit number. I used to rent space there years ago."

"Thank you. I appreciate you telling us that."

Joe held the door for the man as he exited.

"I'm Doctor Cleavers."

Joe explained. "We're trying to find information on Bubbles' owner. Mary Johnson is in a coma, and we can't locate any family. I'm Joe Wade, Kansas City Police." He pulled out his wallet and showed her his police ID. "I can get a warrant, but we're trying to cut through all the red tape."

"I understand. That's not a problem since I know Hayden."

"I remember when we had to put down my Ginger," Hayden said. "I never wanted another dog after that. Couldn't go through that again."

"Here's Bubbles' chart," the girl handed the folder to the vet.

The vet thumbed through the record. "Her information sheet." She pulled it out and handed it to Joe.

Joe shook his head. "Same information that's on the microchip. What's this cell phone number at the bottom? It's not the same as the other phone numbers."

"I don't know. We copy down any information we can get. We never know, like now, when we'll need it."

"Excuse me, I'm going to call the detective on the case." Joe stepped over to the door and called Ronnie.

"What's the cell number on the phone we found on Mary?" He waited a minute. "Okay. I've got a different number here. Track this number down." He read her the number. "She may have a burner phone, although I can't imagine why. Look, I need a warrant for a storage locker. Turner's on Blue River Road. Unit fifteen-fifty. I'm guessing it's probably under Mary Johnson's name. We'll meet you there in a half hour."

He handed the paper back to the vet. "You've all been a big help. Thank you."

"Do let us know how Mary is doing?" Doctor Cleavers asked.

"I'll be sure to call you," Hayden said.

A half hour later, Lea and Joe met Ronnie and two deputies at Unit 1550. Joe greeted Ronnie with a nod. "Sis."

"Bro." Ronnie grinned.

"Uncle Jim called and said that nothing in the information we sent him on this woman has anything to do with witness protection. Let's hope we find some answers here. I got her keys out of evidence, but none of them fit the lock."

"I got a bolt cutter in the back of the pickup." Joe retrieved the cutter and cut the lock.

"You know that what's behind this door could cause you to buy me dinner," he said as he leaned down to lift the door.

"You know," Ronnie said, "that there may be nothing behind that door."

He lifted the door. His hand fumbled along the wall until he found the light switch and flicked it on.

Lea stood next to Joe. "What is this?" she whispered.

After tugging on latex gloves, Lea, Joe, and Ronnie entered the eight by ten unit. Four long folding tables, littered with notebook binders and papers, were stationed lengthwise in the center of the unit. Large plastic tubs and boxes were strewn along the right wall of the unit. But it was the back wall that captivated them.

Large poster boards taped along the back wall held pictures of children taped on the boards in organized columns. Ronnie and Joe gaped at the pictures and skirted around the tables to the back of the room.

Joe shrugged. "Who is this woman? Is this some kind of kidnapping ring? Look at all of these pictures of little girls."

"Not all pictures have names, but all pictures have dates," Ronnie said, pointing to the display.

"Goes back years," Joe said. "Sixties, eighties."

"All little girls," Ronnie observed.

"Why would you display kids' pictures in a storage locker?" Joe wondered out loud.

Lea opened a scrapbook on one of the tables and slowly flipped through the pages. As she read the newspaper articles fastened to the pages, her heart sank. She picked up another notebook and read the latest entries in what seemed to be a journal.

She focused on the last entry the day before the attack. *Try to get something for DNA. John will help. But I can't mess up. Whatever I do, I can't mess up this time.*

Lea went back to the scrapbook and read another article posted from two thousand and five.

"I wonder where these children are today." Joe mumbled. "If they were kidnapped, who has them, now?"

Ronnie looked closer at the pictures. "Do you think she has contact with them? With whoever took them?"

"Wait a minute." Joe pointed to the last row of pictures in the middle of the wall. "That's Terrie Foster, Lynn's child." Six pictures of Terrie were taped in the last column. "What are her pictures doing here? Was this woman planning on kidnapping her?"

Tears stung Lea's eyes. "How could I have been so wrong?" In Lea's mind, Mary Johnson was a monster, a woman who put her mother in harm's way.

"What did you say?" Joe asked, examining two side-by-side pictures on the back wall.

"I was wrong about Mary Johnson."

"How were you wrong about her?" he asked, still gaping at the pictures.

Lea said quietly, "She's looking for her granddaughter."

16

10000

"What?" Joe whirled around and faced Lea.

Lea held up the large scrapbook. "She's looking for her granddaughter."

"What are you saying?" Ronnie came around the table and read over Lea's shoulder.

"These newspaper clippings are of a carjacking in Houston a little over seven years ago. She lost her granddaughter, and she thinks she's found her." She handed the book to Ronnie and picked up a three-inch wide binder and slowly thumbed through it. "These journal entries date back in descending order to July 2005."

Joe stepped up next to Ronnie and studied the pages with Ronnie. "She thinks Terrie Foster's her granddaughter?"

Lea nodded and handed another binder to Ronnie.

Ronnie read articles on several pages. "News stories about the carjacking," she paraphrased.

"It will take time for all of you to go through this," Lea said, "but it looks like her daughter and son-in-law were killed in a violent carjacking almost eight years ago in Houston. The two-year-old baby in the back seat of the car was never found."

"Joe, here's a newspaper article." Ronnie pointed to a page in the scrapbook. "Benjamin and Carly Dean making a plea to the kidnappers to return the baby. The baby is Emma Norris." Ronnie handed the book to Joe and returned to the back wall.

"These pictures." Ronnie pointed to the wall studying the columns. "This first column is Carly Dean, AKA, Mary Johnson. Slightly obese woman with long, curly hair. She doesn't resemble the woman in a coma in the hospital. Mary Johnson's pencil thin with short, straight hair. The pictures are clusters of Carly at ages five through twelve. The next column is her daughter, Kate Norris at the same ages. They're very close in likeness. These six pictures are Terrie Foster."

Lea looked closely at the pictures. "A lot of similarities between Carly, Kate, and Terrie at ten years old."

Ronnie sighed deeply. "With a woman Mary's age, something should have popped. She was too careful hiding her past. I figured an abusive husband or a boyfriend. I would never have thought this. It's a whole new investigation."

Ronnie stood with her arms crossed in front of her. "If Terrie really is Emma Norris, how did Lynn Foster end up with her?"

"Lots of questions," Joe said, behind her.

"Yes, but, Emma would only be nine years old now," Lea said. "Terrie's twelve."

Ronnie shook her head. "It wouldn't be that hard to fudge a couple of years. The girl's very bright, and if her parents were tall, she'd be about the right height for sixth grade."

"Why isn't the FBI involved?" Lea asked. "Why is she looking by herself?"

"Case probably went cold," Ronnie replied. She turned and looked again at the back wall. "I do admit, this is ingenious. Facial recognition between family members at the same age."

"Is she looking for proof?" Joe asked, removing the lid from a plastic tub. He pulled out a birthday gift, wrapped for a child. He read the card, and a lump formed in his throat. He looked at another gift. *Happy Birthday, baby Emma. From Grandpa and Grandma.*

"What's all of that?" Lea pointed to the boxes.

Joe gently set the gifts in the box and closed the lid. "Birthday gifts for each year she was missing," he said in a hoarse whisper.

Joe nodded to the table. "What's that blinking light?"

Lea pulled a cell phone from under a pile of papers. "Cell phone face says, Ben."

"Don't answer it," Ronnie warned.

Joe pulled notecards out of his jacket pocket and checked the cell phone number. "Same number the vet had. There was the clue to Mary's identity all that time, and we didn't know it."

He handed the phone to Ronnie. She waited until the phone went quiet and opened the call history. "Her husband's been calling every day several times a day. He doesn't know she's in the hospital." She set the phone down.

Joe thumbed through a notebook. "Some kind of journal. Notes reminding herself to not mess up again. Be careful. The 'don't mess up again' worries me. What did she do before?"

He set the book down and glanced around the room. "Boy, this revs the investigation up a notch."

Ronnie stepped to the door and surveyed the unit.

"So, is this why the women were attacked?" Lea asked. "Mary Johnson, or Carly Dean was getting too close to finding her granddaughter?"

Ronnie tucked her hair back behind her right ear. "It's possible, but we also have to consider the possibility that the attack may be completely unrelated. In these investigations, you have to keep an open mind to all possibilities."

"Also, the Gleasons joined Dylan's Games just after Mary Johnson," Joe pointed out. "Could be a connection there, but I don't know where. Mary's from Houston and the Gleasons from Minnesota. That's a stretch."

Ronnie studied the pictures in the back of the unit. "Let's focus on Mary Johnson or Carly Dean for now."

"How you want to handle this?" Joe asked.

"As quietly as possible. Nothing on the radio that can be picked up on police scanners. I don't want that girl disappearing in the night with the child, if in fact, this is Emma. We'll dig deeper into Lynn Foster and Sam Preston's background. They're both pretty tight.

"If this turns into a kidnapping case, I'll have to notify the FBI, but first, I want to know what kind of mess I'm stepping in."

She nudged Joe's arm. "I need you to go down to Houston and interview Benjamin Dean. We need to let him know his wife's in a coma. See how he reacts." She glanced over at Lea, who was leafing through the scrapbook. "Why don't you take Lea with you? She's good at reading people."

"Not a bad idea."

Lea stepped back from the table. "Ronnie, I'm not a police investigator."

"You're good at watching people."

"What about Mom?"

"We'll take care of her. Mike's out of town. We'll have a sleepover like the old days. You two leave this afternoon, you can be back by tomorrow."

Joe grinned at Lea. "Road trip."

Ronnie thumbed through the journal again. "We'll interview Ben Dean first, then we'll go from there."

Joe left to get a notepad from his truck.

"What are you doing?" Lea screeched at Ronnie.

"You two will get in a little bonding time. Be good for both of you. Besides, I do need someone to focus on Ben's reactions to Joe's questions."

"Erick," Ronnie addressed her deputy, posted outside. "Here're my keys. Take the squad car and pick up my car and come back here. Park two rows over. I don't want anyone to notice any activity at this unit. We don't know who all's involved in this. Ask for a forensic team. Nothing on police radios. I'll call the captain." She pulled out her cell phone, called her captain, and filled him in on what they'd found.

Joe peeled off his latex gloves. "That's a smart move to keep this quiet."

"The girl gets spooked and takes off with the kid, we may never find her again."

"If it's really Emma."

Joe had a smug look on his face. "I might not be buying dinner after all."

"It's not over until it's over," Ronnie said. "I thought you had a plane to catch."

Joe started toward the pickup and said to Lea, "She's worse than my boss lady in Kansas City."

"I heard that," Ronnie said, loudly.

17

10001

Joe pulled up across the street from a two-bed-room house on a quiet street and parked. "Pickup in the driveway."

Lea scanned the area. "Nice neighborhood."

"Let's go hear what Mr. Dean has to say."

Joe rang the doorbell. A minute later, a man opened the door. He was a tall, older man with thinning hair, dressed in pressed jeans, a blue shirt, and tan coat jacket.

"What can I do for you?"

"Benjamin Dean?"

"That's me."

Joe held up his police badge and his ID. "We'd like to talk to you about Carly Dean."

The man's face fell. "Is she all right?"

So he admits to knowing her. This might be easier than he thought it would be. "May we come in?"

"Sure. Sure." He swung the door wider.

The room opened to a large sitting room with a kitchen in the back.

"Have a seat," he pointed to a sofa.

Joe and Lea eased down on plush, thick cushions, while Benjamin perched on the edge of a chair. "My wife okay?"

Joe noticed a suitcase and a carry-on bag against the wall next to a large dog pillow. Joe looked the man in the eyes. "Carly Dean was attacked a week ago. She's stable in the hospital, but she's in a coma. We had a hard time locating any next-of-kin."

Benjamin punched his left hand with his right fist. "I knew it. I knew something would happen some day." He scooted back in the chair and closed his eyes.

"Mr. Dean, can you tell us what's going on with your wife? Maybe there's a way we can help her. She's presenting herself as a Mary Johnson."

The man in front of them seemed to age fifty years. He looked up at Joe. "It's the baby... she can't let it go." He stood and went to a buffet on the far wall and removed a family album from a drawer. He returned to his chair and opened the book.

"This is our little Emma." He handed the book to Joe and opened it to a picture of a pretty little girl with a birthday hat on sitting on Ben's knee. "She'd just turned two. We had Paul's parents and everyone over for a big party that afternoon."

He took a minute and looked up at Joe and Lea. "We never knew so much happiness and sadness in one day. The kids left around ten that night. Somehow they crossed paths with carjackers."

His shoulders sagged. "I still remember like it was yesterday the policemen knocking at the door at midnight. We were finishing up the dishes in the kitchen..."

Joe had seen victims relive crimes twenty years later with emotions as fresh as the day the violence first happened.

"They killed my daughter, Kate and Paul, her husband. Took off with the car and the baby. Police found the car a week later, burned in a ditch. They combed through the rubble again and again and said there were no human remains. The baby wasn't there."

Joe let him talk it out. It's always better to let them talk.

"Got a couple of prints, but never could match them to anyone. Anyway," he took out a handkerchief and wiped his face, "Carly couldn't leave it."

He looked up at Joe. "She lived, you know. My Kate. We stood by her bed at the hospital. She asked us to find her baby and then took her last breath."

Joe closed the scrapbook and set it on the coffee table. He gave the man a minute to deal with his grief. "We found a storage unit with pictures of girls taped on a wall," he said quietly.

He nodded. "She does that. When she thinks she's found Emma, she rents a unit and starts collecting information. She matches the girl's pictures with herself and Kate. She's done this two other times. One time, we had enough evidence on a girl, that the FBI ordered DNA tests on the child. The girl couldn't account for her life around the time the child was born and for the next three years. She was pretty heavy into drugs at that time. DNA proved the girl wasn't Emma. It's pretty upsetting for a mother to be told her daughter may have been kidnapped and force them to go through tests to prove their identities. We can't make that mistake again."

"Mr. Dean, your wife's involved with a group of online gamers."

"You can call me Ben. She does that, too. After a couple of years, the case went cold. Three years ago, a man was arrested for a violent home invasion. His name was Frank something. I can't remember his last name. He was in jail, awaiting trial when the prints popped for the carjacking. Hoping for a lighter sentence, he told the whole story. Gave the name of the man who shot Kate and Paul. Andrew Watts. An accomplice with them was a Sandra Coulter. Says the girl tried to stop the shooting, but Andrew fought her off. He was going to sell the baby to someone up north South Dakota or Minnesota, I can't remember."

Joe's mind made a lightning fast connection between Minnesota and the Gleasons.

"But this Sandra disappeared with the child," Ben went on. "He thought she was hiding from Andrew. The boy was convicted of the home invasion and sent to prison. He died six months later from a brain tumor."

"Did they ever find the other man?" Joe asked.

Ben nodded. "Watts was arrested two years ago on bank robbery charges. He was also a suspect in the death of a policeman in Las Vegas.

"The FBI questioned him. They said he got pretty violent and threatened that the police better get Coulter before he did. Still, behind bars, threatening to kill the baby. They were putting together a case to charge him with my daughter's death, but he was stabbed in a prison yard fight and died."

"So, you've been searching on you own?" Joe asked.

The man sighed deeply, looked up at the ceiling and back at Joe. "We spent over a million dollars of our own money on detective agencies. Mostly, they were just taking our money. They were always getting close and just needed ten thousand more dollars." He shook his head. "We gave up on detectives and started looking on our own. I have a good job with an oil company. I work things from here." He took another breath. "When Carly didn't call me back last week, I should have known then that something was wrong. I got an eight o'clock flight to Lincoln tonight."

"Where did the gaming come in?" Joe asked.

"I was getting to that. The FBI profiler said that this Sandra Coulter was obsessed with online MMORPG games. He explained to us that sometimes a person in hiding can't give up their habits. The other two girls that Carly followed played online games. They had shady pasts, so it made them suspects."

"Those games are hard. I've been trying to learn. How did she do it?" Lea asked.

"She paid teenagers in the neighborhood to teach her. Took a course at a community college. Got really good. She really thought that she would find Emma through gaming clubs. She was playing with a group in Lincoln and said she located a girl that looks like Emma at this age. She was taking her time. She didn't want to be wrong again.

"She was collecting information to turn over to the authorities when she got sick last winter. Had to come home here and have her gall bladder out. She was real sick for a while, but recovered. I tried to get her to give it up, but she went right back to it. Can you tell me what happened in Lincoln?"

Joe finger combed his hair. "I think the attack was unrelated to this case, but because of the attack, we were able to locate you. Carly, and Lea's mother, Hayden Curtis are in the run for a one hundred fifty thousand dollar prize the end of this week. A week ago, someone hit Carly and Hayden in the head with a blunt object. Hayden recovered, but Carly's in a coma. She's breathing on her own. If we don't turn up a relative, they'll transfer her to a nursing home."

Ben stood and paced by his chair. "Carly doesn't care about the money. She just wants the girl. I've got to go to her."

"Why don't I change your reservation to a ten o'clock flight, at the police department's expense? I could use that time to talk to you some more and find out everything I can about this case. We put our heads together, maybe we can solve this kidnapping."

"What about Bubbles? Our dog?"

"She's at my mother's house," Lea said. "Mom's taking good care of her."

"I'm so relieved."

"I got a file here in a big box of all the police reports. Also, the FBI did a complete DNA workup from items that were Emma's to DNA from the parents and all four grandparents. Once we find Emma, it won't take long to prove it's her. I've been working with an Agent Hawkins. He's been real helpful. Any time I ever called him, he'd drop whatever he was doing and make time for us."

"That's a good start," Joe said. "Ben, we have every reason to believe Carly will wake up. I can't promise you that the girl is Emma, but we'll know in a few days."

Ben had a faraway look about him. Joe felt the man's grief. A lot of cops distanced themselves from feeling for the victims, but Joe wanted to feel something. Keep it under control, but wanted to always care about the people he served.

"I'll get you that box, and then I got to get to Carly."

18

10010

Patty Gleason called her husband at his work number. "Carl. I wanted you to pick up some ice cream on your way home."

"Remember, I told you that I was working late tonight? We've got that audit on a bank coming up. I can't get away from here until late."

"I'm sorry. I forgot. I'll try and get out later. Bye."

She clicked off. She just wanted to be sure he was at his office.

She returned to the computer and worked her computer controls to phaser the Gorribog in front of her and then she turned her attention to the next one. She was glad it would all be over Saturday, and maybe they'd be one hundred and fifty thousand dollars richer.

A momentary lapse in concentration, and a Gorribog clubbed her from behind, and Patty's online character crumpled to the ground. "I can't believe this."

Patty slogged her way out of the swamp and raced back to the village. Working alone, she made quick work of the threats and set up for an assault at the next village. She'd complete that quest later.

She brought up the gamer standing's page. As expected, Hayden Curtis and Mary Johnson were still holding first place. Sam and Lynn were only a few hundred points behind. She pursed her lips and stared hard at Brian and Cody's standing above hers.

She had to win. Think of it, her on the television news. Her picture all over the Internet. She'd win the game and have a victory party. Invite all their neighbors, and they would congratulate her on how intelligent she was.

It wasn't fair that Jon was picking on her because they were new to the game, micromanaging every move they made online. He didn't watch the others that closely. Besides that, he was letting new people in the group so close to the end. He probably wasn't even doing a background check on them like he did the original gamers. If she didn't win one of the prizes, she'd claim fraud and demand an investigation. If the new players didn't have a complete folder, she'd sue and get more than one hundred fifty thousand dollars.

She returned to the game page and slouched back in her chair. She thought that after the top contenders were eliminated that it'd make it easier to move up, but then Jon let two new gamers take their place. The girl wasn't much of a threat. It was that Joe Wade who presented the challenge.

Who was Joe Wade? Mary's nephew? She Googled Joe Wade in Los Angeles. "This is impossible. Thirty-nine million Joe Wades." She cleared her screen. She got up and stared out the window at her perfectly manicured lawn. Mary never mentioned any family. Said her husband died and moved here to start a new life.

There had to be a way to knock out Joe and Lea. She was sure she could get through Sam and Lynn's defenses to the top. What would make Joe and Lea give up? Joe was rock solid. He wasn't going anywhere. But Lea, she was weak. Stupid girl. At her age, unmarried.

True, she was married to an imbecile, who'd still be working changing tires at that auto shop where she'd met him if it weren't for her pushing him to get an education and make something of himself. He whined all the way through business school and finally got an MBA. He complained incessantly about his boring job. He wanted to take their hard-earned winnings next week and dump it all into building a swimming pool in the back yard. What a myopic man?

It was up to her to be sure her boys worked hard in school and got good grades. Did well in sports. They wouldn't become the loser that their father was. But kids tied you down.

Hayden's daughter was like her husband. No ambition. Why couldn't this ridiculous girl make something of herself? What would make her give up?

Her mother. She was devoted to that old woman. If her mother had an accident, no matter how minor, she might back out.

A knock on the kitchen door. She put the game on pause.

"Hey gorgeous." Bruce Schupe entered the kitchen, embraced Patty, and kissed her.

Patty kissed him and stepped back, waving her finger in his face. "Business before pleasure."

She fixed him a drink, and they settled in front of the computer. He took over her husband's character in the game, and they were scoring points. She had promised him half of their winnings. Carl was used to her having her own private bank account. He'd do whatever she wanted with the money they won. What a mouse.

Now Bruce, there was a man. Tall, muscular—and smart. He had an engineering degree and was brilliant with the games. He was everything her husband wasn't. And he loved her. Couldn't get enough of her. She only wished that he'd come into her life years ago.

Carl was safe. A dependable, predictable worker in an accounting firm. She had his name, a nice house, and two boys. A decent element of respect from the neighbors at dinner parties.

But Bruce was exciting. Unpredictable. Wasn't afraid to bend the rules. In a couple of years, the boys would be in college, Carl's responsibility then. She'd done all she could with them. She'd convince

Carl to let her put the money they won in savings for the boys' college tuition. When the time was right, she'd leave Carl and take the savings with her.

For now, they had a game to win—her and Bruce.

It was always her and Bruce, now. When she was working the game with Carl, she imagined Bruce next to her at the controls. When they were eating dinner, she imagined Bruce at the head of the table.

"We going to win this thing?" he asked.

"Of course," Patty said, shadowing him, watching for attacks. "In a few years, the boys will be gone, and it'll be just the two of us."

"Two years is a long time." He looked over at her, gazing into her eyes. "What if I don't want to wait?"

"Waiting's half the fun. It's an adventure. Finding new secret places to meet. Our own private quests. Makes our times together more exciting."

He liberated another village.

She gasped. "We did it! We blasted through Sam and Lynn's defenses. By tomorrow, we should be in first place."

Bruce closed the program. "Business is done."

19

10011

Home from the doctor's office, Hayden dashed into her bedroom and donned her sweats and running shoes. She wanted to get her walk in before Lea got back from Houston. If she exercised and nothing happened, she could use that as leverage for future walks. She adjusted her sweatband around her head and returned to the kitchen.

"What are you doing?" Edna asked.

"The doctor said I could start walking today."

Edna held up her hand. "Wait a minute, he said a couple of times a week, and absolutely no jogging or running. Why don't you wait until Lea gets back?"

"Let's just tiptoe around the block and see how I do. If I don't get dizzy, we can go again tomorrow."

"I'm afraid something will happen to you, and I'll have to face Lea—alone."

"Edna, I've walked around these blocks for nearly fifty years. Nothing's happened before, and nothing's gonna happen now. You coming?"

Bubbles pawed Hayden's leg, begging for a walk. "You stay here. We'll be right back. And don't chew anything while I'm out. I'm not sure how many more times I can keep saving you from Lea."

"Let's get this over with." Edna followed Hayden out of the house. "I should have signed some kind of release form, exonerating me from any injuries you receive. You better walk very carefully."

Hayden took off down the driveway.

"Slower," Edna ordered. "You'll be at a full trot in a minute."

Hayden slowed her pace half a step. They walked along the side of the street to avoid the ups and downs of the curbs.

"It's sure great to be outta that house." She took a big gulp of air. "I'm feeling well again."

"How are things between Joe and Lea? Every time I see them, it's all about the game. Do you think they're back together again?"

"I had a good talk with Ronnie this morning. Seems like Joe only came back to patch things up with Lea and then all this came up. It hurt her bad when he took off before, but I think she's softening." She put her hand on Edna's arm. "I'm praying real hard they get engaged."

"That's a good prayer. I'll add that to my long list."

They reached the end of the block. "It's such a nice day, let's just take one more block then go back."

"One more, and that's it," Edna groaned.

"I can't believe they're squeezing a new home between those two. They're so close." Hayden pointed to the new house that was being framed.

"Watch this mud," Edna said, picking her way through the mud caked on the road from the building site.

A white compact car came towards the women from behind, and sped up, aiming for them.

"Is that going to hit us?" Edna screamed, leaping towards the sidewalk.

It swerved towards the women, and Hayden jumped out of the way, falling onto the sidewalk.

Edna fumbled in her pocket and pulled out her cell phone. She got up and ran to the middle of the street to get a shot of the car, but her hands trembled so badly, she dropped the phone. The car turned the corner and disappeared.

"You all right?" She tried to help Hayden up.

Hayden stood and moaned. "It's my ankle. It's a good thing my arm was already in a cast."

"I just knew something would happen. Sit down, let me check your ankle."

"I'm okay." She tried to take a step and grabbed Edna's shoulder. She attempted to move her foot. "Oh. I can't move it."

Edna swung Hayden's good arm around her shoulder, and they headed back towards the house. "Lea's gonna kill me."

A pickup pulled out of the work site and stopped. "You girls all right?" a man called out.

"I just twisted my ankle," Hayden replied.

"I'll give you a lift home."

He dropped them at the house, and Edna helped Hayden into her car. She went into the house and got her purse.

As Edna drove to the hospital, she glanced over at her friend. "Hayden, it's like that car headed straight for us."

"I've been trying to put it out of my mind, but I think you're right. The driver didn't even stop to see if we were hurt. Did you get a picture?"

"No. And, it didn't have a license plate. I thought it was a man driving. He was tall and had on a black cap. I didn't see his face. Did you see anything?"

"Only the car when you yelled." Hayden leaned back in the seat. Someone had tried to hit her with a car. The second attempt on her life in two weeks, and only one day after her daughter and Joe discovered that Terrie Foster had possibly been kidnapped. What in the world had she gotten herself in to? She had promised Lea and Ronnie that she wouldn't say anything about the new investigation, but now Edna was involved.

"Look, Edna, I'll just say that I fell off the curb, walking. I'll tell Lea what happened when she gets home. There's things about that investigation that I have to be careful about."

"I understand. Just as long as you tell Lea."

"I will."

20

10100

Lea threaded her way through the arrival area at the airport and was surprised to see Ronnie waiting for them. It was nearly midnight. "Hey, Ronnie."

"Howdy. Welcome back." Ronnie gave her a hug.

Joe introduced Ben Dean to Ronnie.

"I was just at the hospital a few hours ago. The neurologist said that Carly's dreaming and movement during her dreams are a faint sign that she may be waking up. He was careful to explain that waking won't be like when we wake up in the morning. Just a heightened awareness of life for her. But it's the first encouraging movement in her in a week."

"Thanks for telling me that."

"I have a car and driver outside waiting for us."

When they were in the SUV, Ronnie turned to Lea in the seat behind her. She had waited until Lea was strapped in so she wouldn't get all wild. "Lea, your mother had a fall today. I wanted to tell you myself, not in a phone call or email. She sprained her ankle."

"She still gets dizzy, not as bad as last week, but pretty often."

"Unfortunately, it wasn't a dizzy spell. She and Edna went for a walk in her neighborhood, and a car came out of nowhere and tried to run them down. They dove to the side of the road, and the car sped off."

Lea covered her face with her hands. "Oh, no."

"She's fine. Just a sprained ankle. She's at home. Officer Theresa Myers is with her."

"Is Edna okay?"

"She wasn't hurt. She tried to get a picture, but couldn't. She said that the car didn't have a license plate. I also stationed a guard outside of Carly's room."

"This is awful," Lea cried, tears forming at the corners of her eyes. "Mom would never hurt anyone. She doesn't deserve this."

"Lea, we're taking every precaution. She's fine," Ronnie tried to reassure her friend. When Edna called from the hospital, it made Ronnie physically sick to her stomach. "We'll have a police detail on her until we figure this thing out. The driver had to pass by a convenience store, and we got a good pic of the side of the vehicle and a figure of what appears to be a man driving the car."

The driver dropped Joe and Ben off at Mary's house. Lea told them to come over for breakfast. The driver pulled in Hayden's driveway.

"It's late, and I'm going home. I'll stop by on my way to work tomorrow."

"Ronnie, thanks for everything."

Lea entered the house. She found her mother, dozing on the couch with Bubbles' head on her leg.

The officer introduced herself. "I'm Theresa. She's fine. I'll be in the kitchen."

Lea nodded. She sat on the edge of the coffee table. Bubbles ears perked up, but she didn't move. Hayden opened her eyes. She reached over and grabbed Lea's hand.

"Oh, Mom." Lea leaned forward and kissed her mother's forehead.

"Honey, I'm just fine. Really."

"Mom, you can't stay in that game. We've got to pull out."

"Lea, that's what they want us to do. I'm not a quitter. We're going to finish this game if I have to crawl around the outdoor quest on all fours to complete it. That little girl's life is at stake if she really is this Emma child. Lynn may have legally adopted her and doesn't even know she was kidnapped. We got to keep this up for Terrie's sake."

"I love your spirit, but it's getting too dangerous." Her mother was always willing to believe the best about people. Only she would believe that Lynn didn't know that her daughter wasn't her daughter.

"It'll all be over Saturday. I'm confined to the house, so what can happen?"

A lot.

"What's that you got?" Hayden pointed to the scarf Lea had in her hand.

Lea reached over and scratched the dog behind her ears. "I brought Bubbles a red Texas bandanna."

"She has a way of getting to you, doesn't she?"

"Ben Dean explained about the day his daughter died and the baby disappeared. This dog is the only link between him and his missing granddaughter."

"I'm going to sleep here. I already got my spot all warmed up. You get some sleep. We'll be all right."

Lea made sure Theresa was comfortable and told her to help herself to the food in the fridge. She changed into her nightgown and snuggled deep under the covers. She was emotionally charged and couldn't sleep. Who was doing this?

A gamer disrupting the game?

A person who kidnapped a baby years ago?

If it were about the kidnapping, then Terrie Foster was Emma Norris.

21

10101

The next morning, Joe tapped at the kitchen door and entered with Ben Dean. "Morning."

"Hi," Lea said, taking a pan of cinnamon rolls out of the oven. "Mom's injury spawned a whole new wave of food deliveries."

"Good Morning, Ben. Why don't you sit here," she pulled out a chair, "and I'll get you some coffee."

"Thanks."

Lea heard Bubbles scratching across the floor. Mom must be up. Bubbles scratched into the kitchen and sniffed at her food bowl.

"Hey, Bubbles."

"Ruff. Ruff. Ruff." Bubbles bounded over to Ben and hopped up into his lap.

"Hey, girl, I missed you." He scratched behind her ears.

Bubbles whined and licked his face, unable to contain her excitement.

Hayden hobbled into the kitchen, fully dressed and ready for her day, her left arm in a sling and her left leg in a soft bubble cast. "You must be Mary's husband," she said, shaking Ben's hand. "I'm so glad you're here."

"I'm sure glad to meet you. You're all Carly talks about when she calls."

"We're praying real hard for her."

Lea set a pot of coffee in the middle of the table. "I got hot rolls and a scrambled egg and cheese casserole coming." She set the rolls on the table.

Joe slathered butter on a roll and took a bite. "That's good. You know, I was thinking, let's all keep Mary's alias she's currently using. I don't want anyone to slip up and accidentally call her Carly." He turned to Ben. "Is there another name we can use for you?"

"My middle name's Arthur. I never use it. Arthur Smith?"

Joe nodded. "That's good, Uncle Art."

"I do hope that's your little granddaughter, but I can't imagine Lynn as a kidnapper. She's a really sweet, smart girl. Maybe she legally adopted Terrie and didn't know she was stolen."

"We'll know in a few days," Joe said, pouring more coffee.

Ben sipped his coffee and watched the group around the table interact. From his discussions with Joe last night and meeting the family here, their concern for Carly overwhelmed him.

When they first lost Kate and Paul, the response from the community was staggering. Then over time, it trickled away, leaving Ben and Carly searching by themselves. Eventually, their isolation from society became the norm. John Hawkins called him every month. They'd have lunch. There was never any new information.

When Carly started calling from Lincoln, she sounded better than she had in years. Even if this wasn't Emma, Carly had crossed paths with some wonderful people. A lump formed in his throat. It had been a long time since he'd had a sense of family.

Bubbles wouldn't leave Ben's lap. He fed her bites of egg.

Lea sat next to her mother and scooped egg on her plate. "Where did the name Bubbles come from? That's a little odd for a dog."

Ben took a sip of coffee and set the cup down. "Emma. Kate and Paul got Bubbles a few months before Emma's second birthday. She was just starting to put words together. They asked her what to name the dog, and she insisted on Bubbles. They tried different dog names, but Emma wanted Bubbles."

"Bubbles is a great name for her," Hayden said, reaching over and petting the dog.

"This is actually the first Bubbles' pup. The original Bubbles is pretty old now. We gave her to Paul's parents—something of Emma's they could keep. Before she got too old, they let her have a litter, and we got one of the females."

The group around the table was silent for a few minutes.

"Joe, they got me confined to the house for the duration of the games."

"It's for your protection," Joe said.

"As long as I'm under house arrest, could you reconnect my treadmill?"

"Mom, your ankle."

"I know I won't be able to use it for a day or two, but I'd like to know that I can use it when I'm ready."

"I'll do it before I leave. I'm taking *Uncle Art* to the hospital. He's going to stay with Mary today. I'm going into the police department and work with Ronnie. We'll send over a relief for Theresa when I get there."

After the men left, Lea cleaned up the kitchen and found her mother in the back bedroom. Joe had moved all of her computer equipment in there and hooked it to the wireless router. "Whatcha doing?" she asked her mother.

"Just skimming for points. Jason's coming over later today, and we're going to work on the game some more."

Lea took her place next to her mother. She watched her mother eliminating villains. This game that had brought so much danger into their lives could be the event that might return a young girl to her family.

"Wait till you see my secret weapon," Hayden giggled under her breath. "Jon Mathers designed this for Mary and me."

Abbirah poised on a slab of rock. A mangy Gorribog approached slowly, his huge club raised to strike her.

"Mom, he's going to get you." Lea resisted the urge to grab the mouse out of her mother's hand.

"He won't."

Hayden tapped a few keys. Abbirah stuck out her chest and put her hands on her hips.

"Hold down CTRL+C and then hit enter."

Abbirah's voluptuous bust wiggled, and the Gorribog dropped down dead.

Lea let out a squeal and burst out laughing. She hugged her mother. "You're full of surprises."

"Try that tonight when you and Joe are playing. When you're done and before you close down the game, get his character to face you, and you can knock him out." A yellow light blinked at the bottom right of the screen. "What's this?"

"What's that blinking light?" Lea asked.

"Means a message from the GMs." Hayden clicked on the gamemaster message board.

"Social gathering for tomorrow night at Burelli's at six o'clock. Details for final quest will be explained."

"Ronnie must have talked to Jon. She wanted a time when everyone was together. She's going to reassure them about additional security."

Lea left her mother working on the game. She cleaned up through the house. This time she had spent with her mother, they'd grown closer. They were always close, but there was a deeper bond between them now.

It saddened her that it took something so frightening to wake her up. She was beginning to take it for granted that her mother would always be there for her. Our relationships can become so predictable. She sank down on the edge of her bed, closed her eyes, and prayed for her mother and Mary that God would deliver all of them—and little Emma.

22

10110

Joe carried the heavy box of police reports in and dropped them on a table in the large conference room at the Lincoln Police station. A half-dozen police officers were combing through files or working on computers.

Ronnie studied a computer screen of financial data. "How's Hayden?"

"You know Hayden. She hobbles around like nothing happened." Joe took off his jacket and rolled up his sleeves. "What you got going here?"

"Doing a thorough background check on Lynn Foster and Sam Preston. Sam may not be involved, but he and Lynn are close friends. Also, we're doing a check on any possible link between the Gleasons and Carly Dean."

Joe pointed to the box on the table. "I have all of the FBI and police reports that Ben Dean had access to. We need to pick one person to become an expert on that box."

Ronnie pointed to Erick. "Erick. Box. Memorize all of that data. He's practically got an eidetic memory," she said to Joe.

"I'm on it." Erick began pulling file folders out of the box and organizing them on the table.

"Ronnie, I got some financials on Sam Preston." Patrick Collins handed Ronnie a spreadsheet. "Seems he's made two five thousand dollar deposits into his bank account the last two weeks. I can't trace the origins."

Joe raised his eyebrows. "And that's the couple we thought we didn't have to worry about."

"I'm still not convinced the attack on the gamers and the kidnapping are related. Lynn and Sam were too far away from Brian VanDeer to get through our security, club him, and get back to their area."

"So, we both win?" Joe grinned at his sister.

"It's not over until it's over," Ronnie reminded him.

Joe grimaced. "Somebody got through the security at the park the other day."

"Ronnie, Joe," Chief Williams addressed them. "I need to see you in my office."

Joe and Ronnie entered the chief's office and nodded to the two men present.

Chief Williams closed his door. "This is Agent Greer from the FBI and Agent Michelson from the DEA in Omaha."

Agent Greer spoke. "Your chief has briefed us on the case here, and we agree completely that a kidnapped child has precedence over every other case in the state, but we've got a problem."

Joe had dealt with the FBI's attitude before. This could be a big problem, and it wasn't about the crimes involved here. "Which is?"

"Tomorrow morning we're taking down a multi-state drug ring. Among other ways this bunch procures drugs, one way is to threaten a pharmacist at a major drug chain. They not only want computer printouts of patients' prescribed marketable drugs, but want shipment dates. If the pharmacist doesn't cooperate, a family member is put at risk. We picked up a flag on Sam Preston's bank account that law enforcement was investigating him. I need all investigations of him dropped. He's working for us."

Michelson spoke up. "If these people are watching Sam, they're also watching his money. Our whole operation is at risk, not to mention Sam's life and his son's."

Joe understood what the men were saying. "This is happening tomorrow?"

"We've got twenty-five multi-department agents in two states ready to go at five a.m. tomorrow morning. Sam's cooperated with us fully. We'll have a watch on his house for his protection."

"What were the money deposits in his account?"

"We allowed the payments from the drug group to keep up his cover."

"Sam's not really who we're after," Ronnie said. "The focus is on Lynn Foster. But I'm worried with stepped up police involvement, and if she really is Sandra Coulter that she'll decide the money isn't worth waiting for and take off with the kid."

The chief nodded slowly. "I'll authorize additional surveillance."

"I can send you some help with your investigation," Agent Greer offered.

Joe rubbed his chin, pondering the turn of events. "If we back off Sam, we'll have to back off Lynn."

"Not necessarily," Ronnie said. She turned to Greer and Michelson. "We apologize for interfering. We had no idea."

"After noon tomorrow," Greer said, "any additional law enforcement you need for your assignment, don't hesitate to call us. We'll have plenty of agents leftover until they're reassigned."

The chief opened his office door. "Thanks, Ronnie, Joe. I'll let you get back to work."

Ronnie pulled Patrick and Jason to the side. "Something's come up. Stop looking into Sam Preston, at least, for now."

"Whatever you say," Jason said.

Chief Williams escorted the men to the elevator and then stepped into the conference room where Ronnie and her team were hard at work.

"Where are you with all of this, Ronnie?"

"Pretty good. Ben Dean contacted the FBI agent in charge of their case. He's gotten to be good friends with him. He's flying up from Houston with another agent to handle the possibility that this is Emma Norris. We needed to get the gaming group together so that Joe can get DNA from Lynn Foster and Terrie. Also, we're not telling anyone about Hayden's attack yesterday. I just explained that I wanted to reassure everyone about the outing Saturday, and that we'll have volunteer law enforcement in plainclothes scouting the area."

"You know, I've got an idea," Joe said. "What if we do a fake arrest?"

"Huh?" the chief questioned.

"We arrest someone for the attacks on the women and Brian. That will take the pressure off Lynn. No more police. We'll still keep up security for the outing to guard against a copycat, but there wouldn't be any more invasive police questioning of the gamers."

"Who would we arrest?" Ronnie asked.

"I know someone," Jason said. "My older brother's an armchair detective. He's sat through some stakeouts with me."

"I didn't know you had a brother," Ronnie said.

"He's four years older. He picks up roles as an amateur actor in some of the community theaters here and in Omaha. He'd love this."

The chief shook his head. "I don't know."

Ronnie furrowed her forehead. "We arrest him and book him for assault. But then what do we do with him? If we get him bailed out, people will wonder why we didn't keep him in jail until the games were over in a few days."

"We could put him in isolation. Keep him away from the other inmates," Jason suggested.

"I don't know," the chief said. "I hate keeping an innocent man in lockup. Too risky."

I have an idea," Ronnie said. "Arrest him. My uncle, who's a retired U.S. Marshall, can pick him up on a fake federal warrant. Take him to his farm outside of Omaha until Saturday."

The chief shut his eyes tightly. "How much paperwork we talking about?"

"Miniscule," Joe said. "I did something like this before to catch a pedophile on the run. Arrested a cousin of one of our officers, and the real pedophile emerged from hiding. Nabbed him that same night."

"I wouldn't do this, but if there's any chance in the whole world that that little girl is Emma Norris, I don't want the Foster girl taking off with her. I'd hate to get this close and lose her."

The chief's gaze bore into Ronnie. "Get Jason's brother in here. Use a phony name. Stage an arrest scene. But make sure all legal documents are signed. I don't want him suing the department because he got a paper cut signing an arrest document."

"This might work," Ronnie said to Joe. "But the real attacker will know we have the wrong person."

"Who's he or she going to tell? It might force his hand. Embolden him so he'll make a mistake."

Ronnie sighed. "Jason, call your brother and get him in here."

"You know what's bothering me?" Joe said.

Ronnie picked up a folder of Lynn's financials and studied the spreadsheets. "What now?"

"I think we should clue Jon Mathers in to what's happening."

Chief Williams shook his head. "Joe, the more people who know about this, the more chance of someone slipping up."

"If this gaming operation unravels, a lot of research money would disappear. We owe him. He's been completely up front with us."

Ronnie closed the folder and set it on the table. "What about Jon and Shelly, only?"

The chief thought for a minute. "It's only fair. We may need his cooperation in the future, and we don't know where all this investigation will take us. When does this game end?"

"Saturday," Joe said.

"Talk to him after the social tomorrow night. I want to hold it off as long as I can."

Ronnie's cell phone chirped. "Ramsey here… She is?…That's great… I'll be right over."

She flipped her cell closed. "Mary Johnson woke up. She's sitting up in bed talking to her husband."

"Wow. That's super. The first good news we've had all week," Joe said.

"Ronnie, you go ahead," the chief said. "I'll keep an eye on things here."

Ronnie shouldered her purse. "Joe, we need to get together and strategize later."

"Get together at Hayden's at five."

23

10111

Ronnie entered the hospital room. A guard was still posted outside the door. The shades were drawn and lights were dimmed. She stepped slowly over to the bed. She knew that people coming out of severe head injuries needed reduced stimulus. Ben stood next to the bed, holding her hand.

Carly turned her head slowly toward Ronnie.

"This is the detective I told you about," Ben explained.

Ronnie moved over next to Dean so that Carly wouldn't have to move her head so often. "How are you, Carly?"

"A little confused, but I'm okay."

"Good. Do you remember anything about that night?"

"No. Not really. I just remember me and Hayden getting dressed. Snatches of things. I remember combing her long hair... that's all."

"That's fine. Don't worry about any of this. We've got everything under control. You just get well."

"Is Hayden okay?"

"She's perfectly fine. Walking again." Ronnie didn't mention the incident yesterday.

"She likes to exercise. I've been healthier since I've been around her."

Carly looked up at Ben. "Probably should leave Bubbles with Hayden until I get out of here. They get along real good."

"Honey, you don't have anything to worry about."

Carly's face turned red and she teared up. "I thought I found her. I really thought I did this time."

Ronnie put her hand on Carly's arm. "Mrs. Dean, we've got a full police force watching Lynn Foster and Terrie. We'll know in a few days who Terrie Foster really is. I want you to put this out of your mind and concentrate on getting well."

"Thank you for helping." Carly clasped Ronnie's hand.

"I need a word with you," Ronnie whispered to Dean.

They stepped into the hall.

"I've asked the attending physician to keep Carly's name as Mary Johnson. Also, we'll address you as Art. I got a call on the way over here that the FBI team from Houston arrived and are working at the police department. We'll pick you up in a few hours and bring you home for dinner. You need to get away for a bit just to rest."

"I got it. Thanks for everything."

"We'll see you in a few hours."

Ronnie climbed into her car and headed back to the department. This really could be their little granddaughter. None of Lynn Foster's information tracks farther than six years. Exactly as far back as they could track Mary Johnson's information. We know about Mary now.

She just needed to focus on Lynn. Lynn had told the other gamers that she was living in Louisiana and their records were wiped out in Hurricane Katrina. There were no records on file in any state offices in Louisiana of a Lynn Foster or Terrie Foster that matched the social security numbers Lynn had on file in Nebraska. She was glad that the FBI was now involved. They had access to computer data systems that local police departments didn't have.

What was Lynn hiding? Lynn's financial records with social security information would have been preserved, and there're no work records of Lynn Foster with her current social security number back beyond four years ago. *Please, God. Give me and my team the wisdom to solve all of this.*

24

11000

A few minutes before five o'clock, Hayden opened the kitchen door for Ronnie and Agent Hawkins. "This bad ankle brought us good luck. It generated a whole slew of new casseroles. We've got five casseroles and six pies."

"It smells good in here," Ronnie greeted her friend. "How's Mike?"

"He's bowling in his office league tonight. Hayden, this is Agent John Hawkins. He worked on the carjacking seven years ago and has been following it ever since."

"I'm so glad to meet you. Ben Dean's in the living room."

Agent Hawkins eyed the woman's arm in a sling and the bandage around her ankle. "You've been through a lot."

"I'm pretty tough. It's all for a good cause."

"News is coming on," Joe called out from the living room.

Everyone piled into chairs in the living room to watch the evening news.

The reporter began. "An arrest was made earlier today of a man who brutally attacked three online gamers on quests in parks in Lincoln. Chad Sonders was arrested and charged with three counts of assault. Sonders attacked gamers raising money for childhood cancer—"

"That's my brother," Jason laughed.

Hayden stared at the man with long hair and a scraggily beard, dressed in bulky clothes. "He sure looks scary."

"It took us an hour to get that beard glued on."

"Does Jon Mathers know this isn't the real attacker?" Lea asked.

"Yes," Ronnie said. "I only told Jon and no one else. I explained to him we were arresting someone to take pressure off the group. That might cause the attacker to make a mistake. We've used this strategy before to ferret out criminals. He said to go ahead. He's desperate to salvage these games."

Ben asked, "So, Jon doesn't know that Joe's a policeman?"

"No. He knows nothing at all about this kidnapping investigation either."

Jason's phone chimed. "This is great." He passed his cell phone around so they could view his brother sitting beside Ronnie and Joe's uncle's pool, sipping a soda.

"We got food," Hayden announced from the kitchen.

"Mom, you've got to get off that foot. It'll never heal."

"I'll rest next week when all this is over. Me and Edna's been talking about taking a vacation at one of them Dude ranches in Colorado. Lots of hiking trails."

Ben watched the group around the table and a lump formed in his throat. For nearly eight years, he and Carly had carried this boulder around on their backs. For the first time, their load seemed lighter. Even if it wasn't their little girl, he felt he wasn't alone anymore.

Bubbles sat quietly next to his leg with her paw up in the air, begging. He cut a small piece of meat, placed it on a bread and butter plate and set it on the floor. He sat back and sipped his iced tea. He stole a memory from his heart. One that he'd kept locked. Emma sitting in the grass, the late sun lighting her blond hair, giggling at the puppy licking her feet.

He coughed and locked the memory for later.

After dinner, the women made quick work of the dishes. They joined the group in the living room. Jason had set up dry-erase boards on easels.

"We've got a lot of work to do," Ronnie announced, while Jason passed out notepads and pens.

"We've still got to figure out who's attacking the gamers and now, this kidnapping."

Hayden sat next to Ben, waiting for the others to get settled. Bubbles sat on Ben's lap for a few minutes, then crawled into Hayden's lap.

"She doesn't know where to settle," Hayden chuckled. "Ben, how's Mary, I mean Carly doing?"

"Real good. The doctor got her up walking around the room. He did an hour-long neurological exam. He doesn't see any issues."

"Can she talk all right?"

"Speech is a little slow, but okay. Doctor said that she'll have bouts of confusion for the next few days."

"I want to go in to see her, but I'll wait until you think it's a good time."

"She's been asking about you. It might settle her if she sees that you're all right."

"Let's start going through this," Joe said. "The kidnapping's more serious."

Ronnie nodded. "We'll take it first."

"We've got no past history on Lynn Foster going back beyond six years," Jason said.

"We'll have DNA tomorrow night," Joe pointed out.

Bubbles crawled back into Ben's lap. "How long before we'll know?"

Hawkins spoke up, "We've got the markers loaded into the computer in Kansas City. We just need Terrie Foster's DNA to match with Emma's. Forty-eight to seventy-two hours for a preliminary match. We'll have enough to pick her up."

"I thought it took longer," Hayden said.

"They'll do a more in-depth study, but we'll have enough to go on in a few days."

"We've got round-the-clock surveillance on Lynn Foster. First sign she's packing her car, we'll grab her and take her in for questioning."

"There's not much we can do until tomorrow night," John said.

Ronnie pointed to the board. "Next on our list, the gamer attacks."

"That's a toughie," Lea said.

Ronnie uncapped a dry-erase marker. "Suspects?" She listed the game members in order of their current standings.

"I'm casting my vote for Hayden Curtis," Joe said, nudging Hayden sitting next to him.

Hayden raised her good arm. "I confess. I done it."

Everyone laughed as Ronnie drew a line through Hayden and Mary's names.

"Sam and Lynn."

Lea shook her head. "They were too far away from Brian. They would have had to run past us, get through security people, clobber Brian, and get back to their area."

"Somebody got past security," Hayden reminded her.

Ronnie drew a circle around Cody's name. "He found Mary and Hayden. He found Brian."

"I don't think so," Hayden said. "Cody's a nut job, I'll give him that, but he liked Brian's mother. Felt bad that she was deteriorating. He'd get her picture books of flowers or zoo animals and take them over to her. She liked to look at the pictures. I can't see him doing something that would put her at risk."

Joe reached over to pet Bubbles, who growled at him. "One hundred and fifty thousand dollars can change a person's heart. I've arrested family members who've killed for as little as four hundred dollars. We just don't want to overlook anything."

"I'll leave his name up there. The Gleasons."

"Now we're getting somewhere," Lea said.

"Carl's a bit of a softie," Joe pointed out. "But, Patty—classic textbook narcissist."

Lea got a pillow for her mother and helped her prop up her leg. "Like Sam and Lynn, they were a ways from Brian. They hadn't texted their codes and were frantic to find the last clue. As determined as she was to win, I can't see her leaving Carl alone, beating up Brian, and getting back in time to find the clue."

Ronnie slumped down in a chair and sighed.

Joe screwed up his face. "It's about the group." He studied the board for a minute. "What changed in the group dynamics? Sam and Lynn, Brian and Cody have been in the games from the beginning. Mary Johnson came in a little over a year ago. She played a couple of short quest games and won the respect of everyone in the group. She recruited Hayden eight months ago. From my discussions with the game-masters and the players, everything was fine—until the Gleasons."

"I've studied some of their past game activities," Jason said. "Patty Gleason's a good gamer, but so determined to beat everybody else out, she takes big risks during the plays and loses points. Not a fair player, she creates bots and farms resources. Hacks other players' games. Sends her sons out to disrupt players' dig quests."

"She is aggressive," Ronnie said, "according to Jon and Shelly."

Ronnie picked up her cell and speed-dialed her office. "Erick, it's late tonight, and I know that you were moved to the kidnapping case, but tomorrow morning, very early in the morning, I want you to find whatever you can on Patty Gleason and Carl. Where they lived before here? Where Carl worked? Why did they move? Problems at work? Problems, and particularly, problems with the boys in previous schools?"

"Thanks." She clicked off.

Ronnie studied the board. "What interests me is that Brian was taken down with pepper spray. A woman might use that to subdue a man larger than herself and then clobber him with something."

"Did Brian remember anything about the attack?" Agent Hawkins asked.

Ronnie shook her head. "Nothing. He remembers arriving at the park, but nothing after that."

Joe yawned loudly.

"Years and years of teaching you good manners, and this is what we get?" Ronnie laughed. "This is as much as we can figure out for tonight until we get the DNA tomorrow."

"I hate to ask this," Hayden said, "but, what if it isn't Emma? What if Terrie really is Lynn's daughter? What if Lynn's running from an abusive husband or boyfriend?"

"That's a fair question," Agent Hawkins said. "I was working with Carly when she found the other girls. I know how terrified the one women was when we had to do tests on her and her child and proved that in fact her daughter was her own. The girl had a shady past and couldn't properly account for her life around the time the child was two years old, but the child was hers. I won't let that happen again. We'll get proof of who Terrie Foster is before we proceed.

"All we have now to go on is a high school photo of Sandra Coulter we've had for years. She's now in her thirties. We ran some photos of Lynn Foster taken at club socials against the picture of Coulter. Technicians say the markers are very close. Too close to ignore. If after all of our technological evaluations are completed, we determine that this really isn't Emma Norris, we'll interview Lynn Foster just to fill in the gaps." He looked at Ben. "Then, we'll keep searching for Emma. But, I think our search is over."

Hayden reached over and petted Bubbles. "I got me a mountain of praying to do."

"Agent Hawkins, I'll drive you to your hotel," Jason offered.

"Thanks," John said, standing. "I'm really impressed. You people do great work."

The house quieted after everyone left. Hayden waited at the kitchen door for Bubbles to finish her run.

"Lea and I are going to work for some points tonight," Joe said, cutting them slices of apple pie.

"You just want to play with that gaming machine." Hayden smiled at him. "Help yourself to whatever you want. I'll make you some coffee."

"That's okay. We'll go with milk."

"Joe, what's going to happen to Terrie if she really is Emma? I can't bear the thought of her being dragged away from Lynn. She's the only mother that she's known. As wonderful as they are, she doesn't know Mary and Ben."

Joe sighed. "It's a tough situation. You'd be surprised how resilient kids can be. You're right, she's had a good life, but Lynn may not be her mother. Terrie will be turned over to family services and assigned a case worker. She'll get the best psychological help in the world. Once it's explained to her where she came from, visits will be set up with Mary and Ben and the bonding process will begin."

"What will happen to Lynn? Will she be charged with the murders?"

"According to police reports, she tried to stop them. But she was an accomplice in a kidnapping. It will all depend on her, how she behaves when she's arrested. If she cooperates fully with the investigation, doesn't lie, the courts may go easy on her."

Hayden opened the door, and Bubbles rushed in. Hayden closed and locked the door. "I'm going to bed. I got me a pile of praying to do. Good night."

Joe hugged Hayden. "It'll be okay. Good night."

Hayden hobbled off to her bedroom, Bubbles scratching after her.

Joe plopped down next to Lea and set her pie and milk on the table next to the computers.

"Can you believe this? The Gleasons are ten points ahead of us."

"We got to change that, don't we girl." Joe gently stroked the side of the machine.

"You're a total geek."

Lea entered the game and checked her backpack. She gawked at Joe. "Captain America? Mm. What an irresistible hulk of a man!"

"If I'm going to win this game, I need a male figure I can identify with."

"Abbirah, the Strong One and Captain America. What a team."

The chat room lit up at the right of the game. Gamers gave a thumbs up for Captain America.

"So, what's this quest?" Joe asked. "I've been away from this for a few days."

Lea orientated him to the screen. "I hate this, it's a jungle and you never know where something's coming from. Anyway, a rift volcano has opened up and is threatening the Narel Kingdom. We have a golden key and have to get to the dam in the mountains above the volcano and unlock the dam.

The waters will flow down into the gorge and stop the lava flow from the volcano, thus saving the kingdom.

"The problem is that the Narels are being attacked by Yeekun warriors."

Joe took a bite of pie and gulped his milk. "Fun."

"This jungle terrain is swampy and those vines hanging down may wrap around you, squeezing you to death. I got killed twice last night."

"Why don't you take the lead, and when I adjust to the terrain, I'll move ahead."

Lea worked the controls, and Abbirah surged ahead, slogging through swamp and eventually rose to a dry area. She carefully threaded over and around huge tree trunks in a northwesterly direction. Captain America followed behind, removing threats as he went.

The jungle became darker, which slowed her down. Eventually, it opened up again, but the foliage was dense. "That smoke ahead could be a Yeekun campfire. They come at us in groups of seven."

"I'll take the lead."

Captain America surged ahead, his weapons drawn. They circled around to the east side of the camp. Eerie animal screeches pierced the jungle scene.

"They set up against that hill and have nowhere to run. The other side is a drop off. We'll split them up in the middle. You get the three farthest to the left, and I'll get the other four."

"You ready?"

"Yes, Captain."

Captain America crashed forward and made quick work of two Yeekuns, who were taken completely by surprise. To his left, Abbirah deftly took out her three warriors. America got the last two warriors, but suffered a serious blow.

"Heal me," he cried out as Captain America collapsed to the ground.

Abbirah brandished her scepter and held it toward America. A cloud of yellow healing mist floated from Abbirah and enveloped America. In another second, he stood.

"That was close," he said.

They took out two bands of marauders and another group of Yeekuns. Captain America ran right into an enormous spider web that Abbirah had to phaser him out of.

"We're two hundred points ahead of the Gleasons. Let's take out one more detachment of warriors."

Yeekun warriors had surrounded a cabin at the edge of a village. America made quick work of the four warriors in the front of the hut, and Abbirah got the two in the back.

"There's one hiding behind a shed to your right."

"I got 'em. Watch this."

"So, we'll know in the next few days little Terrie's fate," Lea shook out her hands and moved the Strong One to face the warrior.

Joe raised his phaser. "It won't take long once we get the DNA. She's a sweet kid. The short time we've know her, she has a way of making room in your heart for her."

"I just dread what she has to go through. Tearing her away from Lynn."

"If they handle it right, they can reduce the trauma the girl suffers. If Lynn stays calm and doesn't put up a fight, it won't be as bad."

Lea watched the screen as the Yeekun slowly moved toward Abbirah, brandishing a huge saber and growling, his teeth glistening. Lea glanced over at Joe and waited until the warrior was close enough. She tapped CTRL+C. The Strong One's hands dropped to her hips. Her chest wiggled. The warrior dropped dead.

Joe burst out laughing. "Where did you get that move?"

"Hayden says it's her secret weapon."

"Come here," Lea said, turning Abbirah towards America. Captain America moved toward Abbirah. Lea tapped CTRL+K and kissed him. She moved back a few spaces, hit CTRL+C and dropped Captain America—dead.

"And that's how it's done!" she tossed her mouse on the table.

"You killed me," Joe whined.

The chat room lit up with messages approving the kiss of death.

Joe faced Lea. "You're not getting away with that." He scooted his chair over to Lea and planted a kiss on her lips.

At first she put her hands on his shoulders to playfully push him away, but then put her arms around his neck, savoring his kiss.

He moved his hands to the sides of her face and tipped it up. "I love you, Lea."

Lea gazed into his eyes. She could see the softness of his eyes, the love he had for her. Could he see her love for him?

"I love you, too," she whispered.

25

11001

Lea and Joe entered the banquet hall and ducked as a paper airplane sailed over their heads. Sam caught it and sailed it across the room to Cody. A banner hung across one wall said, "Good Luck Dylan's Gamers." The mood was definitely festive. Gamers and their families laughed and teased one another.

Lea took a seat next to Brian. She felt guilty for trying to separate Brian and Cody, but last week she was desperate to get at the attackers any way that she could. Cody was huddled in a corner with Carl Gleason making a point about something, gesturing with his hands.

"How are you feeling?" Lea asked Brian.

"Better. Really good. I'll start back to work next Monday."

"How's your mother handling all of this?"

Brian nodded. "Good. She hasn't really figured out that anything happened. She's happy that Meals on Wheels is bringing so much food. She seems to like the women that visit. I can't thank you and Hayden enough for all you've done."

"I'm glad we could help."

He shrugged. "Mom got so bad that I quit going to church. I felt guilty about leaving her when I worked. I realized this week how much I missed everybody and worship. A couple in church are going to stay with Mom Sunday during the first service, so I can start going again."

"That's really great. When Mom's fully recovered, maybe we can help with that, too."

"Thanks," he said, catching the paper airplane and aiming it at Carl.

Lea noticed that Patty was uncharacteristically quiet, no opinionated ramblings. She focused on Terrie Foster at the table across from her. The child did have facial similarities to Carly, her wide forehead and chin. But children changed so much during these years. She looked similar to a dozen other people's children that she knew. How were they going to sort all of this out? Her heart ached for the little girl with such happy eyes. If she really was Emma, her world as she knows it was about to crumble to pieces.

"May I have your attention, please?" Jon Mathers' voice boomed from the front of the room. He waited a few minutes for the room to quiet. "With all of the problems we've had during these games, the team thought it would be good to get together one last time before the final outing on Saturday. Good news, Mary Johnson is awake and speaking."

The kids shouted and clapped, and the others joined in.

"She walked around the ward today. She has no memory of the attack, which is just as well, but is progressing nicely. Her brother, Art is with her.

"As you saw on the television last night, the police arrested a man who confessed to the attacks. Just to be on the safe side, we're keeping up security in case there's a copycat out there who wants to disrupt the games.

"Now, for the standings. You're all neck-in-neck, just points away from each other. We may have a surprising upset by the end of the week. As far as this week's pics of gaming shots, the wall behind me shows the top five."

A few of the video clips showed children having a picnic with Gorribogs, who began swinging through the vines of the jungle with the kids clinging to their backs. The next video depicted five Yeekuns advancing up a hill towards Cody, who rolled himself into a ball and took out all five like bowling pins. The number one video of the week was Abbirah, the Strong One kissing Captain America and taking him out with her secret weapon.

The gamers screamed with laughter. Lea noticed that even Patty laughed out loud.

"I hope you enjoyed our show. On Saturday, meet here promptly at two-thirty. For security reasons, you will be driven to a secret location for the final outing. Please enjoy the food and fellowship."

The gamer filled a plate with salad and two slices of pizza, grabbed a can of soda, and returned to the table.

The gamer watched the people in the room interacting and took a gulp of soda. So they caught someone. Why would he confess? It made no sense. By the time the cops figured out that they had the wrong guy, the games would be over. Maybe they won't look for the attacker anymore since Mary's recovered. The statute of limitations for simple assault ran out in four years. If everyone recovered and there weren't any new attacks, the police would give up the case.

What worried the gamer was that Jon didn't mention Hayden's accident. That was weird. Maybe they hadn't connected it. Just a random hit-and-run.

The gamer was safe, for now.

Joe let the people fill their plates and begin eating. Sam and Lynn were in deep discussion about game strategies. Cody turned around and gave them a few pointers and turned back to his food. Joe wished people would quit interrupting Terrie so that she'd finish her meal faster.

"I got a laptop set up on the front table," Shelly announced. "If any of you want to type a message to Mary Johnson or share any pics with her, I'll leave it here for you."

Terrie and Kevin raced to the front of the room to type a note to Mary. "Mom, can you bring my tablet?"

Lynn grabbed Terrie's tablet and went up front.

"Now or never," Joe stood. "You run interference."

Lea made her way to the front of the room.

Joe sauntered to the table where Lynn and Terrie had been sitting. He deftly dropped Terrie's empty soda can in a bag and her plastic utensils. No one was paying any attention to him. Sam was facing Carl behind him. Joe collected Lynn's soda can and plastic utensils. He escaped to the main restaurant, unnoticed.

In the men's room, he handed the bags off to FBI Agent Will Brickman.

"I'll have these in Kansas City before you get home tonight."

"Thanks."

To cover Joe's actions, Lea began randomly cleaning off the tables. Joe returned to the room. No one took notice of him.

Jon stepped up to Joe. "Now that Mary's better, are you going back to California?"

"I'll finish the game on Saturday. My uncle's going to stay for a week. She can't really be alone when they discharge her the first few weeks."

"I'm so relieved that she's come out of it so well."

"You ever have trouble like this before? Don't these kinds of games attract a certain type of character?"

"That's a misconception with the public we're trying to change. We have very strict rules for our gaming, specifically designed to weed out overly aggressive players. The *no foul language* rule knocks out ninety percent of undesirable players. We're a family-oriented gaming group, and I'm determined to keep it that way. We'll review everything after the games are over Saturday and find ways to improve our security for future games."

"You've got a good group here. I hope it works out."

"Jon," Kevin said, "the computer froze up."

"I'll get it."

"Did it go all right?" Lea asked.

"The package was delivered," Joe smiled.

26

11010

The servers had cleared out the food and plates. Jon shoved his laptop into its bag. Shelly and Lea rolled the last of the streamers and packed them in a box.

Ronnie entered the room and waved to Jon.

"Detective Ramsey, don't you ever sleep?"

"It's top secret, but I'm really a police singularity. I only need recharging once a week in the motor pool."

"You do look rather robotic," Joe said.

Jon set his laptop case aside. "You got any new information about the attacks?"

"Yes. Let's sit and talk."

Joe sat with Lea, and the Mathers sat across from them. Ronnie took a seat at the head of a table.

Ronnie began. "I never fully introduced Joe to you. This is Joseph Wade of the Kansas City Police Department, and my brother."

Jon and Shelly gaped at Joe. He pulled his identification out and passed it to them. "Sorry about the deception. Hayden's like family to Ronnie and me, and I couldn't walk away from her."

"You're not related to Mary?" Jon passed the credentials back to Joe.

Joe shook his head. "I'm on loan from the Kansas City Police Department."

"Are you a robot, too?" Shelly asked.

"No. I built Ronnie years ago for a science project in school," Joe replied.

Shelly studied Ronnie and Joe. "You two do look alike."

Ronnie smiled. "Additional facts about the attacks have surfaced, and I thought it only fair to pass the information along. As far as the attacks go, we're focusing on a female. Whether it's one of the finalist or someone outside the games, we don't know. Pepper spray was used on Brian. A woman would use that to subdue an attacker larger than her. I'm hoping we'll have this solved before the outing on Saturday."

"That's good," Jon said. "No one knows that you arrested a man who didn't do the attacks?"

Ronnie shook her head. "No one knows."

"I'm starting to feel better about all of this." Jon said. "I sure don't want anything else to happen."

"Something else has happened," Lea spoke up. "My mother was attacked again a few days ago."

"Oh, no," Shelly gasped. "Is she all right? I didn't know."

"We're not telling anyone. A car purposefully swerved to hit her and a friend as they were walking near our home. They jumped out of the way, and Hayden sprained her ankle. She's recovering at home."

"That does it." Jon slapped his hands on the table. "We've got to stop the games now. This has gone too far."

"We can't stop," Joe said.

"Why ever not?" Shelly asked.

Ronnie sat up straight. "While we were investigating the attacks, we accidentally uncovered a second crime. This is more serious than the attacks. A baby was kidnapped almost eight years ago during a violent carjacking in Houston, Texas. The parents were murdered—"

"That's terrible," Shelly gasped. "How's that related to our games?"

"We believe that Terrie Foster is actually Emma Norris, the baby that was taken."

Shelly covered her mouth with her hands. "It can't be." She looked at Jon. "That's not possible. We've known Lynn and Terrie for years."

The color drained out of Jon's face. "Are you sure about the kidnapping?"

"We'll know definitely in a few days. We're running Terrie's DNA and should know by Saturday or Sunday."

Shelly sat back in her seat. "I just can't believe this. I just can't. How did you come across this kidnapping?"

"We can't divulge all of the details. It's an ongoing investigation," Joe said. "We felt that you had a right to know. We may have to make some adjustments in the next outing. We can't pick up Terrie or arrest Lynn until the results of the DNA tests come back—"

"For the child's sake, you can't reveal to anyone what we've told you," Ronnie said. "If Lynn gets any hint that we're closing in on her, she may flee with the child, and we may never get this close to finding her again."

"And, there's also the possibility that Terrie isn't Emma Norris," Joe said.

"What makes you think Terrie is the child you're looking for?" Shelly asked. "I've known them too long to believe this."

Joe glanced at Ronnie then back at Jon and Shelly. "You can't divulge this to anyone. Mary Johnson has been searching for her granddaughter for seven years. The girl that took her is addicted to online games. She tracked her here until she was beaten into a coma. While we were researching her past, looking for a next-of-kin, we came across documents she'd collected."

"So maybe that's what happened to Mary?" Shelly asked. "She was getting too close and Lynn did this. I just can't imagine Lynn Foster trying to kill anyone."

Ronnie spoke up. "We're still investigating this as a separate incident. Lynn was at work when a driver caused Hayden's injuries two days ago. Also, she was too far away from the women the night they were attacked."

"So, Mary Johnson's the grandmother?" Shelly asked.

"Yes," Ronnie said.

Jon held out his hands. "I'm stunned by all of this. Ronnie, Joe, whatever can we do to help?"

"First," Ronnie said. "You absolutely must keep this information to yourselves. Out of fairness to you, we felt you should know. You've got a great organization you've built here, and we want to protect it.

"Second, you may want to hold the final outdoor quest in a more secure place than a park."

"You've been up front with us, so I'll let you know that we've obtained permits to hold it inside the shopping mall. None of the gamers will know where it's going to be held until we bus them there."

"A large team of law enforcement officers were involved in a drug sting that you'll see on the news, if you haven't already. Since the arrests have all been made, the agent-in-charge is assigning the officers to our department until the games are over Saturday. We've got all of the security you need."

Jon sighed, closed his eyes, and slumped back in his chair. After a few minutes, he looked at Ronnie. "You've got my number. Let me know if you need anything at all. I'd like to know what happens with little Terrie. She's been the light of our lives for years. Lynn's been like a daughter to us."

"You got it. I'll be in touch before the games. Thank you for your time." Ronnie stood.

Joe stood next to Ronnie. "Look, I joined the game under false pretenses. If your rules require me to be disqualified, you can do that, but I need to stay in the games until the kidnapping case is resolved."

Shelly looked drawn and tired. She looked up at Joe. "Your standing is sound. Is your real name Joe Wade?"

"It is."

"Are you currently employed by any gaming group?"

He shook his head.

"Then, you're in. We just don't allow people registering under a false name."

"What about Mary Johnson?" Lea asked.

"We're keeping her real name a secret," Ronnie said, "but the FBI provided her a legal alias of Mary Johnson years ago when she began searching for Emma on her own."

"I don't need to know her real name," Shelly said, "but if Mary Johnson is a legal name that she legally procures a driver's license under and pays taxes under, then that's legal enough for us."

"We're sorry we dumped all of this on you," Ronnie said, "but in all fairness, we thought you should know what's going on."

Jon smiled at Ronnie. "I appreciate that. Gives us a better focus for our prayers."

Jon watched the group leave. He reached over and clasped Shelly's hand.

"I feel like all the energy's sucked right out of me. That poor girl. And Lynn. Surely, Lynn didn't steal that girl."

Jon shook his head. "I just can't see it. They're so close. She works hard to provide for that child and has done a great job raising her."

Shelly closed her eyes. "My mind's kinda frazzled. What do the police want us to do?"

"Continue the games as they are until they prove this thing about Terrie."

She played with a streamer that she was rolling up. "Maybe they'll find that she is Lynn's child."

He felt that helpless feeling like when they were losing Dylan. He knew that his wife was hurting and there wasn't anything he could do about it. He put his arm around her shoulder.

"I love them all equally," Shelly said. "Mary, who's lost her little grandchild. Lynn and Terrie, whose lives are about to be shattered. I want the best for all three of them."

"And the best for them," Jon said, "is for the truth to come out."

He clasped her hand tightly. "We must through much tribulation enter the Kingdom of God."

"Much tribulation," Shelly echoed.

"God will provide mercy and grace for Mary Johnson. He'll provide mercy and grace for Lynn, and he'll provide an extra measure of mercy and grace for Terrie. Let's pray."

A half hour later, Joe pulled into Hayden's drive. "I'll come in and check on Hayden."

Lea pointed to a truck parked out front of Mary's house. "That police department pickup's been there for two days. It hasn't moved."

"It's a pickup that needs repairs, and the part hasn't come in. We're using it to deter anyone from breaking into the house."

"Look at the moon," Lea pointed.

"The end of May, it's a full moon."

Lea crossed to the back patio and settled on a bench near the flower garden. She stretched her legs out in front of her. Joe dropped down next to her.

"It's been a wild couple of weeks. You never got any vacation."

"Hanging around with Hayden's adventure enough for me."

"You going back... to your boss?"

Joe sighed. "Don't say anything to anyone. Ronnie knows, but I put in papers for a transfer to Omaha's gang division. I'll be the liaison officer for Lincoln if the transfer's approved."

"That's a big change for you."

"I've had a lot of experience with gangs in Kansas City and can be a huge help here."

"Be good to be close to family."

Joe waited a minute, then said, "It'd be good to be close to you."

He thinks he's won me over. "Where are we going, Joe?"

"I know I messed up and hurt you bad. But the truth is, I want you in my life. The question is, what do you want?"

What do I want?

She let a long minute pass.

"You, Joe."

He reached down and clasped her hand. "Let's start there. Take our time. Take it slow."

The kitchen door opened, and light poured onto the patio. Bubbles raced down the steps and up to Lea, barking.

27

11011

Friday morning, Lea took Hayden to visit Mary. When they entered the room, Mary was dozing in a chair.

Hayden set a bouquet of mixed spring flowers on the window sill.

"Hayden." Mary raised her head.

Hayden gave Mary a gentle hug. "I missed you."

Lea got chairs for them.

"Lea, it's nice to see you again." Mary shifted her position in the chair.

"I'm so glad you're doing better," Lea said.

Hayden settled in a chair. "You look so much better."

"The doctor says I may be able to go home next week. I'm still a little unsteady on my feet. What happened to your foot?" She pointed to the ace bandage around her leg. "Did you hurt your leg in the attack?"

Hayden had removed the soft brace on her wrist so as not to worry Mary. But she couldn't walk without support on her ankle. "The doctor and my daughter," she shot a glance at Lea, "confined me to the house. He lifted the ban yesterday, and on my first day out, I stepped off a curb wrong and sprained my ankle. I had big plans for my first day of freedom, and now this."

"I'm so sorry." She looked at Lea and then back to Hayden. "Hayden, Ben told me that you know about our troubles. About little Emma. I'm so sorry that I never told you. I started to a few times, but couldn't.'"

Hayden put her hand over Mary's. "It's okay. I always thought there was a deep sadness in you, and spent a lot of time praying for you. I promise you, it's all right. We'll let the police handle this. All you and I have to do is focus on getting well."

"You're such a great friend." A tear slid down her face. "After a while…in Houston, most of our friends distanced themselves from us. We were so obsessed with finding Emma. It's all we could talk about. I realized last summer how much I missed having a good girl friend. I guess I was so lonely here and missed Ben so much."

"I'll be your friend forever," Hayden squeezed her hand. "I was so worried about you, Mary. Here, I brought a few pictures of Bubbles. I wanted to bring her to see you, but the doctor didn't want you getting too excited."

Mary laughed as she took the pictures from Hayden. "Bubbles has a way of raising your blood pressure. These are great." She laughed out loud. "I like the one with your slipper in her mouth. She looks like she's doing fine. Thank you."

"Everybody from the games sends their love."

"Shelly stopped by for a few minutes earlier and gave me some printed papers with messages from the group. My eyes don't focus too well, so I'll look at them later. Tell Terrie that I love the little bracelets that she made." She tapped the bracelets on her arm. "You know, these really could be from Emma."

"You need to let that rest until we know the truth."

Mary nodded. "You're right."

"Lea and Joe have us in first place."

"I heard. Lea, have you ever played these games before?"

Lea shook her head. "Never. Your mother and Joe have been coaching me."

Mary leaned forward and whispered, "Did she show you how to work our secret weapon?"

Lea laughed. "Oh, yes. I've used it a few times."

Mary sat back and chuckled. "I do miss the games, but my eyes won't focus for long."

"It'll be great to have you home." Hayden could see that Mary was tiring. "You been sitting up for long?"

"A few hours. I think I'll get back into bed."

Lea and Hayden helped Mary into her bed. Lea put up the side rails. "We're going to go and let you have a rest. There's no telling how Bubbles has rearranged things at the house. We're going to pray for you before we leave."

Hayden clasped Mary's hand and prayed a long prayer that the police would locate little Emma. She prayed that Mary would be at peace and recover her health.

"Thank you."

Hayden tucked in her blanket. "You just get well."

28

11100

Lynn and Sam settled in front of the computers on Lynn's kitchen table. She inserted new batteries in her gaming mouse.

Terrie poured a thin stream of hot sauce over the nachos. "Mom, we're making you some brain food."

"Nachos, with hot sauce. That'll stimulate your brain cells," Kevin reported.

Sam plugged in his keyboard. "I'm not leaving anything to chance. I can't believe the Gleasons are ahead of us. They must have cheated somehow."

"We'll smoke them today," Lynn said, studying the standings.

"That's great that Mary's gonna be all right."

"It's a miracle that she lived. From what Shelly said, she really got clobbered."

Terrie set a big platter of nachos between her mother and Sam.

Kevin set sodas next to the gamers. "I'm just glad they caught that guy, so you two won't get hurt."

"Without all those police around, maybe we can settle down and get some real gaming done." Lynn focused her attention on the screen in front of her. "Grab that bow and arrows for your pack. We may need them."

"They'll slow us down."

"Nah." Lynn studied the paths through the jungle. Dense foliage gave way in the distance to a foot bridge across a ravine and more open spots ahead where they could be ambushed.

She was relieved that the police were no longer involved with the games. She had a backdoor set up in her online checking account and no one had been snooping, so far. She could relax now and finish the game. If there were no more problems, she'd stay put. But if anything else happened, she'd stay long enough to get her money out of the game and this summer plan their next move. She glanced at Terrie, cleaning the kitchen counter. She had to keep her safe.

Kevin watched his father setting up their game. "So, you got food and sodas. Want us to massage your necks while you play?"

Sam waived Kevin off. "Last time you massaged my neck, I couldn't move my head for three days."

"You kids go find something to do," Lynn said.

"Mom, can we borrow the keys to the car?"

Lynn faced Terrie and furrowed her eyebrows at her.

"Just checking your mental stability," Terrie teased.

"C'mon, squirt," Kevin said. "Let's let them work. I'll teach you the finer skills of algebraic solutions."

"Leave your door open," Lynn called, bringing up her character. "I hate this jungle mess."

"It's too unpredictable, but that's what good gaming skills are all about."

Sam checked his pack and clicked it onto his character's back. "You want to take the lead and switch off later."

"Works for me. We're half way there, and only have until tomorrow night."

"We'll make it." Sam eliminated a python about to attack Lynn.

Lynn moved stealthily ahead. "Sam, do you ever worry about Kevin? I mean what would happen to him if something happened to you?"

"I've thought about it a few times. Watch that pile of leaves ahead. Could be a hole."

Lynne circumnavigated around the mound.

"My brother lives in Boston and travels all the time for business. He couldn't care for Kevin. My mother's terrific, but she wouldn't know how to handle Kevin. After Dad died last year, she's retreated into herself. Kevin would have to raise himself and take care of her."

"My parents are dead and Terrie's father never wanted her. I don't have a clue where his parents are. I can't imagine Terrie ending up in a foster home."

Sam moved under a tree in the shade. "Okay, two clusters of Yeekuns ahead. Hm." He tapped on his mouse, thinking.

"We could set off those boulders on the cliff above the left group. That'd keep them busy while we take out the other group."

Sam studied the area. "Okay. I'm going to jump up, cause a slide. You take out any Yeekuns that escape."

Sam hit the "j" key and landed on the shelf above the warriors. He loosened the boulders and jumped down to aid Lynn.

"Got 'em all." Lynn moved in position to battle the next group. She quickly eliminated the last two warriors.

Sam sank down to his knees. "Heal me!"

Lynn shot a healing mist, which enveloped his figure. Sam finished off the second group.

"I'm thinking that clearing ahead is an ambush."

Lynn nodded. "We'll sneak through the brush and take them out."

They worked in tandem until all the warriors were eliminated.

"Let's pause and consider how to handle the foot bridge," Lynn sat back. She filled a plate with nachos.

"I understand your concerns about Terrie. Why don't we each have a will written making us guardians of Kevin and Terrie? If anything changes in our lives later, we can just change the wills. At least they'd be covered for now."

"You wouldn't mind taking on Terrie?"

"You know I wouldn't."

"Let's get through the games this week, and work on the wills next week."

Sam figured out a plan to cross the gorge without using the foot bridge. He shot an arrow into a tree across the gorge and constructed a zip line. They were across in minutes, avoiding the dangers on the bridge.

Lynn felt better. The cops weren't nosing around, and she'd have Terrie covered next week. Having a will done was risky. The school accepted the birth certificate that she'd designed. She claimed all of her records were destroyed in the flood. No body questioned anything. Would a lawyer scrutinize her birth certificate more closely? Probably not. They'd just want lots of money, and she'd have it in the next month.

She'd always planned to take Terrie back to Houston and return her to her grandparents. But with Andrew still after her, that wasn't an option. Only she knew how insanely violent he was. He shot Terrie's father and laughed. He didn't flinch when he shot her mother.

She moved her character along the path behind Sam. She shuddered to think what Andrew would do to Terrie if he ever got hold of her. It would be a long, tortuous death. And her grandparents. He'd spare no mercy.

No, she was safer here.

29

11101

"Let's finish off the game and be done with it." Lea dropped down in a chair in front of the big machine.

Joe wiped lint off the front of the computer.

"You know, you're going to have to give that back to Jason's friend next week."

"He won't be back from training for another month."

"So, it wasn't me you wanted after all; it was the computer?"

"Shhh, she doesn't know she's a machine. Her name's Lola." He positioned his huge mouse in front of the screen.

"She has a name?"

"You're jealous, aren't you?"

Lea shook her head and brought up her screen character.

Joe had added an anthem to his character that played every time Captain America made his appearance.

"It's four o'clock, and we're almost there." Lea moved into position.

"The last battle's always the fiercest. I don't want to be dumped in the swamp now."

"That's the dam up ahead. We've got to climb the mountain in order to get to the flood gates."

"Easier said than done." Joe checked their standings. "I'd avoid the battle altogether, but the Gleasons are right behind us in points."

"I'd just hate it if Patty won first prize, or any prize." Lea studied the computer screen with renewed determination. "Eighteen Yeekuns. Yikes."

Hayden hobbled into the room and set steaming cups of coffee down and fresh peach cobbler. "Brought you some nourishment." She studied the computer screen over Lea's shoulder. "Don't forget your secret weapon."

"That smells great," Joe said. "Thanks."

"Boy, that's a tough quest. Mary would pause the game and scribble notes on a pad until she came up with a solution."

"I'm more of an action kinda guy." Joe scooped cobbler into his mouth. He leaned forward, focused on the computer. "Our best chance of survival is to stay together."

"I can hold the others off while you scoot around the group and get to the dam."

Joe narrowed his eyes and shook his head. "We stay together. He clicked on the "v" at the bottom right of the screen. "We've got sixteen villagers who can aid us. I've been saving them just for this. We station them by twos around the Yeekuns, you and I can get around them and reach the mountain."

Lea sipped her coffee and finished her cobbler. "Mom, that was great."

"I'm gonna go in the other room. This makes me too nervous."

Joe positioned the villagers. "Stay sharp. A Yeekun may get through and come after us."

Lea sat up straight and shook out her hands. She closed her eyes for ten seconds then opened them. "Let's do it."

Joe hit the play button and moved forward to the left of the fray. He and Lea had to work the keyboard and mouse to distribute the villagers and move ahead to the mountain.

One hairy Yeekun broke through and came after Abbirah. Lea fumbled the controls. She couldn't believe that she was actually shaking.

"Duck!" Joe yelled.

Lea hit "d."

Joe phasered the Yeekun. "Let's get to the mountain."

They moved ahead, breaking out of the jungle and climbing up a high mountain. They reached a narrow path that snaked along the mountainside and abruptly ended at a wide scree field.

"This isn't good," Lea whispered.

"Take it slow." Joe clicked on walking sticks in his pack. "Slide with the rocks and stop. I'll go first."

Joe moved ahead slowly. A quarter of the way across, a huge bird, screeching loudly, dive-bombed them. As Abbirah phasered it, she toppled over and started sliding with the rocks.

"Don't do anything. You try to scramble up, it'll make the slide worse.

In a second, the sliding stopped.

"Click to stand and slowly make your way up to the path."

Abbirah made it to the path and they stumbled to the end of the scree. Another huge bird screeched at them, circled overhead, and landed on a boulder ahead of them.

"It could start a slide." Lea tapped her mouse nervously.

"We could circle above it," Lea suggested.

Joe shook his head. "When it moves, it could still cause a slide."

"Maybe it won't move if we sneak by it."

"Too late," Joe said. Rocks above them slid their way. "Run."

Lea turned Abbirah and moved back to the middle of the rocky field. Rocks and boulders tumbled down the mountain behind her. She turned and Captain America's leg was trapped under a boulder.

Joe clicked his keys and handed Abbirah the golden key. "Get to the dam and open the gates."

Lea moved Abbirah forward past America, carefully picking her way across the scree field. She slid a few times, but made it to the packed path ahead. She climbed up the hill. Before her, a huge door blocked her entrance to the dam. A keyhole glowed.

Lea tapped her mouse on the key and the keyhole, and the door swung open. Abbirah pulled a huge lever and the floodgates opened below. Water poured out of the dam into the gorge, which caused a crust to form over the lava. Vapor rose up from the gorge.

The computer screen flashed, "Congratulations! You've completed your quest."

Lea slumped back in her chair, still shaking.

"We did it," she said in a small voice.

"You're amazing." Joe pulled her to him, kissing her.

She rested her head on his shoulder. "I'm exhausted."

Joe sat back. "Just the quest tomorrow, and we're done."

"Ruff. Ruff."

"Sounds like Ben's here," Lea said.

Joe checked the standings. "The Gleasons just finished. They're ten points ahead of us."

"What?" Lea screamed.

Joe pointed to the screen.

"She had to have cheated."

Joe put his hands on her shoulders. "Stay in control."

Lea entered the living room and greeted Ben. "We're done." She turned to her mother and dropped down on the couch next to her. "Mom, we're in second place. The Gleasons beat us. Sam and Lynn are behind us. Cody and Brian are still working, but they're so far behind."

"I'm proud of you." Hayden hugged Lea. "I don't like the Gleasons being in first place, but with the overall points and the points you'll get with the outing, we can still will. Now you'll know how to do it when the next game starts."

Joe's cell phone chimed, and he stepped into the kitchen. Agent Brickman texted him a progress report every six hours. The tests were still being processed.

Bubbles looked from Hayden to Ben, unsure of which lap she wanted to jump in. She jumped up into Ben's lap and licked his hand.

Hayden laughed at the dog. "I invited Ben to have dinner with us tonight."

"We just ate dessert," Lea said.

"Now you're ready for some real food."

Joe entered the living room. "Good to see you, Ben. Just a text from the lab in Kansas City." He held up his phone. "No news yet. Agent Brickman sends me reports during the day."

Ben nodded.

Hayden stood. "Just take me a minute to get dinner on the table."

"I'll help."

Lea took a chicken spinach casserole out of the oven and set it on the table. Hayden poured iced tea. Bubbles followed Hayden around the kitchen, looking for a handout.

The men took their places around the table. Hayden said grace and passed rolls to Ben. "So how's Mary?"

Ben nodded. "Good. Real good. She did two laps around the whole ward without a walker. Doctor's going to discharge her on Monday. I never told her, but the doctor was watching for evidence of seizures, which are common with severe head injuries. So far, none have developed, so she's out of danger."

"I'm glad. We'll go over and give the house a good cleaning," Hayden said. "Get everything freshened up for her."

Joe checked his cell phone face and set the phone next to his plate.

"Joe, you haven't heard anything about the tests?" Hayden asked.

He shook his head. "It may take several more days. They have to build a DNA profile on Terrie before they can match it to Emma's profile."

"I always thought it took months for those DNA tests," Lea said.

"We were able to get it in right away. It only took four hours to prove Osama bin Laden's DNA. This is a little more complicated. I'm thinking we'll know tomorrow."

Ben cut into his casserole. "We've waited seven years. I guess we can wait one more day," he smiled at the group.

"You all have so much courage," Lea said.

"We've got a lot of grace from God. It's just that Mary's worried now, if we're doing the right thing. If it is Emma, the girl's taken good care of her, and the man threatening their lives is dead. She wonders if we should just leave it." He shook his head. "Our worry is will Emma recover from the shock of hearing the truth about her little life? Will she reject us?"

Joe sat back. "It's a hard thing, but it's better that she know the truth. This girl has done a great job with her, but if it isn't her daughter, what protection does the child have? What if Lynn is killed in an accident? Who gets the child? Foster care? If you step in later and lay claim to the child and tell her you knew the truth all along that may be a greater difficulty to overcome."

"The truth is always better," Hayden said. "God can do more with the light in truth than with the darkness in a lie. She'll have the security of a loving family."

Ben nodded. "You're right. We already got a child psychologist lined up if this is Emma. She'll take her in, and Emma won't have to go to an institution."

"We'll know before long," Joe said.

Joe's cell phone face lit up. He opened his messages and shook his head. "New pictures of Jason's brother slouching by the pool, playing tennis, and horseback riding."

"When will they let him go?' Hayden asked. "He can't stay there forever."

"I'm not sure that he wants to leave. But he's free to go after the games are over Saturday night. Sunday he'll return to the city and melt back into the population, no one the wiser."

Lea watched the others talking and laughing. Tomorrow, it would all be over. If Terrie was Emma, her little world would change so much. She had the same trepidation in the pit of her stomach when tornado warnings were announced on the news. The stillness of the heavy air outside. The insects and birds quieted. A green tinge formed on the horizon...

30

11110

Joe arrived at the police station at ten in the morning, summoned by his big sister. There were no texts on his cell phone that the DNA results were back.

"Whassup?" he asked.

"You're not gonna like this," she grinned. "Looks like you owe me dinner. A woman called and is on her way in with information about the attack in the park last week. She sounded pretty solid on the phone."

"Like you said before, it's not over until it's over."

A few minutes later, Ronnie and Joe entered the family conference room. "Good morning," Ronnie said, pleasantly.

A young woman with two little girls sat on the couch. "Hi," the woman said.

"I'm Detective Ramsey, you can call me Ronnie. This is Officer Joe Wade. Officer Kim will wait by the door in case you need anything."

The woman nodded. "We've never been in a police station before."

"You're on the good side of the police station, so you don't have to be afraid. Your name is Pamela Grooves?"

"Yes. These are my daughters, Nicole, who's ten and Lila, who's six. They wanted to go to the park today since school is out now, and I told them that someone was beaten up in the park and that they couldn't go without me. Nicole asked that if the police caught the person who did this, could they go to the park? Then she told me what happened last week."

Ronnie leaned forward. "Hi, girls. I heard you saw something scary last week."

Nicole glanced at her younger sister and back at Ronnie. "We saw a man get hit in the head."

"At the park?"

Nicole nodded.

"Why don't you tell me exactly what happened." Ronnie said softly. "You girls aren't in any trouble at all. Tell me what scared you. We just want to catch the man who did this so the park will be safe." Ronnie sat back.

"Well, we were playing in the park, and Lila had to go to the bathroom. Mom always told us to not use the park bathrooms, but with all the policemen around, we thought it was okay. We came out of the building, and a man was standing over a man near the bushes across from a walking path. Another man was kneeling on the ground, crying. He had his hands on his head. The other man hit him real hard with a baseball bat—"

P. Ryan Hembree

Lila started crying. "He begged him not to hit him, and he did it anyway."

Ronnie gave the girls a minute to let them calm down. "How do you know it was a man?"

"He had a black hat on his head and was skinny and tall. Me and Lila were scared, so we hid in the bushes."

"What did he do next?"

He ran over to his car and threw the bat into the trunk of his car. Then a woman came out from behind a tree and started talking to him."

"Can you describe her?"

Nicole shook her head. "I couldn't see her very good. She was shorter than the man. She had a hat on. A dark blue shirt and jeans. I never saw her face."

"You're doing really great." Ronnie looked at the girls' mother. "I wish adults were this observant." She focused on Nicole. "Did the woman get into the car with the man?"

"No, she ran up the hiking trail." Nicole pulled a cell phone out of her pocket. "I got a picture of the man, but it isn't very good."

God bless you girls.

"May we copy these pictures?"

Nicole nodded.

"That's fine with me," her mother said.

Ronnie handed the cell phone to Joe and asked him to copy the pictures. She pulled a map out of a folder and set it in front of the girls. "Do you use maps in school?"

"I do," Nicole said. "I'll be in fifth grade next year."

"You must be very smart. This is where the bathrooms are near the children's play area." Ronnie pointed to the area on the map. "Can you trace with your finger where the man was?"

Nicole pointed to the position, and Ronnie marked it. "After the man threw the bat into the car, where did the woman go?"

Nicole pointed the path.

"You girls have been a really big help. I have an idea who this person is, and we'll have him locked up in a few hours."

"Detective Ramsey, my girls won't have to testify in court will they? They're so young."

"Absolutely not. We have enough other information about this person. I just needed confirmation of whom we were after. There is a reward for information leading to the arrest of this person, and I'll see that you get it."

"We don't want a reward," Nicole said. "We just want our park safe."

"And you'll have your park safe. You girls have been a big help."

"Officer Kim will escort you back to the front entrance. Thank you for coming in and telling us this."

"Also, Kim, I want you to make a note to follow up with the family later in the week to be sure the girls are recovering from what they saw. That was a brutal attack they witnessed. If they aren't sleeping or having problems, we can get them some counseling. Also, get them a summer pass to the Children's Zoo."

"Yes, ma'am."

Ronnie returned to the conference room. Joe was checking his phone messages.

She sat the folder on the table and put her hands on her hips, her usual deep thinking stance. "Now, we just have to tie this to the white compact car that came after Hayden."

"And, find out who this man is. That had to be Patty Gleason the girls saw. She and Carl were working that side of the park."

"Could be, but it couldn't have been Carl who did the attack. The man drove off. Carl was still in the park."

"The techs may be able to enlarge the picture of the car enough to get a license plate. It's not at a good angle."

Ronnie stretched and sighed. "I'll have a couple of the men scout around the area and get security surveillance videos. The city approved street cams for the children's area, but they haven't been installed yet. There're gas stations and a car wash in that area. Maybe one of the cameras picked up the car."

Joe stood. "What a break this was. I've got to get to our last outing. I'm glad it's indoors. They've forecasted storms all afternoon."

31

11111

Ben sat with Carly, reading excerpts of the newspaper to her. He hadn't told her details of the investigation so as not to worry her. That they'd obtained DNA from Terrie. But maybe the news blackout worried her more. He just didn't know what to do.

Agent Hawkins and Doctor Walsh entered the room. Hawkins closed the door.

Ben nodded to Agent Hawkins. "John, it's good to see you."

He stepped over and shook John and Carly's hands.

"Carly," Dr. Walsh said, "I'm thinking that if there aren't any problems this weekend, we'll do a quick neurological exam Monday morning, and let you go home."

"I'd like that," Carly said. "I do miss my home."

The doctor stood aside and let Agent Hawkins speak.

Agent Hawkins pulled a chair over and sat across from Carly. He reached up, took her hand, and looked into her eyes. "Carly, it's her. You found Emma."

Carly sat, frozen in time for long minutes. "You ... sure?" she whispered.

He nodded.

Ben put his arm around Carly's shoulders.

"We found her," Carly whispered. Tears cascaded down her face.

"You got the report back?" Ben choked.

Hawkins nodded, wiping a tear from the corner of his eye. "Preliminary tests are conclusive. It's Emma Norris."

Tears formed in Ben's eyes. "Our little girl."

"My purse," Carly whispered.

Ben pulled her purse out of the nightstand and handed it to her.

She fumbled opening the purse and pulled out a picture of Kate and Emma taken a few hours after Emma was born. She held it up in front of her face so she could see her daughter. "We found her, honey. I promised you we would." Fresh tears splashed down her face. She was trembling.

"Carly," Ben said into her ear. "You have to stay calm. Take a deep breath." Ben stuffed a huge wad of tissue in her hands.

Carly nodded.

"Try to breathe slow."

Ben looked up at John. "So, what happens next?"

"We have a team on their way over now to pick up Lynn Foster and Terrie."

"Oh, that poor girl," Carly sobbed. "She'll be so hurt. Maybe we should have let her alone."

""She'll come out of this just fine," John said. "In a couple of years the girl would have applied for a driver's license and those fake identifications that Lynn was using wouldn't have withstood the scrutiny of valid IDs. The truth is always better. I've seen this before. Children always flourish in the truth."

Carly looked up at John. "Will you let us know when you have her? If she's all right?"

"Of course. Dr. Hayes has a room all ready for her."

32

100000

"Mom, what should we take?" Terrie asked, stuffing her good-luck bear in her back pack. She was excited that she and Kevin could participate in the quest.

Her mother called from the living room. "There won't be any digging. Just a bottle of water. Maybe your camera."

"Good idea." Terrie slid a fresh battery in her camera and dropped it into her pack.

"Where are we going?"

"We won't know until Jon takes us to the site."

"I like mysteries," Lynn said, scanning her room to be sure she hadn't forgotten anything.

The doorbell chimed.

Lynn opened the door. "Detective Ramsey."

"May we come in?"

Lynn swung the door open wider for the detective, her officer, and a woman in a business suit.

"Where's Terrie?" she asked lightly.

"Getting ready in the bedroom." Lynn's heart began to pound. This wasn't right.

In a quiet voice, Ronnie said, "Sandra Coulter, we can do this quietly and minimize the trauma to Emma. Your choice."

She hadn't heard her name in years. The room seemed to spin. Lynn grabbed the back of a chair to steady herself. Tears formed in the corners of her eyes. She whispered. "Don't hurt her...I...did this, not her."

Lynn was sick to her stomach. "Terrie, honey, come here." A wave of nausea washed over Lynn. She sank down on a chair and pulled a waste basket over and vomited.

"Mom?" Terrie dropped her pack on the floor and knelt next to Lynn.

Lynn reached up and stroked Terrie's hair. "Honey, I'm...I'm real sick. They're going to take me to the hospital. You go with that lady; she'll take care of you."

"Mom, I want to go with you."

Lynn put her hand to her head. She thought she'd faint. "I'll be all right." She reached for Terrie's hand and squeezed it. "I love you."

Terrie hugged her mother's neck. "I love you, too."

Ronnie helped Lynn up. She was shaking, fighting back tears.

Be strong. Be strong for Terrie.

Ronnie escorted Lynn out to the waiting squad car.

Terrie stepped outside. The police lady was helping her mother into a police car. Lightning flashed around her and sheets of rain poured down. Something wasn't right. Four police cars? She pulled her arm away from the woman, who tightened her grip.

"I have to tell my Mom something."

The car her mother was in sped up the street.

"Mom!" Terrie screamed.

The woman opened the back door of a police cruiser. "Get in and buckle up."

Terrie pulled away. "No. I wanna go home."

"Terrie," a voice from inside the car called to her, "get in the car."

She ducked down and looked inside. "Hayden?"

"Get in, honey, you're getting wet."

Terrie crawled into the back seat. "Where'd they take my mom?"

"Let's buckle up." Hayden clicked the child's seat belt.

"I have to know where my Mom is."

"They'll explain everything at the house."

"What house?"

The car lurched forward.

Terrie clutched the seat belt. A searing crack of thunder shook the ground. A familiar terror gripped the child. She put her head down and cried.

Help me, God. Please, help me.

33

100001

Lea and Joe climbed out of the pickup and waited by the SUVs to be taken to the quest site. Her heart wasn't in it. All she could think about was how destroyed little Terrie's world was. She nodded at Cody and Brian. No costumes today. The games were all business. Patty and Carl and their two boys stood nervously waiting to start the quest. Lea spied Sam and Kevin coming out of the restaurant with Jon Mathers and Ronnie. Sam looked pale.

"I see we're all here," Jon said. "Lynn and Terrie can't make it. Something's come up. Let's get into the SUVs, and you'll be taken to your secret destination. We have spotters in the SUVs. Anyone texting or using any communication device we haven't authorized will be automatically eliminated."

Lea noticed that Jon's gaze bore into the Gleason boys. "If you think the temptation might be too great to resist, you may want to leave your communication devices here. We'll keep them locked up until the quest is over."

Patty snatched the cell phones from her boys and handed them to Shelly.

They boarded two SUVs. Lea and Joe were in the same vehicle as Sam and Kevin.

Joe whispered to Lea. "I better keep up a normal appearance."

He leaned forward to the seat in front of him. "Where's Lynn?"

Sam shook his head. "She never said. Some legal issue. She wrote me a note, apologizing. Told us to make her proud. Said she'd call me tonight. It must be serious. She'd never ditch a quest."

"Guess we'll know later," Joe said. He patted Sam's shoulder.

This man's courage impressed Joe. He coped with his wife's death and raised his son on his own. He foiled a major drug operation, and now this. Who was the real Captain America?

Ten minutes later, the SUVs pulled up to the main entrance of the Gateway Mall. Jon ushered the contestants inside to the center of the mall.

"Gather around." He waited for the groups to cluster around him. "Each team will be assigned a specific wing of the mall. The clues are very different. Geometric signs and shapes of objects you have to notice. For example, that sports shoe store." He pointed to the store. "Can you see the arrow, cross, or mountain symbol?"

"An arrow pointing up between sports and shoes," Kevin said.

"The tape at the top of the arrow would hold your next clue," Joe said. He read them a list of dos and don'ts. "Also, everyone must wear an orange ball cap. That's how the store clerks know to respond to the gamers in the quest."

Shelly passed out caps, wing assignments, and cell phones with the first clues.

"Questions?" Jon asked the group.

Lea heard Patty mumble, "This is ludicrous."

"Food court," Joe smiled. "My favorite wing."

Joe and Lea headed towards the carousel in the middle court. "He said the signs are a linear run. No zigzagging, like the park the other day."

"The Gleasons have the length of the center court."

"For good reason, Jon wants to keep an eye on them."

"Why didn't they arrest Patty?"

"Until Agent Hawkins interviews Lynn, we still don't know if anyone else is involved. It's possible there's a connection between the Gleasons and the kidnappers. We have to know that the Gleasons aren't tied into the kidnapping in any way. They're still trying to find the man in the park. Agent Hawkins wants the games to proceed normally."

Joe stopped. "First clue, bear tracks." He handed the cell phone to Lea.

"Bear claws." She scanned the area. "I have no sense of spatial recognition. I'd make a terrible pilot." She couldn't concentrate. Joe was so relaxed and into the game as if nothing happened. She was angry with him for being so calm—for being a cop.

Joe studied the wall designs, ceiling, floor, and store displays. "This is tough."

To heck with the game. I'm in a shopping mall. Think I'll shop. Lea gaped at a jewelry display case in a window. "That emerald bracelet's pretty."

"Remember, we're not shopping."

"It's hard to focus on anything right now."

"Concentrate on the game," Joe said.

Like I could.

Lea glanced over the jewelry in a window display, again. "The birthstone for May is emerald. Joe, look at that necklace with the twists of chains hanging down from a golden half-moon, embedded with tiny emeralds." She took the cell phone and turned it upside down. She held it up to the display window next to the necklace, comparing the clue to the necklace.

Joe shook his head. "You're right. You have no sense of spatial recognition. We're wasting time." Joe started up the court towards the next shop.

Lea backed away from the display. She turned away from the display and closed her eyes. She did an about face and stared at the necklace. She nodded.

She entered the store and asked the clerk to see the necklace. The man grinned and handed her a red note. The next clue.

"Thank you." She quickly texted the code on the paper.

Lea caught up with Joe, who was lying on a bench studying the high ceiling. He pointed to a light fixture above him. "What do you think?"

Lea sat down and shoved his feet off the bench. "Our next clue, a heart." She handed him the paper.

He narrowed his eyes at her as he took the paper. "Show off."

He read, "A heart."

She could do this, now. She'd do it for her mother, for Mary. She jumped up. "Follow me."

They scoured the ceilings, walls, and floors, as well as shop displays. "Lots of obvious hearts in the candy displays and gift shops."

Joe caught sight of a mountain clothing store. He gawked at the hiking boots.

Lea shook her head and tugged the sleeve to his shirt. "C'mon." His weakness for hiking boots surpassed her weakness for jewelry.

He pointed to the display. "They're having a sale on mountain trekkers."

Lea glanced at the shoes. Joe's birthday was in July. Maybe she'd come back later. He stepped away from the display, put his hands on his hips, and scanned the kiosks.

"Wait a minute," Lea said.

"What?"

"Those hiking shoes," she pointed. "Look at the odd lacing pattern." She stepped back from the display, closed her eyes, and opened them again. "The outline around each side of the tongue... could be a heart."

"I doubted you once, and I'm ashamed." Joe entered the store and asked the clerk to see the pair of hikers in the window. The man smiled and handed Joe a red note. Joe thanked the man and quickly entered the codes. "By the way, how much are they?"

"These are on sale for one hundred fifteen dollars."

"We'll be back," Lea said, tugging Joe out of the store. "It'll look bad if we lose and show up at home with dozens of shopping bags."

"Next clue, fast arrow." He shook his head.

A half hour later, Joe spotted the store sign with lettered "express shipping." The block print revealed an arrow between the "E" and the "X."

"Last one," he said, texting in the code.

"We've got to win this since the Gleasons pushed ahead of us in the game." She read the clue. "Moving waterfall, but not a real one or a picture of a waterfall." Lea looked up at the ceiling and moaned, "Ugh." She pulled Joe aside and pretended to look at a window display in a dress shop. "Speaking of the Gleasons, why are their boys in our area and not with their parents? And where are their caps?"

"The parents were allowed to bring their kids if they thought they wouldn't be a distraction. They can be anywhere they want to be. But, we'll keep a sharp eye out."

They walked the whole length of their area. "So far, the Gleasons are ten points ahead of us in the quest. Cody and Brian next, with Sam and Kevin at the end. Lynn missing must be throwing them off their game."

Joe put his arm around Lea and pulled her to him. "You're really getting wrapped up in this."

"Mom and Mary suffered so much. I want to win for them."

Joe scanned the area again. "We'll win, trust me."

Lea nodded down the wide aisle. "The only place we haven't found a clue in is the food court."

Joe headed toward the end of the wing. "I'm so hungry, I'm afraid to go there."

Lea, stood in the center of the walkway studying the strings of decorative lights hanging down, not paying attention to anyone around her.

Joe was ahead of her, sniffing out a hotdog stand.

Someone slammed into Lea from behind and grabbed her purse. She saw the figure of a male in a dark blue hoodie and jeans running towards Dillard's.

"My purse," Lea screamed.

Joe was on Lea in a second.

She pointed. "He ran towards Dillard's."

Joe, calling on his cell phone, ran towards Dillard's, gaining on the man.

The man tossed Lea's purse onto the floor, and disappeared into the store.

Joe picked up the purse.

A man flashed a police ID at Joe. "We'll take it from here. Get back to the game."

"You hurt?" Joe asked.

"I'm fine. More angry than hurt."

He handed her the bag. She quickly checked it. "Nothing's missing."

"Let's finish this," he said.

"Yes. Let's." Lea pointed a shaky finger to the ceiling. "I've been studying those strings of decorative lights hanging down. They sort of look like a waterfall."

Joe glanced at the decorations and shook his head. "Too obvious. Also, they're stationary."

"We've got to move fast. You check display windows and building structure. I'll focus on the kiosks."

"One fast sweep," Joe said, "then we'll go through more slowly."

Lea walked slowly along the center row of kiosks, recovering from the attack. It had to have been the Gleason boys. She hadn't seen them since she was knocked down. Ten minutes later, she stood back from a kiosk of scarves.

"You like scarf?" an Asian clerk asked two women who stopped to browse.

"Just looking," one woman said.

"It's cold in here today," the clerk shrugged into a sweater.

The woman pointed to the ceiling. "You're under the air conditioner."

Lea turned back to the kiosk of belts and leather goods, then her eyes caught five scarves, decorated with shimmering beads and sequins, gently swaying under the air conditioner blower. She signaled Joe.

"Those shimmering scarves?"

Joe shrugged. "Anything's possible."

"May I see those scarves," Joe asked the woman.

"Very good. Very good." She handed him a red paper.

"Read me the numbers," Lea said, holding up the cell phone, ready to text in the final codes.

"Prime numbers, twenty-seven, nineteen—"

A boy ran close to Lea, knocking her down, again. "Whoa." She dropped the cell phone. The back broke off and the battery fell out, sliding across the floor.

"Hey, guys, watch it!" Joe yelled to Chad Gleason.

"Sorry, my brother pushed me."

The boys raced off up the center walkway.

Lea got the battery back into the phone, but it was dead. Joe took the phone and lightly tapped it on the counter of the kiosk. The face light lit up. He quickly texted the code and hit enter.

"Congratulations! You're in second place in this quest."

He looked up at Lea, smiling "We're second."

"Who's first?"

Joe pursed his lips together. "You're not going to like this. The Gleasons are first."

"What!" Lea screamed.

People passing by stared at Lea.

"Those brats!"

"Calm down."

"They did that on purpose. I can't believe we're in second."

"It's not over. The total point tallies may put us ahead. Get control of yourself. We've still got to wait for Brian, Cody, and Sam. Let's walk it off."

Joe paused when he passed the mountain clothing outfitter, but kept on going. He bought ice cream cones for both of them, and they sauntered back to the center of the mall.

"Mr. Wade," a man dressed in a jogging suit addressed Joe.

"Yes."

"I'm Lewis Burns. We lost the guy in Dillard's. He was careful to keep his face down from the cameras."

"Thanks for trying," Joe said.

The man tipped his cap and headed towards the Sears store.

Lea did stop to purchase a scarf for her mother and Mary from the lady who was so helpful. She was calmer by the time she reached the group, clustered inside the main entrance, but she fumed inside, watching Patty smiling broadly, recounting how she found the final clue.

It's only a game. It's only a game.

And you're going to get yours, soon.

Cody and Brian arrived. "Before we sign up for the next quest," Cody said, "we're both going to take a course in geometry. We'd have never gotten that last clue if I hadn't tripped over my shoelace and fell. As I was getting up, I finally found the mountain symbol."

"We wanted to give your brains a workout," Jon laughed. "Let's head back to the restaurant. The team at the gaming office will have the final scores tallied up."

34

100010

Ronnie thumbed through the pictures the girls took at the park the day Brian was attacked. The techs had enlarged the pictures, but all that did was make the images grainier. Jason and Erick scanned videos from a car wash and a convenience store blocks away from the park to try to find the car. Although Sandra Coulter was in custody and Agent Hawkins was taking her statement, they had to be sure this attacker wasn't any part of the carjacking years ago.

"Got it!" Jason called out. He tapped feverishly on his keyboard and hit enter. "DMV mug shot belongs to a Bruce Schupe."

Ronnie got up and studied the picture on Jason's computer screen. "Erick, crosscheck any phone numbers for him with all of the phone records for the Gleasons' phones."

Ronnie paced impatiently. Just one call, one eensy connection, and they'd have them both. Long minutes went by.

"You're going to like this," Erick said. "Dozens of calls between Schupe and Patty's personal cell phone."

"What I've got is even better than what Erick has," Jason said. "The day before Mary and Hayden were attacked, ten thousand dollars was withdrawn from Patty Gleason's savings account, and that very same day, ten thousand dollars was deposited into Bruce Schupe's checking account."

Ronnie smiled. "Go get him. And I want him alive," she called to Jason and Erick as they dashed out the door.

Fifteen minutes later, Bruce Schupe was safely ensconced in an interrogation room. Ronnie stared hard at the man. He could be anybody on the street. Clean shaven, short hair. Clean angular face with a long jaw line. His red tee shirt and jeans were clean. He didn't look like the ruffian that she expected.

Ronnie didn't have time for games. She knew what she had on him; she'd bait him and see what he gave up. She marched into the room and dropped down in a chair across from Schupe. She slapped a folder down on the table in front of her.

"Bruce Schupe, I want you to state your name, address, and occupation. This session is being recorded."

"Hey, I didn't do nothin'."

"You're not going anywhere until we talk, so again, state your name, address, and occupation."

He slurred the information Ronnie asked. "What's this all about?"

"Last Saturday afternoon, Brian VanDeer was attacked in the Morrow Running Park. My deputies found a bat in the trunk of your car with blood on it. We also have pictures of the attack taken by people in the park of you hitting Mr. VanDeer. Why don't you tell me what this is all about?"

Schupe's shoulders sagged. She knew she had him, but how long would it take for him to come clean?

"I didn't hurt no one. I was just jogging in the park on a sunny Saturday afternoon."

"The park was closed to joggers that afternoon."

A tap on the door and Jason entered. He handed Ronnie a paper and left. Ronnie scanned the information and tucked the paper into the folder.

"Mr. VanDeer suffered a concussion, which he's still recovering from as a result of your attack."

He shrugged and looked away.

"You participated in a quest three years ago with Dylan's Games. You were sanctioned a number of times and finally disqualified. Is this about revenge?"

He sat for a minute staring at Ronnie. "Lady, you got the wrong man."

"We have a bat with blood on it found in your car trunk."

"I put my car in for service this week. Anyone could have put that bat in there."

Ronnie pulled two pictures out of the folder of the bloody carjacking years ago. She scooted the pictures in front of Bruce.

"What's that?" he asked.

"Seven years ago. A carjacking in Houston, Texas. Paul Norris died at the scene. His wife died in the hospital. We're developing a solid link between the Gleasons and this attack. We already have an established link between you and Patty. We're running your cell phone records now. If we find that your cell phone pinged off a tower in Patty's neighborhood, we've got you. If any motor vehicle records place you in Texas, you'll be charged with first degree murder."

He scooted his chair back. "Hey, I don't know nothing about any killings."

"I already have a connection between you and Patty Gleason. It's just a matter of time before I can tie you into the carjacking."

"I didn't do that. I was never in Texas."

"What's you connection with the Gleason woman?"

He sat, bouncing his knee up and down. He scooted his chair forward and put his arms on the table. "I don't know nothin' about any killing in Houston. Me and Patty, it was all about the computer games. I was helping her with the games. She was going to win, and give me half the money."

"Whose idea was it to attack the gamers, the women and Brian VanDeer?"

He stared hard at Ronnie. His shoulders sagged. "She asked me to do it. Gave me a down payment and the rest after she won the games."

"Why did she want Brian attacked? They weren't in position to win."

He crossed his arms in front of him. "We were mad at the GMs. He kicked me out of the games years ago just when my partner and I were winning. Patty said Jon was picking on her. Jon treats gamers like his kids. She said the best way to get back at him was to go after one of the gamers."

That woman was a sociopath. One final question and if she got the right answer, they'd have her. "Where'd you buy the weapon?"

"She gave me the bat. It was her son's. Told me not to hit them hard, just enough to scare 'em. I just tapped 'em."

"Mary Johnson's been in a coma for weeks. I'd hardly call that a tap."

"The day before Mary Johnson and Hayden Curtis were attacked, ten thousand dollars suddenly appeared in your checking account."

She enjoyed the stunned look on the man's face.

"You know that?"

"Did the tooth fairy leave you that money? I have detectives tracking bank records, searching for the origin of the money now."

"That's the down payment. Said she'd split the prize money when she got it."

"How was she going to give you the money without her husband finding out?"

"Me and Patty," he shrugged, "we're real close."

"Close?"

"You know, close. She was going to leave her husband. We were going to run off together."

Patty Gleason sure put one over on him. She'd never leave Carl for this punk. Ronnie stood, gathered the pictures, and picked up the folder. "Excuse me."

She stepped into the cubicle.

"Good work, Ronnie," Chief Williams said.

"I need to go pick up Patty Gleason before anyone else gets hurt."

"I'll get his statement. You go ahead."

35

100011

At the restaurant, the women took a much needed bathroom break. Lea combed her hair and reapplied lipstick. Patty came out of a stall and washed her hands.

"I heard what happened, and I apologize for my boy's rudeness."

That tone of voice. She wanted to pick a fight. That was her way. Fight over everything and fight with everybody. In the spirit of her mother and Mary's gentle natures, Lea wouldn't brawl with this woman. She turned to Patty. "Thank you for saying that." She abruptly left the restroom and returned to the banquet hall.

The hall was brightly decorated with balloons and streamers. Tables overflowed with pizzas, lasagna, salads, and breads.

Lea's heart went out to Sam, who kept watching the door for Lynn, who wasn't coming. Kevin had lost his best friend and didn't know it. She took a seat next to Joe and turned her attention to Jon and the behind-the-scene staff lined up behind him who had labored so intensely for these games.

Jon called the group to attention and introduced the staff and thanked them for their service. "You contestants have been a great group to work with. We've had some serious challenges this time, but we weathered the storms. In spite of our difficulties, with the donations and other online gamers' wagers, we were able to raise just over one million dollars for childhood cancer research. We're in the black and every penny of that money will go to fight cancer. The funds for the quest prizes were raised through royalties we received by selling our games we design."

The group clapped and stood, continuing to cheer for the volunteer workers.

When the gamers settled, Jon started again. "I know you're anxious to hear the standings. Just to remind you, the checks will be presented at a formal ceremony a month from now once our outside source verifies the points. As always, we can have an upset at the end of a game. Although Hayden and Mary, through their children, played valiantly, the one hundred and fifty thousand dollar first prize goes to the Gleason family."

"Huh?" Lea whispered. Stunned, she turned to Joe. "We lost?"

Joe took her hand under the table. "Stay calm."

A lump formed in her throat. *I won't cry. I wanted so badly to win for Mom and for Mary.*

She took a deep breath and fought for control.

"Second place," Jon glanced at Lea and Joe. "Hayden Curtis and Mary Johnson."

"Third place, "Sam Preston and Lynn Foster. Brian and Cody in fourth place."

"I'm so proud to know each one of you and hope you will register for future quests."

Gamers congratulated Patty and Carl Gleason.

Lea shook Patty's hand. "Congratulations."

"Thank you." Patty grinned broadly.

Lea stepped over to the food tables and dumped salad on a plate, forcing herself to recover her composure.

"You okay?" Joe asked.

"Barely. To think that woman orchestrated the attack on my mother, I'd like to club her."

"As soon as Ronnie has irrefutable proof of Patty's involvement, she'll get what's due her."

Lea filled her plate and returned to her table. She saw Sam, sitting alone. He was texting on his cell phone. Texts that Lynn would never respond to. She should go up and say something to him, but what?

Joe dropped down next to her. "Are they going to tell Sam what really happened?" she asked.

"I don't know. I was only hired to solve the crime about the attacks. Agent Hawkins has taken over the kidnapping."

"Is the case closed now?" Lea asked.

"Not officially until formal charges are filed and a judge makes a ruling in the case."

Joe's cell phone face lit up. He took the call. "Yeah, they're here. Stuffing themselves with pizza. Will do." He clicked off.

He leaned over to Lea. "Something's up. Ronnie's on her way over with a police detail."

She turned her head toward Joe so that no one could see her lips move. "They have Patty? They're going to do that here?"

Before Joe could respond, Ronnie entered the banquet hall and whispered something to Jon Mathers. He left with her.

"Be right back." Joe got up and followed Ronnie out the door.

"You need to hear this, too," Ronnie said to Joe. "Officer Braylin, keep an eye on Patty Gleason. Don't approach her, just be sure she doesn't leave the room."

"Yes, ma'am."

"We found the car the girls in the park got a picture of and got the license plate. We arrested a Bruce Schupe for the attacks. He implicated Patty. We got a search warrant and found baseball bat in Schupe's trunk. We found the black cap the girls mentioned. The pictures aren't very revealing, but we'll use them as bait. Seems that Patty had a boyfriend who's given us enough to arrest her."

"A boyfriend?" Joe asked, "Patty Gleason?"

Ronnie nodded. "Forensics is working on the bat. We've got a picture of Schupe clobbering Brian. We can only charge him with Brian's attack until the lab report comes back. Mary's wig came off during the attack, and her blood may be on the bat, also. And, we found a police report from when the

Gleasons lived in Minnesota. Four years ago, Patty was charged with assault for threatening a neighbor with a baseball bat.

"Schupe confessed to all three attacks and implicated Patty. She paid him ten thousand dollars as front money. Until we can get bank records to prove the transactions, some of this is circumstantial, but with documented money transfers, we can put together a solid case."

Jon shook his head. "It makes me sick that one of these people involved in our games would do something like this. Really sick. I remember putting Schupe out of the games several years back. Detective, do what you have to do."

Ronnie and two policemen entered the banquet hall. Ronnie stepped up to the table in front of Patty. "Patty Gleason, you're charged with assault on Brian VanDeer."

"Stand up, ma'am," Officer Braylin told Patty. He took her arm.

"Get your hands off of me." Patty stood and slapped the officer.

Officer Dodd grabbed her other arm to secure the handcuffs.

"Get away from me. What are you crazy people doing?"

"Ma'am, you have the right to remain silent—"

"I'll not stay silent. It was those new people Jon let into the group who did this."

Officer Dodd snapped handcuffs on Patty.

Earsplitting screams pierced the room. "Carl! Carl! Make them stop."

Carl and the boys followed the policemen out of the restaurant.

Joe stood next to Ronnie. "Good work, Sis."

"I'm sorry we had to do it this way, but I wanted her in custody before she injured anybody else. I still want to link her to the attack on Hayden a few days ago. Schupe confessed that it was Patty that put him up to it, but we'll get the solid evidence before long. I just needed her off the street."

"I'll work on that case with you."

"I want to get back. They've finished processing Sandra Coulter, and I want to talk to her. I'd like you to listen in."

"I'll meet you there."

Jon, looking older, stood in front of the group, asking for their attention. "I apologize for the interruption. Apparently, the police have proof of Mrs. Gleason's involvement in the attacks. It's still an ongoing investigation. We're going to hold off on final game standings until the police have completed their investigation. I don't anticipate any more situations developing, please enjoy your meal."

"How about I drop you at home," Joe said to Lea. "I have to go to the station."

"I've had all I can take of this for now."

Lea thanked Jon and Shelly for letting her take her mother's place.

Jon shook her hand. "I'm so sorry about your mother and Mary. We'll design games in the future to prevent this type of thing from happening again. If they have proof that Patty really caused those attacks, the family will be disqualified. Carl and Patty registered as a team. If a team member commits a felony during a game, they're automatically disqualified. That puts Hayden and Mary in first place."

"Thanks for everything. Ronnie and I will get with you later and explain the whole thing to you. You deserve to know."

A half hour later, Joe pulled into the driveway. "You going to be all right?"

"I'm completely exhausted," Lea said. "I hear Bubbles barking. Mom will still be with Terrie, I mean Emma."

"I'm going in and listen to Lynn's story. I'll be by later."

"Joe, thanks for everything."

36

100100

Joe entered the cubicle behind the interrogation room. Agent Hawkins was there with Ronnie.

"How long's she been waiting?"

"They just brought her in." She nodded to Agent Hawkins. "He only asked her a few questions. We had to be sure no one else in the group was part of the kidnapping. Once we were sure, then we went after Patty."

Ronnie looked at Agent Hawkins. "You want to do this?"

"I think she'll respond better to you. Joe and I'll wait here."

"Did she put up any resistance?" Joe asked.

Ronnie shook her head. "I quietly addressed her as Sandra Coulter, and she crumbled. As traumatic as it was, I think she's inwardly relieved that it's over."

"She'll go through a battery of emotions in the next few days."

Ronnie nodded and picked up the folder off the table. "I'm going in. Pray."

"You got it."

Ronnie entered the room and sat across from Sandra. She handed her a bottle of water.

"It's not a trick. I know you were sick earlier and thought you might be thirsty."

Sandra unscrewed the top and took a gulp. She set the water aside.

Ronnie noticed her hair was still wet. Smudges of fingerprint residue under her nails.

"Is Terrie all right?"

"As well as can be expected. Hayden's with her."

"We're taping this interview. To start with, I'd like you to state your name, age, occupation, and current address."

Sandra stated the facts Ronnie asked for.

Sandra looked puzzled. "How did Hayden know?"

Start with the truth. See how far she deviates from it. "Hayden didn't know anything. It was Mary Johnson. Her real name is Carly Dean."

She let that sink in.

A flicker of recognition in Sandra's eyes. "Her grandmother?"

Ronnie nodded. "She found you. Hayden had no idea who you were until a few days ago. Hayden was worried about Terrie, so we allowed her to stay with her."

"I'm glad she's with her. I never guessed. Mary looked nothing like Mrs. Dean." She shot up straight in her chair. "Look, you don't know what you're doing. You gotta get Terrie protection. He'll kill her. Kill Terrie and kill the Deans. I'll tell you whatever you want, but you have to go now and protect them."

"Protect them from what?" Ronnie asked quietly.

She was nearly hysterical. "Andrew. Andrew Watts. He's crazy. He'll kill them."

"Andrew Watts died two years ago in an exercise prison yard riot."

"He's dead?"

"Dead."

"You sure? You have to be sure about that."

"He was arrested for killing a policeman in Las Vegas. I'm sure."

She slumped back in her chair and stared at the table. "Then she's safe." She looked up at Ronnie, tears flooding her eyes. "Terrie's safe, now."

"Sandra, why don't you start from the beginning, the night of the shooting, and tell me what happened, in your own words."

She took another sip of water. "Years ago, I got in with a bad group. Andrew was the leader. The guys broke into rich houses. In most homes the security's set up for downstairs. Andrew worked for a company that installed high-end security in expensive homes. He said they rarely wired upstairs areas because it's so expensive; the homeowners don't want it. They'd get all the jewelry and whatever they could. Sometimes, they'd sneak downstairs while the people were in their entertainment rooms or eating a late dinner and they'd grab laptops and cell phones, wallets, purses.

"One night, they got into a house and got caught. I always parked two blocks away from the house. They got out of the house, but I couldn't get the car started. Andrew said he'd get another car. The three of us got to an intersection, and a car was waiting at a light. He ran up to the car, and held a gun on the man on the driver's side.

"The man got out of the car, and Andrew shot him. I couldn't believe he did that. The woman got out of the car and was trying to get to her baby in the back. I was scared he'd shoot her, too, and threw myself on him. He shoved me away, and shot her. He laughed as she tried to crawl to her baby. He grabbed her by the hair and pulled her away from the car. I knelt down to help her."

Sandra paused and took a breath. "The woman whispered to me to save her baby. Then she died.

"I heard police sirens. Andrew shoved me in the back and got into the driver's seat. Frank got in the front. He took off."

"You didn't see anyone around? No people on the street? No other cars?"

She shook her head. "It was real late."

"We got to the house, and I took care of the baby. I was scared because Andrew was so wild about almost being caught and having to leave his car. They got on Frank's motorcycle and went back and cleaned the car real good and left it parked there. A few days later, they drove the car they stole someplace and burned it. He told me not to get attached to the baby, because he had a buyer for it. He said that if I ran off with the child, he'd find me and kill the baby and kill her family."

"Do you know who was going to buy the baby?"

She shook her head. "He never said."

"He did another robbery and got a jar full of gold coins. He and Frank got pretty drunk that night. The next morning, he told me to clean up the baby. When he got back, he was gonna take her to her new home. He knelt on top of me and put a knife to my throat. He said if I didn't have the baby ready, he'd kill her and me. I didn't think he'd kill the baby because he'd get money for her. But I wasn't so sure about me. Without me, no one could protect her.

"I knew where he hid his coins and money. I took enough for us to live on and got out of the house. I hotwired a car at a movie theater and drove to Dallas. I cleaned the car and left it in an airport parking lot. I settled in Dallas for a year, working jobs as a waitress.

"One day I came home, picked the baby up from the sitter's, and there he was, in my apartment. He came towards me and tried to grab Terrie out of my arms. I grabbed a fire extinguisher off the kitchen counter and sprayed him. When he dropped to the floor, grabbing at his eyes, I bashed him with the broom. I taped his mouth and tied him up. He'd get free eventually, but I needed time to get away."

"Where'd you go?"

"I got a ride on a truck hauling a load to Oklahoma City. From there I took a bus to Denver."

"In view of your fear of him, did you ever think of going to the police? At least leaving the baby with a hospital worker?"

"You don't know this man. If he said he'd kill her, he would, just to get even. That lady begged him to not hurt her or her baby. He shot her and laughed about it."

"So, what happened in Denver?"

"I got a job designing websites and encrypting business data. The couple I worked for were great. She always talked about how good the schools were in Lincoln, Nebraska. Every day, I was scared about Andrew.

"I made up some fake papers and got Terrie enrolled in a preschool program. She was tall for her age, so I told them she was five. Even at three years old, she could say her alphabet and add numbers. I taught her how to write. I told the school, all her records were lost in Hurricane Katrina. Nobody questioned me.

"The next year we moved to Lincoln. I got Terrie in school. She's real smart. Then I started doing the games. Made extra cash to help out."

Ronnie made some notes and put her pen down.

"What's going to happen to Terrie? She didn't do anything wrong."

"She's assigned to a child psychologist. Eventually, she'll be introduced to Carly and Ben. They'll take over her care."

"I should never have gotten mixed up with those guys. Once I found the baby, I just had to protect her." Sandra looked up at Ronnie. "Would you tell them I'm really sorry?"

Ronnie nodded. "Yes. I don't know how this will go. You will be assigned an attorney, and it's all up to the courts."

Sandra shrugged. "As long as Terrie's safe, I'll be all right."

"Emma. Her name's Emma."

"I'm sorry. I keep forgetting."

"I'll let the guard return you to your cell. I've got a lot to sort through."

After Sandra left, Joe and John entered the interrogation room and sat across from Ronnie.

"Wow," Joe said.

"She thought she was doing the right thing. If Carly Dean, an amateur, a clever amateur, could have found Emma, that boy would have found her."

"You look used up. Go home."

"Mike's making dinner. I'm going home to my man."

37

100101

Joe tapped on the kitchen door and entered. Lea was filling the dog's bowl with water and set it down on her mat.

"Hey, loser," Joe kissed Lea.

"Lovely greeting."

"Hayden back yet?"

"No. I'm going to crash in the living room and watch some mindless show. You eaten? Frances brought us a nice double layer chocolate cake."

"Maybe later."

Lea thumbed through the channels and found an old Jane Austen movie. Joe settled next to her on the couch. Bubbles jumped up and tried to find a spot between them. Lea put her in her lap.

"What's going to happen to Lynn, I mean Sandra? Honestly, I can't keep up with all these names."

"She wasn't directly involved with the shooting and did try to stop it, but was an accomplice in the robberies. Statute of limitations has run out on them. She did take a stolen child across state lines.

Although her reasons were altruistic enough, she genuinely thought the baby was in danger, it's going to depend on how the court views it."

"Are they in the same jail, Sandra and Patty?"

Joe shook his head. "Ronnie had them take Patty up to Omaha, claiming overcrowding in the women's unit."

"I still don't get why they attacked Brian. The games were almost over, and he wasn't going to win anyway?"

"Patty wanted to get back at Jon for the way she imagined she'd been treated. Once she started the mayhem, she just couldn't stop herself. If those kids in the park hadn't come forward, we might not have solved this."

Lea shook her head. "I thought she was a little off. But, this was just plain mean."

The kitchen door opened. "I'm home."

"Ruff." Bubbles jumped down from Lea's lap and bounded into the kitchen.

"Hey, girl."

"We're in here." Lea called out.

Hayden hobbled into the living room. "Jason drove me home."

"How'd it go?"

"I'm going to sit in my chair and put my leg up." Hayden dropped down in her recliner and raised the foot rest. She eased her leg down. "Ah, that feels better."

Her mother looked pale. Her short hair, bushed out. No make-up. She hadn't seen her look this bad since her father died.

"I don't mind saying, it was hard. She's so confused, and I can't tell her anything. The doctor's real nice. Works with kids who've been violently abused. Although Emma wasn't abused, it's a rare case, and she's the most qualified doctor to help her. She only takes one child at a time. I got Emma, I have to start calling her that, I got her to eat a little soup. The doctor gave her a mild sleeping pill. I sat with her until she cried herself to sleep."

"I feel so bad for her," Lea said. "When will they tell her about everything?"

"Tomorrow, some time. She's going to give her a little time to adjust to her surroundings and then explain it all to her. She told me I could come over and sit with Emma while she explained everything to her. I told her I'd be there. She says usually the children don't believe it at first, but she'll figure it out. It's going to take time and a pile of prayer."

Hayden shook her head. "All those years Carly's looked for her granddaughter, and now she's got her back. What a miracle. The tenacity of that woman to not give up.

"We made a quick stop at the hospital. They'd given Carly a sedative, wanted to keep her quiet. Ben had just called the other grandparents and gave them the news. Ben's so happy. Crying then laughing then crying again."

"If the attack hadn't happened, we'd never known about the kidnapping," Joe said.

Hayden nodded. "They let Ben in earlier to see Emma. The room Emma's in has a two-way mirror on the wall. They let him observe her while she was eating. I think he'll rest better tonight knowing she's safe."

"I'm glad he saw her."

Hayden sat up straight. "And that Patty Gleason! When I get my hands around her throat, what I'm gonna do to her isn't religious."

Lea chuckled. "Mom."

"By the way, did you hear when they're starting the next quest?"

"You can't be serious?"

"You know how to do it now. We can all be our own family team."

Lea picked up a small throw pillow and tossed it at her mother.

Hayden tossed the pillow back.

38

100110

Lea sank down in the seat in Joe's pickup and buckled up. "I'm glad that's over. They took it well."

She had sat quietly while Joe explained to Jon and Shelly Mathers the proof of Patty's involvement in attacking the gamers. Carl had cooperated with the investigation and gave up the name of one of Patty's few friends that had loaned Patty her car the day of Hayden's last attack. Also, the lab found traces of Carly's blood on the bat. Lea was glad that she was only there for moral support. The news sickened Jon since he was so willing to believe the best about people. He assured Joe that the staff at Dylan's Games would cooperate with the ongoing investigation in any way that they could.

Jon said that with the Gleasons disqualified, Hayden and Mary won first prize. Sam would receive the second prize, and Brian and Cody split the twenty-five thousand dollar prize.

Their duty done, they had the rest of the day to rest.

"They're a great couple." Joe turned south on Twenty-seventh street. "All the sorrow they went through losing their son and turning it in to a way to give money to cancer research."

"I hope they get control of the gamers and can continue on."

"They'll find a way. How about we grab some sandwiches and eat at the park? I thought I'd pick up some rose bushes for Hayden. She lost two bushes in that hail storm last week."

"Sounds good. You're always thinking of Mom. Thank you."

"She deserves something special after all she's been through these last months."

Ten minutes later, Joe pulled into Lincoln's rose park. They made their way to a bench surrounded by rose beds.

"You're limping," Lea observed.

"It's nothing. Just a couple of blisters."

Lea pointed her finger at him. "You went back and got those hiking shoes, didn't you?"

"They're on sale, fifty dollars off regular price," he defended himself.

Lea settled on the bench and pulled the paper back from her turkey sandwich. She took a bite. "It's gorgeous here. Mom would love the whole back yard to look like this—hundreds of roses."

"Lot of upkeep. Mulching, fertilizing, insecticides—"

She slapped his knee. "Stop thinking of all the work and enjoy the beauty. When her leg's better, I think I'll bring Mom here. I haven't done that in a while."

"I was talking to Ben earlier. He's putting the house up for sale in Houston and is moving up here. All of Emma's friends are here, and she's done so well in school. They want to provide as much stability for her as they can."

"Mom will like that."

"Ronnie got permission for Sam to see Lynn this morning."

"I wonder how that will go? He's really in love with her."

"Time will tell." Joe collected the trash from their lunch and dropped it in a receptacle. He sat on the bench and put his arm around Lea's shoulder.

"I like those circles of roses and lavender," Lea pointed. "Roses don't belong in rectangular boxes."

The beautiful floral displays, the warm afternoon sun, the scent of lavender, all worked its magic. Without taking his arm from around her, he pulled a small box out of his left pocket. "Lea, I want us to be together always."

Lea looked at him.

He flipped the box open and held it up to her. "Will you marry me?"

Lea glanced at the ring, glimmering in the box and then into Joe's eyes. "Yes. I will."

He leaned down and kissed her. "I love you," he whispered.

She gazed into his eyes. "I love you."

They clasped hands and inhaled the beauty of the gardens. She knew they'd be together, and it was time.

A half hour later, Joe parked in the drive. Lea unlocked the garage door and rooted for gardening tools. Joe dug out the dead bushes and set the new rose bushes in the ground.

Lea heard a car door slammed. Hayden greeted them.

She looked over the new plants. "Those are beautiful."

"I know how much you like your roses," Joe said.

"They're lovely. Thank you, Joe."

They sat in the lawn chairs, admiring the small garden, Hayden between them.

"Mom, I want to show you something, but you have to promise to stay calm."

"I'm always calm," Hayden grinned at Lea.

Lea held up her left hand so that her mother could see the ring. "Joe asked me to marry him."

Hayden grabbed Joe's and Lea's hands. "My two favorite people. I'm so happy. I love you both so much." She leaned over and kissed Lea and then Joe.

"I'd go inside and make us a big celebration meal, but I'm all outta casseroles."

Joe put an arm around Hayden. "We'll go out to eat. I'll call Ronnie and Mike. We both owe each other dinner, and this is a family event."

39

100111

Carly Dean stood in the cubicle of the visitation room at the women's correctional facility. Ronnie had set up an interview for her with Sandra. She watched as the guard brought Sandra in and instructed her to sit at the table so that she faced the mirror.

Ronnie stepped into the cubicle next to Carly. "I'll be here. At any time you want to end the interview, just signal me."

Carly composed herself and entered the room. She took a seat across from Sandra. Carly waited a minute before she spoke. In a quiet, controlled voice she said, "For eight years, I rehearsed what I'd say to the person who savagely murdered my daughter and her husband and stole my grandchild. I wanted that person to hurt as badly as I hurt. But those words would never make up for the suffering we endured. The suffering that Paul's family has endured."

Sandra sat motionless, her lips pressed together.

"I'd see you at the socials laughing at something Emma said, and my blood would boil. That should have been my Kate laughing with Emma—not you."

Sandra trembled slightly.

It was a few minutes before Carly could speak. "But then, they told me how you shielded Emma from that murderer. Kept her safe all those years... so, what's a grandmother to do?"

"I'm really sorry," Sandra whispered.

Carly's gaze bore into Sandra. Sandra had confessed to her past crimes. There would be no jury trial. The judge sentenced her to five years in prison, eligible for parole in twelve months. Given the extenuating circumstances of the child's abduction and the documented violence of Andrew Watts, she got off easy. Ben and Carly had written a letter to the judge asking for clemency.

Give her the gift, fluttered through Carly's mind.

Her heart burned.

That's the gift.

I understand it now.

Carly reached across the table and took Sandra's hand. "Thank you... for protecting Emma." A warmth of love dislodged itself from Carly's heart and traveled down her arm into the girl's hand.

"I never would hurt her."

Carly released her hand and sat back in her seat. "I know."

"How... how is she?"

"She's a smart girl. She's figuring it out. We took her to the Children's Zoo yesterday."

Sandra nodded. "She likes it there. She likes the tortoises and monkeys best."

Carly studied the girl for a few minutes. She wasn't the hardened, wild girl from years ago. With a little love and acceptance, God could do miracles in her life. Sam and Kevin visited her regularly. Court orders in place prevented Sandra from having any contact with Emma.

"I wanted to meet you in the reality of God's truth." Carly pulled an envelope out of her pocket. "Court orders prevent you from contacting Emma, but your birthday's Tuesday. I got permission to give you this. According to prison rules, it had to be open. Emma wrote you a card." She passed the card to Sandra. Inside was the balm Sandra needed to begin her healing. Emma thanked her for protecting her and hoped they'd meet again.

Sandra took the card in her hand. Tears dropped down, splattering the envelope. She clutched the card to her. "Thank you."

"My time's up. I wish you the best, Sandra."

Sandra nodded, unable to speak. She mouthed, "Thank you," again.

That afternoon, Carly and Ben sat with Emma in the backyard of the psychologist's house. It was a warm day in June and the flowers bordering the gardens were in full bloom. Brick walkways separated the pretty gardens. Tall bushes bordered the yard. Water gurgled in a fish pond to their left. Dr. Hayes made herself scarce.

"We brought you some more pictures of when you were a little girl." Carly pulled out a small photo album. The doctor said to only bring a few pictures at a time so as to not overwhelm the child. "These pictures are of you when you were a baby. I know you don't remember that, but I thought you'd like to see them."

Emma timidly took the album and opened it. Carly could tell that she was still unsure about her and Ben's place in her life.

Emma looked at a picture of a little baby sitting on the floor, playing with a pile of colored blocks. Another picture was of a little girl in a yellow sun dress standing, holding onto a soft chair.

"That's when you first started to walk. You held onto anything soft."

Emma turned the page and gripped the album. "That's my dream." She pointed to a picture of a little girl in a child's blow-up pool in a large fenced-in yard. The little girl was splashing a dog, who was in the pool with her.

"What dream, honey?"

Emma looked up at Carly and then back down at the picture. "I sometimes have these dreams." Emma slowly got up from the chair she was sitting on and nestled between Carly and Ben.

Carly held her breath. It was the first time Emma had initiated any physical contact with them. She exhaled slowly.

"In my dream, I'd be playing in a swimming pool and Bubbles, your dog, would jump in. I'd be laughing. Sometimes I'd wake myself up laughing." Emma looked at the picture and back up at Carly and Ben.

"You really are my grandparents, aren't you?"

Carly swallowed. *Keep it together.* "Yes, Emma we are. Kate and Paul Norris were your real parents."

Emma sat back, leaning against Carly. She stared directly ahead at the fish pond. "What about Lynn?"

Carly put her arm around the child. "I don't know this for sure, but I think God sent her to you as a guardian to protect you. The courts don't see it that way, but I do."

Dr. Hayes crossed the lawn to the family. "How are you doing?"

Carly stood. "Good."

Carly faced Emma. "Emma, we have to go now, but we'll be back tomorrow."

Carly and Ben turned toward the house to leave.

"Bye, Grandma and Grandpa."

Carly turned and nodded at Emma. She smiled, fighting back tears. "We'll see you tomorrow."

July 25, Emma's tenth birthday

"You grab that cake, and I'll take this one," Hayden instructed Lea. "Joe, can you carry those paper plates for me?"

"Got 'em."

They paraded across the street to Carly's house and entered the through the kitchen door. Ben and Sam Preston were out back, stringing lights.

"Put those on that folding table," Carly said.

"This all looks great." Joe gazed hungrily at the mounds of food.

"We may have thunderstorms later, so I set the food up inside."

"Where's Emma?" Hayden asked.

"Downstairs. She and Kevin are playing a new game Jon sent them. Jon and Shelly will be over later. It's hard to believe that she's been home for nearly a whole month."

"I wanted to come over," Hayden said, "but I thought you all needed time to yourselves."

"She's doing great. It was a little awkward the first few days, but she's settled in nicely. She enjoys her Sunday school class at church. She told me the other night that one of the worst things about all of this was finding out that she was only nine years old. She thought that she was almost grown up."

"I'm only across the street. You know if you ever need anything where to find me."

"Thanks. I know that. I appreciate your friendship more than I can say. Paul's parents are coming up next week. The doctor said to introduce the family slowly. We linked up a video on the computer last night and introduced Emma to her other grandparents. Emma told them that she can't wait to meet them."

"Hey, everyone." Brian VanDeer entered the kitchen, carrying an aluminum tray of barbequed chicken.

"Donna, welcome," Carly greeted Brian's mother.

"Thanks for inviting her. She'll sit in the living room looking at magazines. She won't be no trouble."

Joe returned with another cake.

"Bing Crosby." Mrs. VanDeer pointed at Joe.

"Hey, beautiful." Joe kissed her forehead.

"Are you going to sing?"

Lea slapped Joe on the back. "Yes, Bing, croon a tune."

He put his arm around Donna's shoulders. "What would you like to hear?"

"White Christmas."

Joe narrowed his eyes at Lea. He took Donna's arm and gently danced her into the living room, singing as he went.

"Brian, where's your partner?" Hayden asked.

"I thought he'd take his money and build up his business; instead, he's been on one Caribbean cruise after another. Got a Facebook post last night from Antigua."

The back yard began to fill up with guild members and their families.

Emma and Kevin emerged from the basement. "We're going to take Bubbles out to play."

"Go easy on her," Carly said, "she's carrying puppies."

"We will," Emma called out over her shoulder, heading towards the back door. She stopped at the door, ran back to Carly, and threw her arms around her. "I love you, Grandma."

"I love you, too, honey." Carly kissed the top of her head.

Seconds later, Emma was out the door.

Hayden put her arm around Carly as she wiped her eyes. "Every now and again, I'm overwhelmed that we found her. I promised my daughter as she was dying, I'd find her. Emma's been like this all week, so loving."

"I'm so happy for you."

Carly watched the kids in the back yard. "Sam said that Sandra's doing better."

"Does Emma still ask to see her?"

"She knows that she can't. But I don't discourage her from talking about her. If Sandra keeps herself straight, once she's released, I may allow a visit. I never told anyone this, but I was hurting so bad after Kate died. I was praying one day, and it was only for a second, but I had my eyes closed, and I saw her. Like she was floating above the grass. 'Give her the gift,' she said. I didn't know what that meant.

"When I was visiting Sandra in the prison, I felt my heart warming, like the gift of love that God gives mothers for their children at special times. That was the gift. Give Sandra the gift of love. I'd kept the love I had for Kate locked up inside of me. I unlocked it, and that ache in my heart I'd carried for so long disappeared. It's all going to be all right now. As Christians, we view redemption as God does. That woman will have a family waiting for her when she's released from prison."

"Yes," Hayden said. "God is our Redeemer."

In the back yard, Emma fell to the ground laughing. Bubbles jumped on top of her, licking her face, making her laugh more.

Acknowledgment

Thank you, Lisa Norman, at Heart Ally Books for your hard work publishing my books. I'm forever grateful to you.

About the Author

P. Ryan Hembree is the author of three novels and two novellas. She is a member of the American Christian Fiction Writers and the Christian Writers Guild. Ryan makes her home in Beatrice, Nebraska with her eighteen-year-old cat, Macey. You can visit Ryan's website at www.pryanhembree.com or follow her on her Facebook page at P. Ryan Hembree Author.

Coming soon from P. Ryan Hembree

For the Love of Power

A Mitch and Gladys Series

Mitch Dryden and Gladys Byrne learn of their friend, Nate Glaser's murder. While comforting his grieving widow, Irene Glaser, they're pulled into the events surrounding Nate's death. A manuscript Nate presented to his publisher before his death details secrets of Braxton Nugent's past, which will stop his campaign for a congressional seat in Dallas, Texas.

Sylvia Nugent's husband is a powerful attorney and a decorated war hero. She isn't going to allow anyone to stop her husband's campaign and fears the damage this book can do to her husband's career, their marriage, and family.

Irene Glaser learns of her husband's book and becomes the focus of Sylvia Nugent's attacks. Where Irene recognizes Sylvia's wealth and dominance, Irene has her own power—her faith in God. As this powerful political family launches its attack on Irene and her children, Irene digs deep into her faith to bring out her spiritual arsenal to guard her family.

Two powerful women. One God.

Also by P. Ryan Hembree:

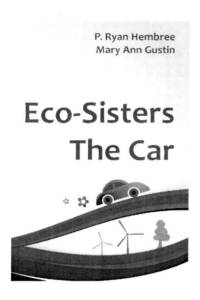

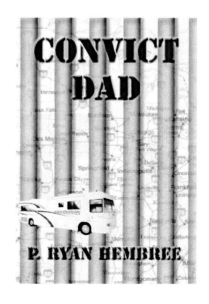

CPSIA information can be obtained at www.ICGtesting.com
Printed in the USA
BVOW01s1110130414

350519BV00004B/63/P